"Grace," Mica said with a sharp edge of irritation. "What are you doing here?"

Her heart slammed violently in her chest. Her hands were shaking. She had to do this quickly.

"I brought you something."

"You what?"

Grace leaned into the back seat and unhooked the straps in the baby carrier, lifting Jules.

She straightened and shut the door with her hip. Mica stared at her and then at the baby. "Hold out your arm, Mica."

He was speechless as she walked up to him, but he took Jules when she held him out.

"He's yours, and it's your turn to take care of him."

Mica's blue eyes blazed with mistrust and something akin to revulsion. "You've got to be kidding."

"Does he look like a joke?"

"No." His surprise and mounting anger hit her like shotgun pellets. Sharp, painful and deep. She'd thought she'd prepared herself for his reaction, but seeing Mica and remembering what it was like to be in his arms... Grace hated herself for being the bad guy. There wasn't a single thing she'd done since last October that merited his trust, love or respect.

"I don't have a son," Mica said and started to hand the baby back to her.

"Yes, you do. This is Jules."

Dear Reader,

Mica Barzonni never questioned his fate until an accident paralyzed his left arm. He'd always assumed he'd inherit his father's successful farm. Despondent and frustrated, Mica wasn't looking for love when Grace Railton came back to Indian Lake to help her aunt Louise at the ice cream shop. But he *was* looking for comfort.

It had been over a decade since the summer Grace lost her heart to Mica. She'd never forgotten the kiss they shared in his parents' swimming pool. Mica didn't remember much, except that Grace was a silly beauty pageant contestant. Now she's an up-and-coming fashion designer in Paris. Little can distract her from her career. Except Mica.

After a romantic October in Indian Lake, Grace returns to Paris. And Mica doesn't hear a word from her for fourteen months...until she shows up on his doorstep and shocks him to his soul.

She presents Mica with their son.

Mica is angry that Grace has kept six-month-old Jules from him, but now that he's met his baby, he wants to keep him—forever. Grace is still looking for one thing and one thing only: Mica's love.

I hope you like *His Baby Dilemma*. I must admit I had fun writing the comic scenes in this story. Not only has Mica never changed a diaper, but he must do it one-handed! As poignant as the love story between Grace and Mica is, there were strong moments of insight, even for me.

Please send me your thoughts and comments at cathlanigan1@gmail.com, follow me on Facebook and Twitter, @cathlanigan, or visit www.heartwarmingauthors. blogspot.com.

Catherine Lanigan

HEARTWARMING

His Baby Dilemma

——

Catherine Lanigan

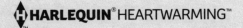

Recycling programs
for this product may
not exist in your area.

ISBN-13: 978-0-373-36865-5

His Baby Dilemma

Printed in U.S.A.

Catherine Lanigan knew she was born for storytelling at a very young age when she told stories to her younger brothers and sister to entertain them. After years of encouragement from family and high school teachers, Catherine was shocked and brokenhearted when her freshman college creative-writing professor told her that she had "no writing talent whatsoever" and that she would never earn a dime as a writer. He promised her that he would be her crutches and get her through his demanding class with a B grade so as not to destroy her high grade point average too much, *if* Catherine would promise never to write again.

For fourteen years she did not write until she was encouraged by a television journalist to give her dream a shot. She wrote a six-hundred-page historical romantic spy thriller set against World War I. The journalist sent the manuscript to his agent, who then garnered bids from two publishers. That was nearly forty published novels, nonfiction books and anthologies ago.

Books by Catherine Lanigan

Harlequin Heartwarming

Shores of Indian Lake

Love Shadows
Heart's Desire
A Fine Year for Love
Katia's Promise
Fear of Falling
Sophie's Path
Protecting the Single Mom
Family of His Own

MIRA Books

Dangerous Love
Elusive Love

Harlequin Desire

The Texan

Visit the Author Profile page at Harlequin.com for more titles.

This book is dedicated to my late husband, Jed Nolan, my hero and best friend. I will love you to the moon and back, and throughout all the galaxies and universes.

Acknowledgments

This year has been a difficult one for many authors and editors. For the family of Heartwarming authors, we must say goodbye to our extraordinarily talented, warmhearted and savvy senior editor, Victoria Curran. Granted, she may not be part of our line any longer, but, Victoria, you will always be a part of my life and my future. For those authors like me who have been in this business, decade after decade, we've walked through these valleys and this I know... you are never alone. Editors are not simply work colleagues. For an artist, an author, an editor is part of our brain, heart and soul. It isn't possible for me to put a part of my heart on a shelf and say, "Be seeing you." Instead, I will say, "Let's talk soon."

To Claire Caldwell, there are no words to express my appreciation for your insights and my downright giddiness when we brainstorm and pull yet another story together. With each story, we have more and more fun. And that's the way it should be.

To my agent, Lissy Peace, to whom I've been "joined at the hip" for over twenty years—it's been a ride!

PROLOGUE

Fifteen months ago

GRUMBLING AT HER travel-weary reflection in her palm-sized mirror, Grace Railton used a cotton swab to clean away the mascara smudges under her eyes. Jet lag. *No sleep and a seven-hour time difference between Paris and Indian Lake are not your friends, Grace.* She peered into the mirror. Nope. Not by a long shot.

"Next stop—Indian Lake. Indian Lake!" the conductor announced as he trundled down the crowded aisle.

Grace inhaled—for courage or stamina, she didn't know. *Almost there.*

"Indian Lake!" the conductor shouted again as he passed Grace's seat.

Grace reached out to touch his sleeve. "Excuse me, would it be possible to get some help with my bags when we stop? I've been traveling for nearly fourteen hours and—"

"Not my job," he barked back and started to move away.

Grace gripped his sleeve. "Sir. I'm most happy to pay for the service and I—"

"We don't take tips." He peered at her, taking in her clothing. "You're not from around here."

"I just flew in from Paris."

"Let me guess. You're the one with the huge bags blocking the exit?" He glared at her.

Grace wasn't about to be shut down. "I only need help off the train."

He continued to glower at her. Hard.

"Thirty dollars?"

"I'll meet you by the door." He looked down at her high-heeled boots. "Think you can manage the steps in those things?"

"I'll be fine," she assured him with a bright smile.

Grace wasn't sure if the man was angling for more money or if he was criticizing her apparel. Either way, she'd gotten what she wanted out of the bargain. Her bags were overloaded and overweight—and for good reason. She would be staying in Indian Lake for over a month, helping her Aunt Louise at The Louise House ice-cream shop while she recovered from back surgery.

Aunt Louise's request was one that Grace wouldn't have dreamed of declining. Louise was the only family Grace had left. Grace's father, Jim Railton, had died when she was very young and her mother, Amanda, had died the day after Grace's high-school graduation.

However, Aunt Louise was always a prominent part of Grace's life and all of Grace's happy childhood memories featured Aunt Louise's quirky presence.

Louise had always treated Grace as the daughter she never had, and because Grace had dreamed of a career in fashion design, Louise had insisted that only Parsons, one of the best design schools in the country, was good enough for her talented niece. Grace had already saved nearly half the tuition from her Junior Miss Illinois and Miss Teen Illinois pageant winnings. Since Grace had grown up in fashionable, urban Chicago, the competition for the crown was stiff, but her determination and talents had bloomed early. Louise had generously offered to cover the rest. Once she graduated, Grace had diligently sent Louise a check every month, though she'd never asked to be repaid. Grace was no longer in financial debt to her aunt, but she wasn't sure she could ever repay the kindness and support

Louise had given her over the years. Helping her at the ice-cream shop was merely a drop in the bucket.

The train rumbled past a riot of autumn-bronzed trees and rolling farmland, golden now with harvested corn shocks and soybeans. The land was serene and lush with abundance, and Grace realized she'd never quite felt the same about any other place. Not even the South of France, with its vineyards, cobblestone streets and outdoor cafés, held the allure for her that Indian Lake did.

Odd, it's taken so long for me to return here.

The last time she'd been in Indian Lake she'd been two months shy of her sixteenth birthday. Her mother had still been alive. Grace had been the first runner-up in the Miss Teen Illinois contest. After winning the crown for Junior Miss Illinois in prior years, Grace was blindsided by her near miss. She'd been certain she would win. Her piano performance was impeccable. The gowns she'd designed and that her mother had helped her make were perfection. She'd delivered answers to the judges' questions with insight and flawless diction. She should have won. But she hadn't.

That summer was a turning point in her life. After that summer, Grace had altered her goal of becoming a model and directed her ambition toward fashion design. It had been a summer for growing up. That much was certain.

Grace ran her palm over the lapels of her jacket, making certain they lay flat.

Nervous habit, she groused to herself and dropped her hands. She'd worked hard on the design she was wearing. Her fingers traveled over the wool fabric she'd snagged at a bargain price from Johnstons of Elgin. The cashmere was from Nepal, but Grace believed the Scots knew how to weave it best. As comforting as her black jacket and slim skirt were, she was anxious.

She leaned her head against the hard seat and exhaled. She had to calm down.

"You coming back home?" the man across from her asked.

Grace had been so deep in thought, she'd barely noticed anyone else on the train at all.

"Yes. No. Yes," she replied, looking at him. *Attractive* was an understatement. He was tall and trim in his well-tailored black business suit, white cotton shirt and conservative tie. The clothes were not expensive, off the rack. He had a good eye for putting himself together and watching his budget. She liked that.

His blue eyes danced and a wave of thick chestnut hair fell over his forehead.

"Can't decide, huh? Think you'll get off when we stop?" He smiled broadly.

He was observant. She had to give him that.

Grace couldn't hold back her own smile. She was used to men striking up conversations with her in cafés. Trains. Airplanes. She'd worn a rhinestone crown since she was ten, and didn't give it up until she was fifteen. Sometimes she thought men could still see the glimmer, even though the glamour and floodlights had faded for her long ago.

He leaned forward. Just a bit. Not so much that the gesture cut through her personal space. "Dylan Hawks." He extended his hand and she took it.

"Hawks? I know that name. Are you related to Isabelle Hawks?" she asked.

"My sister," he said, lifting his chin proudly. "She's why I'm home for the weekend. Her bridal shower."

"How nice." Grace swallowed hard. She limited thoughts of brides to design projects, never imagining herself in that role. "I'm Grace Railton, by the way."

"Pleasure." He smiled and then continued.

"It's a big couples' thing at our friend's house. Mrs. Beabots."

Grace's spirits lightened. "I know her very well. She was practically my mentor."

"Mentor?"

"It's a long story," Grace replied. After high school, Grace had left for New York and entered Parsons School of Design. While her friends went to parties, she drew, created and studied. When they went to Florida for Spring Break, she wrangled appointments with fashion house assistants and design team members. Over large lattes—which she bought for them—Grace picked their brains and soaked up information. In the summers, she took part-time internships on Seventh Avenue. She hadn't cared how menial the job; she'd only wanted to learn. Like striving for one of her pageant crowns, she had to be the best.

She'd graduated at the top of her class and landed a summer internship at Tom Ford. Grace knew that the very best designers worked in Paris, and she'd believed that until she had a chance to prove her talent in the biggest and toughest arena in the world, she'd never be happy.

Aunt Louise had told Grace of Mrs. Beabots's former life in Paris, where she had "done something" at Chanel, though no one in town was certain what, since Mrs. Beabots was as tight-lipped, as Louise put it, as the seal on a coffin. Grace had gotten to know Mrs. Beabots during her visits to Indian Lake in high school. Grace had taken an instant liking to the older woman and they shared an admiration for beautifully made clothes. Mrs. Beabots had eventually suggested Grace sketch the dresses she envisioned and send them to her. Grace did precisely that. Throughout high school and college, Grace had corresponded with Mrs. Beabots, sending drawings and photos of her designs. Grace had pleaded with her her aunt to enlist Mrs. Beabots's help in making connections in Paris, and by that autumn after her college graduation, Grace was on a plane headed to Paris as an assistant to an assistant at Jean Paul Gaultier. Grace's penchant for perfectionism had gotten her noticed within weeks and she had been challenging herself ever since. Now she was an independent designer with her own team, hoping they would be "brought on" to a top couture house. Under an iconic umbrella, they would have respect, clout and the freedom to create their own line of clothing and accessories, with Grace's name and logo stamped on every ensemble. They would have security and respect. Fortunately, up to this point, her designs had sold enough to keep them all afloat. Barely.

No question about it. If not for Mrs. Beabots, Grace would not be anywhere near where she was now.

"So are you here for the party as well? Odd we haven't met. I would remember you..." Despite racing through his questions, Dylan spoke with a dash of charm that was so light most would miss it. Grace did not.

"What a nice thing to say. Thank you. But no, I'm not invited to the party, though I knew Isabelle years ago." She paused, her mind floating back to that summer, when all of Sarah Jensen's friends hung out together. Barbecues. Slumber parties. Pool parties... Grace wrenched her thoughts back to the present. "Actually, I'm helping my Aunt Louise. Perhaps you know her. Louise Railton?"

He snapped his fingers. "The Louise House! An Indian Lake institution."

Grace flashed him a grin. "I'll tell her you said so."

The train slowed as it neared the town. Blazing maple, oak and walnut trees hugged the crystal blue lake like bejeweled arms. White clouds scudded across the sky, the sun dazzling Grace's eyes.

The train jerked to a stop.

"Indian Lake! Indian Lake!"

Adrenaline raced through Grace's body as she shot to her feet. "We're here!"

"So we are," Dylan replied, putting his iPad in his briefcase. "It was nice meeting you, Grace."

"I'm sure I'll see you around town," she said as she gathered her oversize black fringed purse and two large totes, one of which held her laptop, iPad and sketchbook.

"I'm not here all that often. I live in Lincoln Park and work in downtown Chicago. Prosecuting attorney. In case you wanted to know."

A blush colored Grace's face. "I apologize for my manners. My head's been in another world…"

"I could tell." His mouth quirked in an impish grin.

Dylan slipped out of his seat and walked away.

Way to go, Grace. Nice guy and you blow him off. When are you going to get a life? A real one? She slung her purse and one of the totes over her shoulder, then bumped her way down the aisle toward the exit.

Carefully, Grace negotiated the narrow metal steps down to the pavement. For the first time on her trip, she questioned the importance of her fashionable, but apparently impractical, boots.

The conductor waited until she disembarked before unloading her overweight bags. One by one, he slammed them against the concrete and then sneered at her. "What've you got in there? Rocks?"

"Vitamins." She reached into her jacket pocket and withdrew the cash she'd agreed to pay him.

He touched his hand to the bill of his cap and hopped back up on the train. Grace yanked the long luggage handles out to their full length, hoisted one of the totes higher up on her shoulder and began pulling her load. She felt like a pack mule.

"Grace!" a woman's voice called.

"Grace! You're here!" a younger female voice shouted.

Raising her head, Grace saw Aunt Louise coming toward her, bent over a walker. With her was a blonde woman whose sparkling green eyes she'd know anywhere. Grace stood upright and let go of the suitcase handles. "Aunt Louise! And…Maddie? Maddie Strong?"

"Barzonni now." Maddie beamed.

"Grace! Thank heaven!" Louise's smile was nearly as bright as the sun. Tears streamed down her cheeks. "Grace." She held out her arms.

Grace couldn't remember a more wonderful sight. For an instant, she regretted every minute she'd spent apart from her Aunt Louise. Her life in Paris seemed to melt away and all she felt was a rush of affection for her aunt, and nostalgia for this town and the summer long ago with the barbecues, the swimming pool…and Mica.

"I'VE MADE A lot of changes since you were here, Grace," Louise said as Grace helped her into the shop.

Grace flipped the cardboard door sign to Open, then stood in the entrance, her eyes stinging with tears. "It's just an old sign," she whispered, tracing the crumpled edges of the sign she'd turned over years ago when it had been her job to help Aunt Louise open up and close. Just a sign. A battered, old, faded sign. And suddenly, it meant the world to her because it was part of her life with Aunt Louise.

"Grace?" Louise said.

"Sorry." Grace sniffed. "I was making sure the lock was open." She wiped away her tear.

"Sarah and the kids will be here anytime now. It's Annie's birthday, so they'll want some of my newest creations."

Louise moved her walker over to the chair she'd pulled up to the counter, where the old cash register still sat. It was a monster antique with tabs that would make a muscle-builder's biceps flex, yet her aunt had refused to give up the old thing.

"I see you're not computerized yet." Grace chuckled.

Louise swatted the air with her palm and slapped her thigh as she eased into the chair. "Good heavens, of course I am. In the office. But out here, everyone likes reminders of a bygone era. They come here for this old register. That and the pumpkin-spice and gingerbread-nut ice cream I make every autumn."

Grace's heels clacked against the century-old walnut floorboards. She took off her jacket and hung it on a peg next to the wide window with the gold lettering announcing the seasonal offerings.

"I hate to have to thrust you right into work, Grace," Louise said. "But it couldn't be helped. Sarah and the kids…"

"Please, don't apologize, Aunt Louise. I'll be fine." She shoved the sleeves of her black sweater to her elbows, revealing at least nine bracelets on each arm. She went to the sink and washed her hands. Under the counter glass was a group of photographs of the sundaes. "Let me study these for a sec."

"It's the Monster Mash they love. I serve it in those big round dishes. Six scoops of ice cream slathered in hot fudge with whipped cream piled eight inches high. It feeds four."

"Thank goodness!" Grace laughed as the front door opened and nearly a dozen children rushed in. Maddie held the door as Sarah Jensen Bosworth walked in behind them. The kids raced to their favorite tables and picked up the menus, challenging each other as to who could eat the most ice cream.

Grace hugged Sarah and as much as she wanted to catch up, the kids were shouting out their orders and Maddie said she had to rush to get Louise to her rehab appointment.

"I'd better get to work," Grace said.

"You haven't had a chance to take a breath," Maddie said. "Not even change or freshen up." Maddie's eyes traveled from Grace's seven strings of pearls, crystals and gold ropes around the banded neckline of the black knit sweater, to her houndstooth wool pencil skirt and fringed black boots. "I wish I knew how to put something together like that."

"Thanks," Grace replied, basking in the twinkle of appreciation. "That means a lot to me. A lot."

Maddie hugged her, then tilted her head toward Annie and Timmy Bosworth and Danny Sullivan, who were waving huge spoons up in the air. "They look like they're about to revolt."

"I'm on it." Grace smiled and went straight to work scooping six kinds of ice cream into Monster Mash dishes.

After serving up over half a dozen massive concoctions, her hands sticky and nearly frozen, she lost track of time. She was halfway into the refrigerated bin, trying to dig out the last of the pumpkin-spice ice cream when she felt the counter reverberate.

"Where's Louise?" a raw, deep male voice asked.

"She's at the doctor." Grace lifted her head and looked into the Mediterranean-blue eyes she'd never forgotten. *Mica.* Her heart stopped. She was staring, but she couldn't help it. "Rehab. Her back..."

"I heard," he said sharply. He peered at her, taking inventory. "You're new here."

He didn't recognize her. She should have

figured that one. Why would he remember her? She had changed a lot in twelve years. A whole lot.

With the force of a tsunami, the memory of the pool party at the Barzonni villa hit her. The "gang" had all been there…Sarah Jensen, Maddie Strong and all the Barzonni brothers—football star Gabe, horse-lover Rafe and Nate, who only had eyes for Maddie.

And then there was Mica. The most handsome of all the blue-eyed, black-haired, sun-bronzed boys.

Mica had exuded the kind of perfection Grace had been trying her whole life to achieve. He was strong, quiet and arrestingly handsome.

And after a game of swimming-pool volleyball, Mica had kissed her. She remembered the chlorine smell mixed with suntan lotion, the warmth of his lips on hers. It was a quick kiss. One without passion or longing, and yet, to this day, she'd never forgotten it.

Nor had she forgotten his disdain of her pageant life and his dismissal of her interest in fashion. He hadn't been cruel, but he'd made it clear he thought her pursuits were worthless.

She hadn't known how to stand up to him back then. He was three years older and as much as she had wanted to rebuke him, she'd felt there was truth to his arguments. He and his brothers worked from dawn to dusk on the farm. There was always back-breaking work to do and they did it gladly. Mica considered it a privilege to be a part of his father's legacy.

At Parsons and later in Paris, Grace had learned that Mica was right about one thing: determination and perseverance were everything.

Mica Barzonni had changed her life back then, though he didn't know that. Several times over the years, she'd thought about writing to thank him. But now she saw how truly inconsequential she'd been in his life. Obviously, he didn't remember her in the least. He was a Barzonni, after all. He already had everything.

Even now, her heart hammered in her chest. Suddenly she was that teenage girl again, crushing on the boy in the pool. She hadn't been in love; she'd been too young for love, hadn't she? Mica had given her no indication that she was anything to him other than a pest. Except for that one kiss. She was only a girl he'd met one summer…a long time ago.

She stared back at him. He wore dusty jeans, a faded plaid shirt, an old wool vest that she would have trashed and scuffed boots with dirt clods clinging to the heels. There was an oil smudge on his forehead. He looked like he'd walked right out of the fields. His hand rested on the counter, where he'd dumped a big canvas sack.

"What's that?" she asked.

"Pie pumpkins for Louise. My mother said she called and needed them ASAP."

"She didn't tell me." Grace added a final scoop to the sundae she'd been working on, but the dish was overloaded and another scoop fell out. She shoveled it back in and patted it down.

"You need some help there?" He smirked.

Grace stared at him. "I'm fine." She plunged the dipper into the hot fudge and drizzled it over the ice cream. Glancing at the photo of the Monster Mash, she took a can of whipped cream from the under-the-counter refrigerator and pulled off the cap.

"You're supposed to shake it up first," Mica said.

"I know what I'm doing," she snapped. Grace pressed the top and sprayed whipped cream all over the ice cream, the counter and onto Mica's plaid shirt.

He groaned. "Yeah, right."

"Sorry," Grace said sheepishly, handing him a dish towel.

"You should've shaken the can," he growled. "I would have thought Louise would hire someone with skills."

Under Mica's judgmental gaze, Grace felt as if she was fifteen again. Back when she'd just lost the crown and had felt terribly insecure. She'd given her heart away to Mica and he hadn't known the first thing about her feelings. She'd kept silent. Well, not this time.

"If I want your advice, I'll ask for it. Now, excuse me, please. I have to deliver this." Grace carried her vastly imperfect Monster Mash to a table of four boys, who looked askance at the sundae. "I did my best," she whispered to the kids. She handed them four spoons. "It'll taste better than it looks."

"Yeah," Timmy said and gave her a thumbs-up. The kids dug in with audible glee.

When Grace turned around she noticed that Mica was now leaning against the counter, his hand on his hip as he watched every move she made. No beauty contest judge had ever scrutinized her so intently. She felt as if she still had whipped cream on her face or mascara smudges under her eyes. She should have checked her makeup before the kids arrived, but there hadn't been time. Self-consciously, she touched her earrings. No. They were still in place.

All she could do was retaliate in kind. She let her gaze fall to his boots. She lifted the edge of her lips in a lopsided effort at a sneer. "You make deliveries here often?"

"I do now."

"Then the next time you come, wipe your boots before you enter the shop. Saves me from scrubbing the floor."

He straightened. "I remember you."

"Oh, really?" Grace went behind the counter and took out another dish.

"You're Louise's niece. I didn't recognize you without the rhinestone crown."

Grace gripped the sundae dish to prevent herself from bouncing it off his thick skull. "And you're Mica Barzonni."

"Yeah. Well, tell Louise she can mail the check…for the pumpkins."

"I will."

He started to head for the door.

"Oh, Mica. Why don't you stop off at the grocery store. Pick up some soap on your way out of town. Looks like you've run out." She tapped her forehead.

He reached up to his forehead, rubbed it,

then studied his greasy fingertips. He glared back at her.

Grace ground her jaw, picked up the ice-cream scoop and pitched it from hand to hand defiantly. *One word. Try me, and I'll really let you have it.*

He spun on his heel and stomped out of the shop, leaving a clod of mud and grass on the floor.

"Ooooh!" Grace fumed, wishing she felt some relief from having had the last word.

Sarah rushed to her side. "Was that Mica? I wanted to say hi."

"It was." Every smug, judgmental inch of him.

"You're sure?"

"Yeah." Grace frowned. "You look surprised. Why?"

"Mica doesn't come to town much. Especially since the accident."

"What accident?"

Sarah paused. "You didn't know?"

"Know what?"

"He was in an accident a few months ago that nearly killed him. He was working on his mother's car and it dropped on him. He's lost the use of his left arm. He keeps his hand in his jeans pocket so people don't notice. If he seemed—"

"Arrogant as all get out?" Grace interrupted.

Sarah smiled. "Well, yeah. He's always had that about him."

"I would have thought he'd have grown up by now. Learned some manners. Do you remember when he used to call me silly because I was upset about losing Miss Teen Illinois? He didn't get it. Those pageants were important to me and a huge part of my life back then. I thought I wanted to be a model, but then I realized my real talent was in fashion design. I was heartbroken that I didn't win for a lot of reasons. That win would have given me a substantial scholarship to college. My mother didn't have much money but my winnings all went in a back account for my education."

"Did you ever tell him this?" Sarah countered.

"No…" Grace's shoulders slumped. "I guess I was pretty harsh earlier. Aunt Louise owes him money for the pumpkins. I think I'll deliver it in person."

AFTER LOUISE RETURNED from rehab, Grace got a signed check from her and asked to borrow her car. Then she drove south to the Barzonni farm. It was one route she didn't need a GPS to follow.

She rang the bell when she got to the house, but no one answered. She rang it four more times, but there was still no answer.

Remembering that the family often used the kitchen door, she walked around to the back and knocked. Still no answer. She looked down at the check Louise had written.

It was a flimsy excuse for her to be here, but Grace was ashamed of her remarks about Mica's dirty boots and the grease on his face, and she wanted to apologize. She didn't know why he rattled her cage the way he did, but he did.

She banged on the door. "Hello? Anybody home?"

"What do you want?" Mica asked, startling her as he came out of the apartment over the garage. He stood on the balcony, his right hand on the railing as he glared at her.

"I, uh, brought the check we owe you."

"You could have mailed it," he said, starting down the steps.

He came toward her, and Grace was certain that no male model, no Hollywood star, no European prince, was as drop-dead handsome as Mica Barzonni. His blue eyes seemed to be taking inventory of her every eyelash.

I didn't even check my makeup before I left Louise's! This jet lag is going to be the end of me.

"Here," she said, thrusting the check at him as if it would singe her fingertips.

"Thanks."

"Mica…" She cleared her throat. "I came out here because I owe you an apology."

He stared at her, his expression unreadable. "No, you didn't."

"What?"

"You came out here because you found out about my acci— My arm. Who told you?"

"Sarah."

"Good old Sarah. Well, you would have found out sooner or later. Everybody knows."

"And they shouldn't? Is it a secret?"

"I guess not. Still…"

"Still…what?"

"I'd rather not talk about it."

"Why?"

"Because, little miss preteen, then I see the pity in their eyes like I see in yours. You feel sorry for me." He shot the words at her with acidic bite.

Is he serious? "Actually, I don't feel that way at all. In fact, Mica, I think you're just as self-centered and arrogant as you were when we were kids."

"I was never those things."

"Fine. You are now." She jammed her hands on her hips. "And another thing. My life has never been silly. Okay? I worked hard for everything I've accomplished."

He took another step toward her, his face dangerously close to hers. "I seriously doubt that. You haven't got the first clue what it is to work hard. This farm, this land and all it demands, is hard work. I suppose you still tromp around in a pink dress and smile and wink for some judges and you think that's work? Get real."

"That was a long time ago. And there was more to it than that."

"You know what? I don't have time for this. You live in your world. I'll live in mine. Got that?"

"Got it," she roared back.

"I think we're done here. I'll give my mother your check. She'll be thrilled. Probably fly to Tahiti with all this money."

"You're a jerk, Mica Barzonni."

The anger in his eyes died instantly, as if she'd doused the fire. His face softened and she felt he was seeing her for the first time. His eyes were imploring, seeking. "I'm sorry," he said finally. "That was rude of me."

Surprised at his apology, she stared at him for a long moment. She'd had her shields up and had been ready to wield a sword against him if need be. She held her breath, waiting for the next attack.

"I'm sorry, Grace," he murmured. "I like your Aunt Louise a lot. She's a nice lady. And I don't know anything about you or what you've done with your life. Forgive me?"

"I do," she replied softly, sensing his disappointment in himself.

He moved a step closer. "I don't want to fight with you. Or anyone." He touched his left arm. "It embarrasses me that I'm not... well, who I was."

"Don't say that. You're Mica and that's a good thing. At least I always thought so."

He massaged his arm, then let his right hand drop.

"It had to be painful. Sarah said the car dropped on you."

"Funny. A lot of it I don't remember. But every hour of every day, I'm left with this reminder of my carelessness. It was so stupid," he said angrily.

She reached for his hand, but didn't touch him. He jerked away from her.

"See why I don't like going into the details?"

"It's upsetting."

"More than you can imagine," he replied.

"Then let's talk about something else," she said, smiling at him.

"Like what?"

"We have a lot of years to catch up on. I don't know what happened to you. I mean, not about your accident. I remember you talking about engines and machines and the things you wanted to invent. Did you end up going to Purdue?"

"You remember all that?"

"I remember everything about you." Her words came out as a whisper.

"I got my engineering degree," he said, leaning closer.

"Mica, that's wonderful. I'm proud of you."

"Really?"

"Of course. I always wanted the best for you. I knew you'd succeed. You were so determined and focused as a teen."

Confusion wrinkled his brow. "You thought that?"

"I did." She couldn't stop herself from smiling. "You see, I was paying attention."

"I'm…I'm surprised." He raked back a lock of hair. "*You* surprise me."

"That's a good thing, huh?" She felt a warm glow in her chest.

"Yeah," he said, though he still didn't smile. He glanced back toward the kitchen door. "Hey, I was just about to raid the fridge for dinner. Everybody went out to Gabe's house—"

"And you didn't go?" she interrupted.

"No, I don't usually…"

"Why not?"

He placed his right hand on his left arm without looking at it. His eyes were focused on her. Grace liked the attention Mica gave her. A lot.

"I wasn't up to it." A dark shadow clouded his sky blue eyes.

Understanding cracked like a bolt of lightning across Grace's mind. "Mica…are you asking me to dinner?"

He blinked as if he remembered where he was. Who he was with. "Yes. Yes, I am."

"Great." She beamed. "I'm starving. I spent the afternoon surrounded by sugar and ice cream and didn't steal a bite for myself."

He took two steps back. "This way."

Inside the kitchen, he went straight to the large refrigerator and began withdrawing plastic covered bowls. "Manicotti. Salad. Mixed fruit. Ooh, and Mom's herbed Italian bread."

He spooned pasta onto two plates and put the first one into the microwave.

Once the food was heated, they sat at the kitchen table.

The garlic and basil aroma made Grace's mouth water. She finished her pasta long before Mica. She looked up. He held his fork midmotion as if he'd forgotten to take a bite in the process of watching her.

"What?" she asked.

"You give hungry a new meaning." He still didn't smile, and only gave her that enigmatic, distant look that she'd always assumed to be arrogance.

She grinned, hoping to crack the wall of ice he kept around him. "I'd like to blame the jet lag, but the truth is…I eat like this too often. Definitely not healthy."

"Why?"

"Because I work for six, maybe eight hours nonstop. I'm so immersed in my designs that I forget to eat. Or sleep."

"It's that way for you, too?"

She lowered her fork and wiped her mouth. She kept her eyes on his. "Uh-huh."

"I thought it was just me. I thought it was depression from the accident."

"Tell me how it's been, Mica."

She'd barely uttered the words and he started talking without taking a breath.

"It's not the accident—the pain or even this bothersome rehab that's so hard. It's like every aspect of my life is withering away. One day I was the hero on the farm, able to fix every piece of equipment. I have more tools in the mechanical shed than they have at Home Depot. Whatever Rafe could do, I could do as well and faster. Once Gabe left, Mom was sure we'd have to cut back on production. But we didn't. We simply went on." He snapped his fingers. "Like that. Everything changed. Rafe and Mom want to replace me—"

"You can't mean that."

"They do."

"But you're Mica. You're..."

"As insignificant as humanly possible," he interjected, lowering his gaze.

Grace pushed her chair back and rose slowly. She placed her hands on either side of his face. "Look at me."

"Grace, you don't have to say anything. I... thank you for listening."

"Shut up."

She kissed him. It was more electric than she'd planned. She didn't pity Mica. She didn't think he was looking for a savior. She just wanted to know if what she was feeling right now was more than the vestiges of a teenage crush.

And it was.

If she were smart she'd leave. Walk away from him the way she had all those years ago. Except apparently she'd kept her emotions hidden back then. Even from herself.

She had to face it. She'd always been a fool for Mica.

And she didn't care about anything except making this moment last.

When she pulled back, Mica gazed into her eyes and gave her a soft smile. "Grace."

He stood and put his arm around her. She kissed him again, not daring to let him take the lead, afraid he might let his melancholy overcome him.

Though she could sense his strength, she also felt his lost sense of purpose. He was floundering, searching, and she wanted to be the rock in the rushing stream that he held on to.

I'm still in love with him.

He broke the kiss and rested his forehead

against hers. "You take my breath away," he whispered.

"I could say that about you."

"You mean that?"

"I wouldn't say it if I didn't."

"Grace, I think we have a lot of catching up to do. It could take...well, a long time."

"Mica..."

He pulled her hand to his lips.

"I'm only here for a month. Just to help Aunt Louise."

"Then what?"

"I'll go back to Paris." He moved closer and she could feel his breath on her cheek. His eyes were unwavering, pinning her, and in that moment she felt the power that was Mica Barzonni. His right arm slipped around her waist and he drew her to him.

"I have to go back..."

"We'll see about that."

His lips on hers were nirvana. She was whisked away from the earth. Her heartbeat pounded in her chest and thrummed at her temples. The only sound she heard was Mica's intake of breath and the deep resonating strains of her name coming from his throat. He kissed her as if he would never kiss her again. She nearly believed he was in love with her. For years she'd daydreamed that one day Mica would love her. This excruciatingly lovely kiss was perfect. It was everything she'd dreamed of and more.

He deepened the kiss and breathed her name again. "Grace."

"Don't talk. Just kiss me."

Her skin tingled as their bodies melded into each other.

Through her hand on his nape, she felt strength surging through his spine and the taut muscles in his shoulders. She sank her fingers into his thick hair and held him. She wanted him to know that she didn't want him to stop. She didn't want this dream to fade.

At this moment, Grace believed that even she might find a happily-ever-after. That for her, the fairy tale was coming true.

CHAPTER ONE

Present day

MICA HEARD IT from his sister-in-law, Maddie, who heard it from Mrs. Beabots, who got it straight from Louise Railton.

Grace Railton was back in town.

He didn't know which emotion to pick first. Anger came to mind right off the bat, but it was quickly replaced with disappointment, hurt and curiosity.

"What's she doing here?" Grace had made it pretty clear when she left town last year that Paris was the only universe she'd inhabit on a long-term basis. Indian Lake was too small for Grace, the beauty-pageant queen.

Mica stared at the tractor engine he was fixing, then tossed the wrench onto the tool bench with enough force to make the screwdriver beside it jump. *Grace.*

For over a year, he'd gone over every detail of his relationship with Grace, if he could even call it that. No matter how many times he re-hashed the events of that whirlwind October, he came up with only one assessment: they were as mismatched as a tuxedo and a pair of cowboy boots.

If he was honest with himself, he'd known that since they were teenagers.

Grace and her mother had been obsessed with beauty pageants. Crowns and dresses—that was all she'd talked about back then. Unless she was criticizing everything he wore.

He hadn't liked the way he reacted to Grace. She'd had some kind of lightning rod stuck to her spine that just made him want to strike. She'd needled him in a way he didn't understand, always picking at what was wrong with him. Asking why he didn't want more for himself than his life on the farm. Meanwhile, she'd talked about New York and Paris like they were Mecca, or the pot of gold at the end of a rainbow. She'd made perfectly clear her opinions about Indian Lake and the people who chose to make it their home.

Which made it even harder to understand the intense month they'd spent together a year ago October. It had been like a switch had been flipped. She was focused on her career and when she talked about her designs, her eyes lit up like fireworks. There were times he thought he could listen to her and never tire of her enthusiasm. She was the kind of person who would always be vibrant. But Mica doubted if he'd ever know whether she had truly wanted him or had simply pitied him.

He traced the gouged edges of the old pair of pliers his father had used to repair their tractors, generators and trucks. Angelo had built this farm with his hands. Hands that never stopped working, and Angelo had taught all his sons to do the same.

Yet now, Mica only had one hand. He was never going to be the kind of empire builder his father had been. He had to find a new path. Since college graduation, he'd abandoned his engineering goals in order to help on the farm. Now the farm didn't need him or want him. He had to find a way to translate his dreams from the drafting table and his computer into a working piece of machinery for people with disabilities.

Mica slumped against the workbench and looked across at the machinery shed, where he spent a great deal of his time lately. Tinkering. That was all he'd done in the past year or so. All he'd done since Grace left town.

Grace... He ran his hand through his hair.

She'd emailed him once after she landed in Paris, telling him that her design team was further behind than she'd thought. They needed her. She'd be working 24/7 to pull off their spring line. He'd told her he understood. But he hadn't. Week after week, he'd sent emails and left messages, but she never responded.

He ground his teeth. Her silence was like a brick wall falling on him. She wanted nothing to do with him. Maybe she hadn't changed as much as he'd thought she might have during the month they spent together.

Her departure—and rejection—still bothered him, but Mica had had more important things to focus on in the past year. With a lot of rehab—and trial and error—he'd learned his way around his new life with only one working arm. He'd had to figure out how to dress with one hand, and even change the way he did chores around the kitchen. Every sandwich bag had to have a slider so he could put the bag on the counter and slide the top closed. No more jars. Pop tops for everything. Pots and pans were simple. He used one at a time. He chopped vegetables in a food processor or used a mandolin to slice them over a bowl. The majority of the time, his mother made plenty of food for him to warm in his microwave.

He couldn't drive the tractor or change the baler. He was of no help to Rafe, so his brother had been forced to take on another hourly worker. When their father had died, Mica and Rafe had agreed to hire extra help. Now they needed even more.

The only work Mica had now was running errands for his mother.

The reality stung every day of his life, shutting out joy and any hope for happiness.

He ran his hand down his numb and limp left arm.

He wondered if he'd ever get used to the fact that his arm would never work again.

It had been a freakish accident that should never have happened, but it had.

Gina—his mother—had wanted to take her BMW to the shop, but Mica had been bored. He loved tinkering with the farm equipment, old cars, anything with a motor. He felt at one with engines, cogs, pistons and gears. Often, when there was nothing left to do in the shop, he would stay up late messing around with mechanical designs on his computer.

Mica had graduated from Purdue University in mechanical engineering, but for years, he hadn't done much with his degree. He'd been needed on the farm. Farming was in his blood. He adored the land that grew acres of food every year. It was miraculous to him that after a killing winter blizzard, spring always came fresh and green and full of promise.

At least it had until the accident.

Spring meant planting season and every piece of equipment had to be tuned up and ready to run smoothly.

"It's not even New Year's and I'm feeling pressure already," he growled.

He pushed himself away from the work-bench and went over to the pickup he'd recently given an oil change. He closed the hood, then hit the automatic garage-door opener. He got in the truck and started the engine. He'd attached a spinner knob, used by many with physical disabilities, to the steering wheel to give him more leverage when handling the pickup. He'd bought it the day he'd gone to the DMV to have a Restriction C placed on his driver's license, though he'd forgone the handicapped parking tag he'd been offered. Yes, he'd lost his arm, but he could still walk just fine, and for that, he was grateful.

Driving a tractor was entirely different from a pickup truck, in that it required strength and both hands. Driving over rugged farmland was complex, dodging dips, mud holes, bumps and gullies. It was difficult for him to handle the tractor, though he'd built the muscles in his right arm considerably over the past year to compensate for the loss of his left.

Often he toyed with the idea of voice-activated farm machinery. He could work the land as he had done before the accident if he could speak commands to the old Allis-Chalmers tractor.

Mica backed the truck out of the shed, pausing to look out over the snow-covered farm. *New Year's.* Of course. Grace was here to be with her aunt Louise for the holiday. That made sense.

Sometimes, he was a little slow to see the obvious. Just because Grace had left him without any follow-up or follow-through was no reason to mistrust her. She'd told him that her world was Paris, fashion and her career. She'd never deviated from that. She'd been honest. He had to give her that.

Mica spotted Rafe in the flat soybean field, riding the sputtering and hitching old John Deere tractor toward the big barn. He wore a leather-and-sheepskin bomber jacket, a cowboy hat and a wide blue wool scarf around his neck. The brothers waved at each other.

Before the accident, Mica had wanted to

purchase a new all-terrain truck for the farm to replace the John Deere. But now that Mica had been injured, he was glad they hadn't spent the $300,000 on new equipment. The family had struggled through the past year, with Mica unable to pitch in. No one had wanted to hurt his feelings, and he appreciated that, but now it was nearly the new year and Rafe was talking about restructuring—and hiring new employees.

As he drove toward their Italian stucco villa, Mica realized he didn't like change. He was still grieving his father's death nearly three years earlier and he wasn't quite used to the idea that Rafe was married. He and his wife, Olivia, had built their own house on the property. Olivia was a nice enough woman, Mica supposed. She and her mother owned the Indian Lake Deli and Olivia was a good cook, as good a pastry chef as his other sister-in-law, Maddie, and she was a talented photographer.

There actually wasn't anything wrong with Olivia or Maddie, Nate's wife, or Liz, who was married to his brother Gabe. Mica had just never been much of a people person.

Mica had always preferred his own company. Rafe had been closest to their father and that had been fine with Mica. Nate and Gabe were very close to their mother. And that was fine as well.

Mica was the loner. Even in high school, Mica had never participated in team sports. He preferred swimming...alone. Running... alone. Working...alone.

Maybe deep down he'd always been the brooding type, and the accident had simply sharpened that trait.

He pulled up to the house and parked the truck. Without thinking, he went to reach for the door handle with his left hand. Natural reflex. But nothing happened.

He smashed the truck's door with his right hand, as if he could open it with sheer force. He kept banging until he hurt his thumb. "Stupid! Stupid! Stupid!"

How could he not have checked the jack when he raised the chassis of his mother's BMW? Sure, it was the old jack his father had used for decades, but it had never caused any issues before.

The jack slipped. He'd heard the metal rubbing against the grooves of the jack throat. As soon as he registered the sound, he'd started to roll out from under the car, but he hadn't been fast enough to spare his left arm and shoulder.

The chassis dropped on Mica. He'd tried to

yell, but the weight of the car had crushed the air out of his lungs. The pain had caused him to pass out.

He'd woken up when the paramedics were hoisting him onto a gurney. Rafe and his mother were there, leaning over the stretcher.

Rafe, coming in from the fields, had found him unconscious under the car.

The doctor's prognosis had been devastating.

Inoperable. Paralyzed. Those were the only words Mica had heard. The doctor had pushed rehabilitation to keep the arm from becoming fully atrophied. Mica had agreed with that, and for the first month, he'd actually believed he could will his arm to move again. He'd tried everything—even hypnosis—but nothing worked.

The second month, his depression had slid deeper into anger. He had begrudgingly and sarcastically continued with rehab, but he knew now that all the exercise in the world would never bring his arm back.

And then Grace had come into his life.

It was impossible not to think of kissing Grace and holding her each time her face flashed across his mind. That month she'd spent in Indian Lake had almost made him feel like himself again. She'd looked up at him with those intense blue eyes and he'd felt more alive and invigorated than he had since well before the accident, if he was honest.

Maybe it was a good thing she'd cut him off. He didn't know exactly where to put all his emotions for Grace.

Mica got out of the truck and hit the remote to lock the doors. He stared at it for a moment. *Why don't they make these to open the door from the inside?*

He tossed the remote up in the air and caught it. "Maybe I should do that."

He walked to the back door that led to the kitchen.

"Mom, I got the truck ready to go for you. The tractor is nearly fin—"

Mica stopped dead in his tracks.

His mother had her arms around Sam Crenshaw's neck and Sam was holding her close, closer than Mica had ever seen his father hold her. And then…she kissed him as if this was the last kiss of her life. Mica averted his eyes.

"Mom!" he shouted.

Slowly, Gina turned.

"Sam?" Mica spluttered. "Mind telling me what you're doing to my mother?" Sam was Liz's grandfather. He was some kind of in-law, but that didn't give him make-out privileges with Mica's mother.

"I was kissing her."

"I see that." Mica's gaze shot to his mother.

Gina blushed, but she didn't step out of Sam's embrace. Though she politely moved a few inches from his chest. She was smiling. Her face glowed, and…was that a tear falling down her cheek?

"Mom?"

"Sam has just asked me to marry him, and I accepted." She withdrew her left hand and twiddled her fingers at him. "Ring and all."

"You're not serious."

Gina's smile withered. In that instant, he realized he'd shot down her joy, killed it. But he didn't care. A year ago, his world had turned black. It was filled with shadows, fear, doubt and pain. Now his world had shifted again. Rafe wanted to replace Mica, and now their mother was replacing their father. He didn't like it.

His eyes tracked to Sam. "How long?"

"How long what?" Sam snapped, squaring his shoulders.

"How long have you been in love with her? Have you been planning this since my father was alive?"

"Mica!" Gina started toward him, but Sam took her arm and shook his head.

"You want the truth, Mica?" Sam asked.

"Yes, I do."

"I've loved her since before she married your father. We were young then. She'd made a promise to him back in Italy and she honored that promise for over thirty years. I never came near her until after he died. I'm an old man. I may not have many years left, but she's agreed to be with me for however long I stick around."

Mica felt as if he'd been shot through the chest. He'd said he wanted the truth, but this was too much. His mother hadn't loved his father? And all her life, she'd wanted someone else, but hadn't done anything about it? What kind of sacrifice was that?

Maybe he'd inherited his penchant for withdrawal from her. Had she brooded over Sam like he brooded over the loss of his old life?

Mica took a step backward.

Gina moved toward him. "Mica, don't be like this. Be happy for us."

Mica stopped. "Be happy for you? What is that, Mom? Happy? How can I be happy about you or him or anything ever again?" He looked down at his arm. "No. I can't be happy. Not for you or for myself."

He turned on his heel and stormed away, slamming the door behind him.

CHAPTER TWO

NEW YEAR'S WAS all about fresh starts. New goals. Rethinking life. At least that's what Grace told herself to justify flying across the Atlantic at the last minute over the holidays.

Yet, here she was, sitting in her Aunt Louise's car outside the Barzonni villa in the freezing cold. The afternoon sky was a slab of blue-gray pewter that was enough to depress the happiest of souls. It did nothing to bolster her courage.

She dropped her forehead to the steering wheel. "I'm out of my mind." She balled her fist on her thigh. She had to do this. Had to. Tears stung her eyes, but she pressed her fingertips to the corners. She couldn't let anyone see her crying. Especially not Mica.

She had to pull it together. She'd felt brave over the past year, but that didn't come close to how heartrendingly brave she was going to need to be once she came face-to-face with Mica.

He's going to hate me forever.

Oh, he'd wanted her on that golden October night over a year ago. Those days had been like a giddy ride on a Ferris wheel. She'd worked long hours for Aunt Louise at the ice-cream shop, while Louise went to rehab, saw her doctors and healed. She'd never known when she'd see Mica from one day to the next because they never actually made dates or scheduled dinners. He had simply showed up at closing time.

He had been battling anger and depression over his injury. She'd cut him a lot of slack, but still, his distance constantly warred with the magnetism between them.

Before the month she'd spent in Indian Lake, Grace had been attracted to Mica—intrigued by the memory of that day in the pool. Yet in the month they'd spent together, she'd grown to care about him. Deeply. She wasn't sure he'd understood just how deeply. He hadn't asked. Mica was a loner. "Aloof" didn't begin to describe his attitude at times. He needed solitude to heal his psyche. Grace knew instinctively when to be with him and when to give him space. Yet she cherished every glimpse of him. Every breath and word he spoke. For her, there hadn't been anything more important than simply spending an hour over a cup of coffee with Mica.

Looking back, the sharp blade of reality was that as much as she'd tried to show she cared about him, Mica had never said he cared about her. Never told her he loved her. Now that she thought about it, he'd never told her that he even liked her. All of which was a flimsy foundation for a relationship.

"Not that we even have one," she grumbled. Grace couldn't pin that one on Mica. She'd been the one to cut off communication.

She'd itched to send him an email, longed to hear his voice on the phone. But she'd had only one thing to say to him. And it was the one thing she couldn't—wouldn't—say.

I'm pregnant.

She had told herself over and over that he didn't love her and only wanted her as a fling. She lived in Paris. He lived in Indian Lake. They were universes apart in just about everything.

A clean break was best, she'd thought. Then she'd thrown herself into her spring line.

Part of her had wanted to tell him—had insisted it was the right thing. She remembered the times she'd stared at her phone, punched in his number, then lost courage before the first ring. Lost faith that he would ever want her. As the months passed and her pregnancy progressed, their time together had started to seem like some strange dream. It would never work in the long run. It was easier, for both of them, this way. Finally, she had come to a decision. She would have her baby and never tell Mica. She was capable and responsible and she could raise her child while fulfilling her ambitions for her career. She could do anything.

So she'd thought.

A door slammed, startling her. Grace looked up, but the villa was still. The sun was fading behind a shield of dense, snow-filled clouds. The timer on the white lights in the doorway garland and shrubs tripped. Thousands of tiny lights turned the villa's facade into a fairyland.

The sound must have come from somewhere else.

She drove around to the kitchen entrance, and there he was.

He was dressed in jeans, cowboy boots and a leather jacket over a cream-colored cable-knit sweater. His hair was a bit longer than the last time she'd seen him. The lights over the doorway had come on and glistened in his ink-dark hair.

He'd stopped halfway across the paved area between the kitchen and the stairway to his apartment above the garage.

He stared at the car disbelievingly.

She opened the door and got out. "Mica."

"Grace," he said with a sharp edge of irritation. "What are you doing here?"

Her heart slammed violently in her chest as she took a step back and opened the back door to the car. Her hands were shaking and she absolutely knew that all the blood had drained out of her body. She probably only had minutes to live. She had to do this quickly.

"I brought you something."

"You what?" He took a tentative step forward.

She leaned down and unhooked the seat belt that secured their son in his infant car seat, then lifted him into her arms.

She straightened and shut the door with her hip. Mica stared at her and then at the baby. "Hold out your arm, Mica. I've brought you your son."

Mica was speechless as she walked up to him. She shoved the baby to his chest.

"He's yours, and it's your turn to take care of him."

Mica's blue eyes blazed with mistrust and something akin to revulsion. "You've got to be kidding."

"Does he look like a joke?"

"No."

"Just hold him. He'll grow on you." She took a step back.

"Hold on." His surprise and mounting anger hit her like shotgun pellets. Sharp, painful and deep. She'd expected this. She'd thought she'd prepared herself for his reactions, but seeing him and remembering what it was like to be in his arms... She hated herself for being the bad guy. There wasn't a single thing she'd done since last October that merited his trust, love or respect.

She would have loved to run back to Aunt Louise's and cry all night—all week. Instead, she stood her ground and steeled herself for what was to come.

"I don't have a son," he said and started to hand the baby back to her.

"Yes, you do. This is Jules."

"Jules? What kind of name is that?"

"It's French. His middle name is Michael. After you."

Mica clenched his jaw as he looked down at the sleeping infant. "What's his last name?"

Grace swallowed hard. Incredibly, she hadn't thought about the name issue. "Railton."

He plopped the sleeping Jules into her arms

with enough force that Grace rocked back on her heels.

"So, if he's my son, why didn't you name him after me?" He drew in a long breath. "Don't answer that. I'll tell you why. I wasn't there. I couldn't sign papers. And I wasn't there because you didn't tell me you were pregnant. You didn't answer my calls or emails. You vanished, Grace. Poof!" He jerked his chin back forcefully. His eyes were shooting barbs at her and she stood pinned to the spot, ready for the assault. She deserved it.

"I didn't. I thought it best we never see each other again."

"You decided," he declared angrily.

"I did."

"But here you are."

"Yes. With Jules." She looked fondly at the baby. "I need to talk to you about him…"

"You sure took your time, but I get that since you didn't want to see me again. Have anything to do with me. A guy with one arm."

Her stomach flipped. How could he think that? On the other hand, why not? She hadn't given him a reason not to believe that. She hadn't spoken to him at all. And now she was hurting him. Insulting him. And it couldn't be helped. "Mica, I'm sorry, so very sorry, for not telling you about Jules. I was wrong and I deeply regret my decision. But it had nothing to do with your arm. I'm here because I can't take care of him. You're his father. I need you to take over. Just for a while."

His words came out in a rush. "You want me to take care of a baby. That's ridiculous. I only have one arm—"

"Which is in better shape than most men's… even the ones with two working arms. Please— try to understand. I thought I could do this by myself, but I was wrong. I don't expect you to forgive me, but we need to do what's right for Jules. I have responsibilities…my team's futures depend on me—"

"And Jules's doesn't?" he barked.

"Of course it does. That's the point. I'm doing the best thing for him, bringing him to you. I've only got a small window of opportunity to make something extraordinary happen. I was nearly there a year ago when I came back here. How I pulled it out of the water after a month away, I'll never know. But I did it. We didn't get the notoriety I'd hoped for. My team members didn't get internships at the big houses, but I did get noticed by Chanel. If I can pull this off this season, I'm in. And my future—Jules's future—is secure. If I don't make a huge splash, the houses will look for fresh blood. They'll decide that I don't have talent and they'll move on. It's now or never, Mica."

He was silent.

"Mica, please. Please don't hold my actions against our son. It's not Jules's fault that I hurt you—am hurting you." As Grace finished she realized how high-pitched and desperate her voice had become.

Mica was unnervingly stoic. His face registered no response whatsoever, and she could only hope he was considering everything she was telling him. Maybe seeing her side of the situation.

"That's why I have to leave Jules with you," she continued. "I need to turn my full concentration on my work. The truly demanding days of his infancy are behind us. He's sleeping nearly all the night. His colic is gone. He took the flight like a champ. I'm really proud of him." She forced a smile at Mica, but when she looked down at Jules, her face softened. "I'll miss you, little guy."

"Then take him back to Paris."

"What?" She met Mica's steely blue gaze.

"I can't take care of him," he growled and leaned closer.

"It's only two months, max. Till the end of the spring shows. You can do it."

"Forget it. If you'd told me about him before he was born, then maybe I'd be better prepared to become a real father. I could have taken Lamaze classes with you. Gone to the hospital with you. Helped you when he had colic. But no. I was robbed of all that. I didn't get the chance, Grace—because you kept him a secret." He let out a bitter laugh. "Guess the joke's on me, huh?"

"Joke?"

"Here's the way I see it, Grace. First, you find out you're pregnant but can't stand the thought of telling me—the dad, the loser with no career and no prospects. Maybe that was your plan all along—use me, string me along so you could have a child all to yourself. Then this baby interferes with your precious career so you decide to pawn him off on me after all. Oh, I get your reasoning. What else do I have going on? I'm just slugging around backwater Indian Lake. Why wouldn't I be available to take on a kid? Well, it's not going to work, Grace."

He whirled around and took off. Grace's heart cracked. She'd made a mistake, yes, but she hadn't used him. She'd given him a piece of her heart when she was fifteen and handed over the rest of it last October. Being with him had been bliss, and in those few, short weeks, she'd been happy. She couldn't blame him for being upset with her, but this angry, judgmental, intractable Mica was not someone she wanted to know. His chastisement cut straight to her soul. She was left speechless.

He spun to face her again. "You must think I have a stupid streak a mile wide. I'm not falling for it, Grace. I'm not!" he shouted.

Grace's mind went black as she faced the onslaught of his revulsion. Before she could gather her thoughts, the kitchen door opened and Gina walked out.

"What's all the shouting I hear?" she demanded. Then she noticed Grace. Her smile was instantaneous. "Grace! How lovely to see…" Her gaze fixed on the bundle in Grace's arms. "Grace?"

Sam Crenshaw stepped out behind Gina. "What's going on?"

"Grace has come for a visit," Mica growled. "But she's just leaving. Aren't you, Grace?"

Grace felt her heart land on the pavement. No amount of preparation could have helped her combat Mica's anger.

True, Grace needed time to concentrate on

her career, but she also loved her baby with all her heart. She thought she was doing the right thing. Jules needed to learn about his father and experience a father's love, too. She couldn't just up and move to Indian Lake, and until she and Mica could figure out some other arrangement, this was the best she'd been able to come up with.

In her daydreams, Grace had thought that once Mica saw how adorable Jules was, he'd love his son on the spot. That had happened to her. She'd expected Jules to bring out the other side of Mica—the one with the heart as big as the sky. This closed-off, defensive and antagonistic man appeared to want a war.

Well, she was here to fight for her future—and their son's. Battle was easy. It was the heartache she hadn't figured on.

Grace lifted her chin and walked over to Gina, still blinking back her tears. "Hi, Gina. I'm afraid I'm delivering a shock, but there's no way around it." She stood in front of Gina and Sam. "This is Jules. Mica's baby."

Gina's mouth fell open.

Grace glanced at Mica, who shoved his right hand in his jeans pocket. He was silent.

"A boy?" Gina asked, reaching out to touch Jules's sleeve.

Sam put his hands on Gina's shoulders and leaned closer, his affection for her evident in his eyes and his gestures. "He looks just like you, Mica."

"Sure he does," Mica said bitterly, turning away from them to stare at the horse barn.

He was shutting her out—and his mother. *That's odd.*

"How old is he?" Sam asked.

"Six months. He's a very good baby."

Gina raised her eyes to Grace. "You didn't tell us." She looked at Mica. "And you didn't, either!"

"Gina," Grace began sheepishly, "Mica couldn't tell you because he didn't know. I never said a word—until today."

"He does look just like you did when you were a baby, Mica," Gina said, ignoring Grace's revelation. Without asking permission, she reached over and took Jules, cradling him in her arms. "It's cold out here. I think we should all go inside and talk."

Sam opened the door and stood back for Grace and Gina to enter. "I'll make a fire."

Grace turned back to Mica. "Are you coming?"

"No," Mica said, then rushed up the stairs to his apartment.

"He's had one too many shocks today," Gina said.

Grace frowned. "You mean there's more than finding out he has a son?"

"Yes. Now come on in. We have a lot to discuss."

CHAPTER THREE

THE WALLS OF Mica's apartment were closing in on him. His heart was racing as if he'd just lifted the John Deere tractor off its tires with both hands. He couldn't catch his breath.

A son?

When Grace had pulled up, he'd been caught between elation and shock. For a brief moment, he'd actually thought she'd come to back to see *him*. That she was back in town to stay. Back in his life.

He'd been a fool.

A baby. How had he missed that? He'd known something was wrong when Grace hadn't answered his texts and emails, though he'd chalked it up to her busy career. And when she'd continued to ignore him, his hurt had turned inward. He should have seen her silence as the red flag it was. Should have pressed her, tried to find out what was going on.

But ultimately, she was the one who should have reached out.

Told him the truth.

And to think only this morning he'd considered her an honest person.

She was about as honest as a cat burglar.

That's exactly what she is. She swoops into town, takes what she wants from me and leaves. Then, when that doesn't work out for her, she flies in again and deposits her unwanted "mistake" on my doorstep.

She was a piece of work.

Mica rubbed the back of his neck. Grace had betrayed him in the worst way. As contradictory as his emotions were, he mourned the loss of those precious days in Jules's life that he'd never get back. How had Mica spent those days? He'd been here, *brooding*, while his son was learning to smile, to roll over, experiencing so many things for the first time. Despite all he'd lost in the accident, Mica had held on to the dream of one day becoming a father. It had been his one remaining beacon of light.

At the same time, Mica was in no position to take care of a baby. Not yet. As the youngest of four, he'd never changed a diaper. Sure, he played with his nephew, Zeke, but when he got cranky or hungry, Mica handed the baby back to Gabe or Liz.

He raked his fingers through his thick hair,

hoping to hold down the top of his head so he wouldn't explode. Grace had to be out of her mind. None of this was logical. Was it?

He paced the room. His mother was right. Jules was one cute baby. And Grace had him dressed in a little navy jacket with a matching hat. Like he was a doll. Mica would have to find baby cowboy boots. They did make them for babies, didn't they?

A baby. My son.

Suddenly, his anger deflated and the liquid steel that had been running through his veins dissipated. He collapsed into his recliner chair. "My baby."

A few moments later, the door swung open. Grace stood in the doorway, hands on her hips and fire in her blue eyes. Her blond hair spread over her shoulders like a veil of gold. She was stunning. He was glad he was sitting down. The pain of her betrayal crept back onto his shoulders like an iron monkey.

"Grace," he said with as little emotion as he could muster. It took all his self-control not to shut the door in her face. "I don't want to see you. Or talk to you."

"I get that." She came in without an invitation and closed the door with a bit more force than he'd expected. "But that's what I'm here for. To talk. All day and night and all week, until I have to go back."

His eyes widened. "You're only here for a week?"

"Nine days."

"Well, isn't that nice. What do you plan to accomplish in nine days?"

"It's all I had."

"And I have all the time in the world. It doesn't work this way, Grace."

"Well, Mica, that's the reality. And I have to make this work. In nine days I intend to teach you everything you need to know about taking care of a baby. Feeding him, diapering, bathing him. Loving him."

"What do you know about love, huh? From my perspective, I see dishonesty. Secrets. Hurting others for the sake of your precious career."

She approached him. Her face softened, but he didn't understand why. "I deserved that, Mica," she said, her voice trembling.

"And more," he muttered.

"Mica, please listen to me…" There was compassion in her tone, and though he was trying not to let her demeanor affect him, he was rapidly losing ground.

He rubbed his neck again. Something just

wasn't right. Was she acting a part? After all, she'd spent most of her life learning how to please the most critical judges. And he was sitting in judgment of her right now. His wariness was well-placed. "I suppose you've sucked my mother into your little scheme."

"Scheme? You think Jules is part of some sinister plot? To what end? To cause you grief? More pain?" She walked toward him, gesturing with her hands. "Come on. I can take it. Give it to me. Tell me about how I'm intent on blowing up your engineering career. How I'm going to cause you to miss out on a sponsor you've been courting for the past year. I want to hear it," she demanded. "Tell me how, exactly, I'm messing up your life."

He let out a harsh breath. "Why are you really here, Grace? You want money? Because that's the only reason I can come up with that makes any sense. You know perfectly well that I'm in no shape to take care of a baby."

"You're wrong on all counts. I don't want your money or your family's money, and there's no scheme. All I want is for you to take care of Jules. Not forever. Just for two months or so. I need this time, Mica. I'm on the cusp of something so big, it will establish me in the fashion world. My career can only grow from there. I just need this spring show. Then I'll come back and take Jules off your hands. You won't have to worry. If it's what you want, you'll never see us again..." she said, trailing off.

"You could have hired a nanny to take care of Jules. Why me?"

Grace grabbed a chair from the little kitchenette table and sat across from him. She clasped her hands in her lap and looked at her thumbs as she worked them over each other. "Because you're his dad. I'm here to tell you that I was wrong to keep Jules from you. I should have called you when I first found out I was pregnant."

"Why didn't you?" He swallowed hard. He wasn't sure he wanted to hear the answer.

She paused for a long moment, her hesitation causing her to look around the room. Was she searching for an excuse or for courage? Either way, she was holding something back. But what?

"I was afraid. I was in denial. I couldn't believe it was happening. Then I was embarrassed. I was overwhelmed with work. My team depends so much on me. If I fail, they'll all lose their jobs, and I won't do that to them." She touched her fingertip to the corner of her eye. "One day of delay in calling you became a week. Then a month. Then four, five months went by and I'd convinced myself I could do all this on my own. What I learned is that I'm not a superwoman. And I feel so guilty for not telling you. I wanted you to know about him."

Mica listened stoically to her explanation, but he was racked by betrayal. Jules was his son, and he felt justified for every spark of anger he felt toward Grace. How dare she keep this secret? And then show up here, unannounced, and shove a baby at him. On top of all that, she intended to leave Jules here for months and then come back and take him away. Probably as soon as Mica had bonded with him.

"You are out of your mind," he said slowly. "I'm not going to agree to any of this." He shot to his feet, and stepped around her as she sat stone-still in the chair, her hands still in her lap.

He could smell her perfume as he walked past. He kept her in his sights as he went to the refrigerator and took out a beer. "No baby bottles in here. See? Not prepared."

Grace's lips had tightened into a narrow line that showed her determination and did nothing to mar her beauty. Or his absurd desire to kiss her. He shook his head to dispel the thought.

"Mica. Please try to understand. I want to help you."

"I don't need your help, Grace."

She crossed her arms. "Apparently, you do because you're not even trying to cooperate. Jules is your son. I need to show you how to take care of him so you don't hurt him!"

"Oh, like I would stick him under a car and let it fall on him?"

"Stop being ridiculous!"

"Me?"

Her eyes narrowed into slits. "You know what, Mica? Your self-absorption is blinding you. If you'd only spend a few moments with him, you'd see how wonderful he is."

"That's not the issue. This isn't about Jules, and you know it. It's about you. You want to pawn him off on me so you can go back to Paris and your fancy career!"

"My career is what will feed and clothe and educate Jules for the rest of his life. I don't want him to lack anything in the future. I want him to have a wonderful life. I want him to know his father." Her voice cracked with emotion.

For a moment, Mica almost lost it. It took every ounce of his inner strength not to go to her, pull her to his chest and comfort her. Maybe kiss away her fears. But he didn't. He was taking a stand. He had to. If he didn't and he fell for her, he would lose all over again because Grace would never live in Indian Lake on the farm with him.

Besides, she'd made her priorities clear. She had no room in her life for him or their baby.

Grace went to the door and reached for the knob. Her hand was shaking. Had he done that to her?

"I'm going to get Jules and feed him. You have my cell number."

She left, her footsteps pounding on the stairs.

His eyes lost focus as he stared at the closed door. How could he be responsible for taking care of a helpless baby when he could barely take care of himself?

CHAPTER FOUR

GRACE FOUND GINA in the kitchen warming a bottle of formula in the microwave. Jules was sitting in an unfamiliar rocking baby seat on the kitchen counter. Sam was at the kitchen table going through Grace's diaper bag.

"Found one," Sam said, holding up a bib.

"Hi, honey," Gina said, looking at Grace and then gesturing toward Jules. "I hope you don't mind that we got him settled here. I have all sorts of baby equipment from when Liz got pregnant with Ezekiel. I can't tell you how thrilled we are to have another grandbaby in the house," she said, gushing. "Aren't we, Sam?"

Okay. I've missed something, Grace thought as she looked from Gina's beaming face to Sam, who was smiling far too brightly.

"We're delighted." Sam chuckled. "As far as I'm concerned, Zeke is grown up already. He's over two now and talking up a storm."

"I love babies. Adore them, really," Gina

said, taking the bottle from the microwave when it dinged. "That's why I had four sons. And now, this little fella. It's a miracle!"

Sam clucked his tongue. "Now, sweetie, don't get carried away."

Grace was sure her confusion showed on her face, but after sparring with Mica, she didn't want to ruffle any more feathers.

"Oh, Sam," Gina continued happily. "It's just so wonderful to have a baby in the house."

"Too bad Mica doesn't feel that way," Grace muttered.

"What are you talking about?" Gina asked, testing the temperature of the formula on her wrist. She picked up Jules and cradled him while he greedily went after the bottle.

Grace was surprised at how accepting Jules was of these strangers. He didn't seem the least upset that Gina was holding him, nor did he flinch at the sound of Sam's gravelly voice. "He doesn't want anything to do with Jules," she explained. "I've never seen him so angry."

Sam swatted the air. "He's not mad at you or the baby. He's mad at us."

"That's right," Gina said.

"Wait, what?" Grace stared at them. "Why would Mica be mad at you?"

Gina smiled softly at Sam. "We just got

engaged. In fact, Mica…walked in on us in here right after I'd accepted Sam's proposal. He wasn't happy about that. He stormed out of here like we'd set him on fire. Then you drove up."

"And hit him with my news."

"Yes. Well, two life changes in a matter of moments would be hard for anyone, and he's been going through a lot this past year."

"He has, hasn't he?"

"And I guess it's even harder for him since he's always been a loner. Living his life in his head. He has a lot of ideas about the machines he'd like to invent."

"Has he invented anything?" Grace asked.

"Not that I know of. He'd have to patent them first and build a working model. He hasn't done that kind of thing since college. And he spent so many years working the farm with his father and brothers. Then since the…"

"Accident?" Grace said, finishing for her.

"Yes," Gina replied sadly, looking down at Jules. "Mica hasn't done much of anything since then." She sighed. "Jules is such a sweet baby. And handsome already. He has my eyes. All the boys do. Even Zeke." Gina winked at Grace. "I'm very proud of that."

"You should be," Sam agreed.

Grace moved over to Gina and squeezed Jules's foot. "Why would such happy news make Mica angry?"

"Jealousy," Sam barked and went back to digging things out of the diaper bag.

"Oh, Sam. He's just in shock is all. And then you told him you've loved me for over thirty years, that was double-shock. He'll come around."

"I'm not so sure," Sam grumbled.

"This does explain a lot," Grace said. "Not everything, but it helps. I can't imagine him being mad at his own mother for long. He adores you, Gina. That much I know. But the rest of it is my fault. I didn't tell him I was pregnant."

Gina's eyes held concern. "That is a situation. Why didn't you?"

Because I'm not sure he cares about me. I'm terrified I was just a fling. "Shame. Denial. My career. A million and one things."

"Excuses, you mean," Gina said compassionately.

"Yes. Poor ones. I spent the first trimester basically in denial, and when I finally had to face the fact that I was going to have a baby, I had to make plans. I was in Paris. Mica was across an ocean. I didn't want to mess up his life any more, considering how the accident affected him. I didn't want him to feel responsible. And for a long time, I thought I could handle everything on my own."

"Understandable," Sam replied.

"Really?" Grace was surprised. Sam was the first person who had explicitly taken her side since this all began. So far, Mica was a write-off. Gina was withholding judgment, but Grace couldn't expect her not to defend her son. And Grace's team in Paris had been less than thrilled by the news. As her pregnancy progressed and she had to cut back on her hours in the studio, they reacted with hurt feelings and a sense of abandonment. That only intensified when she announced her trip to Indian Lake. They were as needy as children. But as much as they needed her, she needed them. They were her Paris family.

"Of course, dear," Gina added, giving Grace another shock. "I can absolutely put myself in your shoes. You're a long way from home. Coming back here to face Mica would take a lot of courage, not to mention the logistics."

"Well, I say it's time to move on," Sam said.

"Sam's right." Gina took the bottle out of Jules's mouth and put a clean dish towel over her shoulder before holding him against it and patting his back. Jules gave a huge burp and giggled. Gina nestled him back into the crook of her arm. "What an angelic face."

"I think so, too," Grace said. *And every time I look at him I'm reminded of Mica. His father. The man I'll always love.*

Her phone pinged with a text.

I'm going into town. Don't be here when I get back. Please.

They all heard the roar of the pickup as Mica spun the wheels on a patch of ice and backed down the drive.

Grace looked at Gina. "Mica's really raw. And I'm just as upset. I should take Jules and go." She reached for him but Gina turned away from her.

"Just a minute. Now, where are you staying? And when do I get to see this little guy again?"

"Gina…" Sam gave her a warning tone.

"Sorry," Gina said. "But I just met him. I need details."

"You have every right to know my plans. I'm staying with Mrs. Beabots. Her apartment is empty and Aunt Louise doesn't have room for us. I'm here for nine days to acclimate Jules to Mica, and Mica to his son. Then I need to get back to Paris. I need to leave Jules with Mica for two, maybe three months until I can get my spring show under my belt. It's a make-it-or-break-it situation. These months will determine the rest of my life!"

"Seems to me your son is determining your life," Gina said.

Grace hung her head. "He is." Then she met Gina's eyes. "I don't know how to explain this without coming off as selfish and self-centered, but I really do want the best for my boy." Grace felt chills scamper down her spine and her eyes filled with tears. Ever since she'd left Indian Lake last time, waved goodbye to Mica, she'd been an emotional wreck. To be fair, she'd been pregnant most of that time. Still, these days, she cried at the drop of a hat. She told herself that it was hormones. Lack of sleep. But deep down, the truth was always there. It was all about Mica.

"And you honestly think you're going to get Mica to care for Jules?"

"I was hoping he'd fall in love with him at first sight, but Mica is so closed off from us... now I wonder if it's even possible."

"Hmm. That is interesting, isn't it?" Gina pondered as she handed Jules to Grace. "I think the best thing is to let Mica cool off, which he will, and then you need to put him through his basic training. He hasn't the first clue about babies. As much as he loves Zeke, he had nothing to do with him when he was an infant. He likes him better now that he can talk."

"So do I," Sam joked.

"Oh, you!" Gina waved her palm at him. "Let's get him bundled up. I'll do what I can from this end to help you with Mica. Though right now, I'm about the last person Mica is going to listen to."

"Yeah. I'm not sure either of us have much sway with him at the moment."

Gina tapped her cheek with her finger. "Grace. Tomorrow, Sam and I are having a New Year's Eve party and we're going to announce our engagement. Please come and bring Jules. All your friends will be here and it will be a good time to show off Jules. Hopefully, when Mica sees everyone's reaction to this little angel, his heart will soften."

"Do you think so, Gina? After today, I'm wondering if that approach isn't such a good idea."

"He knows about the party. You're my guest. He needs to face his responsibilities."

Grace put Jules in his Bundleme as Sam

replaced all her items in the diaper bag. Gina rinsed out the baby bottle and threw away the inner collapsible sack.

Grace said her goodbyes and accepted kisses from Gina and Sam…her son's grandparents.

MICA HAD HOPED to avoid seeing Grace and the baby again by heading into town, but he hadn't guessed Grace would stop at the Indian Lake Deli. Just his luck. And of course he'd been the one to tell her to leave the farm. Grace arrived twenty minutes after he put in his order and sat down.

When she walked in, he watched as people in line regarded her with awe. He'd been too overwhelmed earlier to notice her stylish, black wool coat, with its black faux-fur collar. She carried Jules in a baby carrier and had a black leather bag over her other shoulder. Everything about Grace was attention-getting.

But it was the way her blue eyes latched on to his from the moment she closed the door. Her smile was faint, but it was there, as if she was happy to see him.

He forced himself not to smile back, but nothing could harness the appreciation in his eyes.

She walked over to him. "Your mom was

feeding Jules. Then I realized I hadn't eaten all day."

"My mom…"

"I'd left Jules's bottles of formula in his diaper bag. Your mom and Sam got him sorted while we were…talking. All you do is heat it in the microwave. He likes it at forty seconds. Not too hot and not too cold."

"Like Goldilocks."

"Yeah." She smiled. "It's nice about the two of them." Mica's breath hitched in his chest. His mother and Sam were engaged. They'd been in love for decades. He wasn't sure he'd ever come to terms with that. Yet Grace was immediately accepting of their relationship. Easy for her. It wasn't her mother they were talking about. Grace's mother was dead.

He felt a streak of guilt shoot down his spine. He should be grateful that his mother was still with him, but right now, all he felt was the bite of betrayal.

"I don't want to talk about it."

"They're in love and should be together. Just because people get old, doesn't mean they shouldn't find companionship and someone to share their lives with."

He leaned forward, his eyes blazing. "My mother was devoted to my father…"

"She was. But he died, Mica."

"Stop talking, Grace," he said lowly so as not to be heard by the others around them. "You don't know anything about my family."

"I know a lot about people," she countered. "Apparently, more than you do."

"Barzonni?" Julia Melton called. "Barzonni? You here?"

Mica turned. "We're here."

"Your order is up."

Mica handed Julia cash and she rang up the sale. Mica was glad he had his back to Grace, so she wouldn't see the confusion he knew was on his face. He'd just answered Julia in the plural, as if Grace and Jules were his family.

Mica was no family man. Or was he?

CHAPTER FIVE

ONE OF THE things Grace loved about Indian Lake was how all Aunt Louise's friends welcomed her with open arms. And as usual, Mrs. Beabots was the first to offer.

Grace owed Mrs. Beabots not only her first Paris connections, but now the use of the apartment in Mrs. Beabots's Victorian mansion also. Grace had known she couldn't possibly squeeze both herself and Jules into Louise's one-bedroom apartment above the ice-cream shop. It had been fun to crash on the sofa when she was a teenager, but with a baby who sometimes didn't sleep the whole night through, Grace didn't think any of them would get much rest in such tight quarters. After all Aunt Louise had done for her, staying somewhere else was the least Grace could do.

Normally, Louise left for Florida each winter, but because of her back injury, she hadn't gone the year before and had given up the house she'd been leasing then. The new people had rented it for the next three years at a higher fee. Louise feared that her Florida days were over.

Luckily, Mrs. Beabots hadn't rented her upstairs apartment to anyone and she was delighted to have Grace and the baby staying with her.

Once Grace had unpacked and settled in, Mrs. Beabots invited her for afternoon tea. She'd already invited Louise, as well as Sarah, who lived next door. Sarah had given birth to a baby girl, Charlotte, only three days after Jules was born on July 1, and Grace was looking forward to having her friend so close by.

Jules was still napping when Grace headed downstairs at four, but because he was used to being transported from her Paris apartment to her studio, where designers shouted at each other over the cutting tables and sewing machines whirred, he could just about sleep through anything.

Grace put Jules, in his baby carrier, on Mrs. Beabots's kitchen island just as Aunt Louise walked in.

Louise smiled at their elderly host. "I brought you a plate of brownies I made this morning."

Mrs. Beabots grinned. "Those are the brownies for your brownie-nut-fudge ice cream, I presume."

"They are."

"How generous of you to share with us, Louise. We'll put them out with the pecan and cranberry sandies I made. The tea is nearly ready. Sarah should be here any minute. I thought we'd sit in the front parlor. Luke put in a new heater for me out there and it's quite toasty." She winked. "The babies won't get cold and we can watch the snowfall as the neighborhood Christmas lights come on."

"Sounds lovely," Grace replied, taking the china plate of cookies out to the front parlor as she hefted Jules's carrier in her right hand. She set him on a red velvet Victorian chair. "Oh!" Grace exclaimed, spotting the skinny fir tree in the corner. "You have a Christmas tree out here."

Louise placed the brownies on the coffee table. "Very pretty."

"My big tree is in the library, as usual," Mrs. Beabots explained. "But I spend so much time in here, reading and visiting, that it's a shame not to have some of my favorite ornaments out to enjoy all the time." Mrs. Beabots pointed to the tree. "All these are from Paris. Don't you love the pink, gold and aqua? They were in vogue back in the sixties."

"I'd love to hear more of your stories," Grace said as the antique doorbell rang.

"That would be Sarah," Mrs. Beabots said, placing the teapot on the coffee table. "I'll be right back."

"Uh-huh. Just in time not to disclose anything juicy about Paris or Coco Chanel, huh?" Grace teased.

Louise winked at her niece. "She'll never spill."

"Not even to me?" Grace asked.

"Never. Secrets are her passion. Along with these cookies."

Sarah followed Mrs. Beabots into the room, holding a pink bundle. "Grace!" she squealed. "I'm so happy to see you!" She gave Grace a one-armed hug. "This is Charlotte. Annie's on her way over. She had to walk Beau first. She's dying to talk to you."

"Goodness. I'm flattered, but why?"

"Oh," Mrs. Beabots said impishly as she took Sarah's coat. "You'll see. She's a million questions, that one. Tea, Sarah? You know you can have my mint-and-bourbon tea now that you're not nursing."

"True," Sarah replied. "I'd love some tea." She glanced at Grace. "Are you breastfeeding?"

"No. I had to go back to work five days after Jules was born. I took him to the studio with me, but formula let me be a bit more flexible with his feeding."

"You're kidding. They let you do that? Bring him in, I mean."

Grace smiled. "Summer was a slow time for us and I'm the team leader. Though, once things ramped up in the fall, it was too hectic and Jules could feel my stress. I found a nanny, but she was clearly more interested in becoming a designer than she was in taking care of Jules. I was basically tutoring her while still doing the lion's share of childcare."

Sarah shook her head. "I can't believe you got any work done at all! I've been able to take a longer mat leave, at least, but my whole day revolves around Charlotte. Sometimes I don't even have time to eat, let alone do anything creative."

Grace felt a rush of shame. The whole reason she'd come back to Indian Lake was that she *couldn't* handle it all. How could anyone understand her motivation for leaving her baby here so she could continue her work half a world away? On the surface, she sounded like a heartless monster. She lifted her hand to Jules and let him curl his fingers around her forefinger. He smiled at her and when he did, the pacifier in his mouth wiggled and wobbled like it always did. Grace felt her heart tighten and then burst with love.

"I honestly don't know how I've made it the past six months," she admitted. "Well, year, really. Jules deserves so much more than I can give him right now. It was tough enough working seven days a week and most nights being pregnant." She lifted her eyes to Louise. "Thank goodness I inherited sturdy genes."

Louise's eyes misted as she put a hand on Grace's shoulder. "You're a good mother, Grace, and this decision has to be unbearably difficult."

Sarah shot her a confused look, and Grace explained about leaving Jules with Mica. She kept the part about not telling him until today to herself.

Sarah spread a baby quilt on the floor and put Charlotte on top. She kissed her baby's head. "Kudos to you, Grace. Seriously, I couldn't do what I do if I didn't have Luke and the kids to help. And that's not counting Miss Milse, who practically lives at the house, and Mrs. Beabots, who is the best friend ever."

Sarah reached for Mrs. Beabots's hand and squeezed it. "I have so much support and there you are all alone in Paris…" Sarah shook her head.

The flood of gratitude that engulfed Grace almost moved her to tears. Her throat thickened with emotion. "You all are what I have been missing in my life in Paris. I have my team members, but I'm their boss. They look to me for support. Not the other way around. I'm their rock."

"No wonder you're worn out," Mrs. Beabots said, pouring the tea. "Everyone needs a rock to lean on. And someone who motivates them. Who motivates you, Grace?"

Grace stared at the older woman. She'd never been asked such a question. What did motivate her, other than the goals she'd set for herself? And then the truth hit her. *Mica.*

Yes, she'd wanted to prove to herself that she had what it took to succeed. But deep down, she'd also wanted to show Mica that she wasn't a silly girl prancing down a pageant runway.

And there was Jules, of course. Once she'd discovered she was pregnant, Grace had become driven to succeed for her child. She would have to provide financial security and a good foundation for him. Above all, she wanted to be the kind of person her child would be proud of and would want to emulate.

"Just Jules," Grace finally said. "He's become the center of my heart."

Mrs. Beabots threw Grace an unconvinced look as she sipped her tea and gently placed the cup back on her saucer. "I never had a child, but ever since Sarah was born, I have felt she was almost my own. Now with Annie and Timmy in and out of my house as much as they are, and baby Charlotte, I can understand how a child could be nearly all a woman would need." She paused and lifted her cup once more. *"Nearly."*

Grace's eyes didn't leave Mrs. Beabots's face. She felt as if the octogenarian knew everything about her feelings for Mica. And her passion for her career and her love for her baby. Maybe even more than Grace did herself.

"Why don't you put Jules on the quilt and see if he and Charlotte get along?" Sarah asked.

"Good idea," Grace replied and lifted Jules out of the carrier. She placed him next to blonde Charlotte, who peered at him quizzically and reached out to touch his face.

Jules burst into tears and wailed at the top of his lungs. Grace held him close as she caressed his back. "Apparently, he's not the people person I'd thought he was," she joked.

"Is Charlotte the first baby he's met?" Sarah asked.

"Um…yes, actually."

Louise lifted her chin. "Could be that and the fact that he's teething. Grace said she was up with him for the past two nights."

"I've got some teething gel that Charlotte likes. And she chews on frozen teething rings. I have an extra in my diaper bag. She's going through the same thing."

Grace exhaled and started laughing. She rocked back on her hips and laughed louder.

"What's so funny?" Louise asked.

"This is all so…unfamiliar to me and yet, normal. I haven't had a soul to talk about babies with—what to do or even what to ask. I've been winging it for months. Granted, I read books when I could keep my eyes open and I listened with one ear at the pediatrician's office, but frankly, I was so busy texting and emailing my team that I guess I didn't listen all that well."

"What about Mica?" Sarah asked. "Hasn't he been pitching in at all, even from across the ocean?"

Grace bit her lip, and an awkward silence fell over the group.

Sarah blinked. "What'd I say?"

Louise and Mrs. Beabots both gave Grace expectant looks. Grace sighed.

"I guess everyone will find out soon enough. Mica didn't know about Jules…until today."

Sarah put a hand to her mouth. "Oh, Grace…"

Jules had quieted down, so Grace put him back in his carrier, where he seemed to be perfectly happy. "It's okay. I mean, it's not okay. I messed up." Grace sat back. "He's angry. I guess I hadn't prepared myself enough for his recriminations. But I hurt him. I know it and I wish I'd handled things differently." More softly, she said, "I never intended to cause him so much pain."

Sarah reached over and put her hand on Grace's forearm. "Grace, you've been in love with him since you were fifteen. I've always known that. Maddie does, too. None of us will ever judge you. We love you. We always have."

Grace burst into tears and hugged Sarah. "I don't know what's wrong with me. Why can't I be happy to pull up stakes, move back to Indian Lake and live with all of you? Why do I keep banging my head against the Bastille of Paris design houses?"

Louise put her hand on Grace's shoulder. "Because it's your destiny."

Grace looked up. "Really? You think that?"

"Of course she does," Mrs. Beabots affirmed. "And so do I. Sarah here is lucky that her design work keeps her close to home. Your life is in Paris. You've just got a tiny wrinkle in your plans is all."

Grace turned to Jules, who was playing with a SpongeBob rattle. "I wouldn't say 'tiny.'"

"At the moment, he is. The big problem is blockheaded Mica," Mrs. Beabots said, then she drained her teacup.

Fresh tears sprang into Grace's eyes. "Is he?"

"Absolutely," Sarah replied. "Yes, you should have told him. Yes, he could have been there when Jules was born. But you know, Grace, maybe your situation is just the thing Mica needs to yank him out of this self-centered pity party he's had going on ever since the accident. Maddie and Olivia have both voiced concerns. Rafe wants to hire more help and Mica keeps putting up such a fight that nothing gets done. Fortunately, it's several months until spring planting."

"And then the tension will be even worse for Mica," Grace interjected.

"I'm afraid so."

Have I just added yet another burden for him to bear? Grace wondered. Maybe taking Jules back to Paris was the right thing after all. She had no idea if she was a good mother, if her career goals were admirable or simply selfish.

Stop it, Grace.

She'd worried over this far too long. She'd flown to Indian Lake. She'd taken the brunt of Mica's anger. She'd dug in her heels. There was no going back.

The doorbell rang.

"There's Annie!" Sarah exclaimed. "I was beginning to worry." She jumped up, and Charlotte put out her arms for her mom, a grimace contorting her pretty pink cheeks.

"I'll be right back, sweetie." Grace's heart squeezed painfully. How would Jules react when she left him...not just for a few moments, but for months?

Sarah came back into the room with Annie, who wore a neon-pink parka, white tights, white snow boots and a white sequined scarf around her neck.

She certainly had a stylish streak. Grace

wondered if the questions Annie had for her were about fashion.

"Hi, Miss Grace!" Annie waved. "I'm so happy to see you. Mom said you could help me."

"She...did?" Grace threw Sarah a curious look.

Sarah took Annie's coat, while Annie toed off her boots. Grace noticed that her dress was a slim column of white T-shirt material with sequined collar and cuffs.

Sarah put her hand on Annie's shoulder. "Go ahead and ask, honey."

"What is it, Annie?"

"Mom says you were Junior Miss Illinois."

"I was," Grace said, feeling that old pang of not measuring up. Of not being perfect. She couldn't reflect on her earlier win without remembering how she'd only been runner-up in Miss Teen Illinois. And it made her sad to think that she might be better known around town for her pageant days than her accomplishments in the fashion world.

"I was wondering if you could...or would you, I mean, have you ever...coached kids like me?"

"Coached?"

"Yeah. You know. Like help me with my

gowns and dresses and stuff. Mom says you know just about everything about clothes. Even more than Mrs. Beabots."

"That's not possible," Grace and Sarah said in unison and then laughed.

"Well, almost, then," Annie said.

Grace's spirits lifted. This wasn't just about her past as a preteen beauty queen. "Annie, I would be honored to help you. You do know there's more to it than just the clothes, right?"

"Oh, I do. I've been taking piano and voice lessons for years," Annie said, as if it had been decades.

"She's very good," Mrs. Beabots said. "She sings 'Over the Rainbow' with more soul than Judy Garland."

"Who's that?" Annie asked.

"She sang it before Iz," Sarah said.

"Oh."

Grace stifled a laugh. "The other thing, Annie, is that I'm only going to be in town for a week or so. We'll have to get together very soon. I'll tell you what. Why don't you make up a list of questions and then, even after I leave, you can always text me or email me if there's something we didn't cover."

"Gosh, Miss Grace! That's so nice of you! Thank you. I'll be right next door while you're here, so I can come over anytime!" Annie hopped from foot to foot.

Sarah laughed. "Well, maybe not all the time. Grace does have her own things to do while she's here," she told Annie. Then she hugged Grace. "You're the best. You've made her day…her month, probably!"

"Absolutely." Grace smiled at Annie. "We'll have a blast."

Annie went over to baby Charlotte, still chatting away with Sarah, and with the practiced moves of a highly trained nanny, picked up the baby and cooed to her as if she'd been doing it for several lifetimes. Grace was struck with Annie's maturity. She was only eleven and she seemed more at ease with her sister than Grace often felt with Jules.

They all visited for another fifteen minutes, until Jules started to fuss. It was time to change his diaper.

"You can change him in my bedroom," Mrs. Beabots offered as Grace grabbed his diaper bag and Louise picked up the baby. "You needn't go all the way upstairs."

Grace adored Mrs. Beabots's bedroom, but she hadn't seen it since Sarah's husband, Luke—a master carpenter—had redesigned the room.

Once they entered the elaborately decorated pearl-gray-and-salmon bedroom, Grace froze. In the center of the room was an antique Venetian crystal chandelier. The walls were paneled and crown molded in gold filigree that would have shamed half the rooms at Versailles, Grace thought. There was a huge four-poster bed with a pearl gray satin duvet cover, pillows and sheets. Several beaded, salmon pink pillows dotted the bed. An enormous antique escritoire was filled with books and a French fauteuil chair upholstered in pink brocade was pulled up next to it. Once she'd taken everything in, Grace unfolded the changing pad under Jules, who had started to calm down once he had his mother's complete attention.

"Annie is amazing, Aunt Louise."

"No more than you were at that age."

"What are you talking about?" Grace put the used diaper in a plastic bag and tied a knot.

Louise sat on the bed and smoothed Jules's dark hair. "Grace, the thing about you is that you grew up fast. When you were very young, you were already taking charge of your life, without direction from your parents or me. Annie is like you. She was taking care of her dad when she was six. You kind of did that for your mother. Being on that stage, learning your lines, being judged all the time would be difficult for an adult, let alone a child. But you sailed through it gracefully. Sorry...about the pun."

"That's okay." She chuckled. "But you're right. I knew what clothes and accessories looked good together. I knew my piano concerto was strong. I saw the playing field, sized up the competition and knew how to win. How is that possible?"

Louise shrugged. "Old soul. Talent. Hard work. All of the above. Some people come into this life with gifts. They have a responsibility to use them. We all hope for equal opportunities, but if we all had equal talents, I'd choose to be Beyoncé."

"Wouldn't we all." Grace laughed.

"Instead, I wear silly hats and dance a jig around my shop for a little kid's birthday. All I want is to see that child smile and laugh and come back to see me. For about forty years."

"And they do."

"I hope this little guy will want to come see his old Aunt Louise."

Grace pulled up Jules's navy corduroy pants, then put on his matching navy socks with gold fleur-de-lis embroidered on the top rib. "One of the benefits of leaving Jules in Indian Lake for a while is that you'll get to see him all the time."

"I hope so," Louise replied sadly.

Grace saw the mist in her aunt's eyes. "What is it? Tell me what's bothering you."

"Mica. That's what. He's being cruel, if you ask me. Treating you like that. You did the best you could under the circumstances. I don't know if I would have done any differently, to be honest. If I didn't have the ice-cream shop, I'd take Jules myself."

"Now, Aunt Louise. We discussed this. Mica is his father and he should be the one to step up. Besides, you've only had a few months with your back being nearly normal. I hate to say it, but you're not thirty years old anymore. It's too much to ask."

"Still and all, I'm here for you and Jules," Louise replied firmly.

"And I love you for it." Grace kissed her cheek and started to tear up again. "You've been so understanding and you didn't have to be…"

"Stop that right now. I won't hear it. You're my family. Jules is family."

"And he's Mica's family, too." Grace gathered him into her arms. "It's really kinda scary, isn't it?"

"What?"

"Jules doesn't look a thing like me. He's Barzonni all the way."

"Well, I hope he inherits your sweet nature and none of Mica's arrogance."

Grace chuckled as she picked up the diaper bag. "I couldn't agree more."

CHAPTER SIX

MICA HAD BEEN a jerk to Grace.

Again.

He'd put up his defenses because he was hurt. The shock of finding out he was a father had been one thing. The fact that Grace had not called him all those months ago and told him the truth had cut him in places he hadn't known he had. He'd wanted to hurt her back, but striking at her repeatedly about not telling him the truth now made him ashamed.

He owed her an apology and he had no idea where to start.

He had to move fast because Grace was leaving in a week.

That was another thing. Why did she have to leave so soon? Couldn't she stick around another week? Or three. *How does she expect me to learn to be Jules's dad in a matter of days?*

They had things to discuss. Serious, life-changing decisions had to be made.

He reached for his iPhone and searched his

contacts for her name. When he found it, he stopped.

Instead of Grace, he should rename the contact "Miss Hit and Run." That's what she was always doing, wasn't it? She rolled into his life like an earthquake, stirring up his emotions, and then vanished, leaving him breathless and shaken.

And why was that? For that month they'd shared, he'd hoped to continue the relationship, even if she was across an ocean. He'd expected to exchange emails and texts. Talk to her on the phone. Fly over for holidays. He was more than open to seeing where they would go. But her silence had cut to the heart. For a brief time, he'd hoped that he might have something with her—something that might bring joy to his life.

But her silence told him that he'd lived a dream. And all dreams fade.

Yet now they had a son who would keep them connected forever. Even though it was too late for them romantically, they had Jules.

And it was all…

Because of the accident. No matter how Mica tried to reprogram his mind-set, he couldn't seem to get over the fact that he wasn't the capable man he had been. And maybe

Grace couldn't, either. It wasn't just his injured arm, but the way the injury had changed his life. He was being edged out on the farm. He was directionless. He didn't know what it was going to take to get past that roadblock, if it was possible at all.

Meanwhile, Grace was ambitious, focused and determined to take her career to the next level. No wonder she didn't want to be with him.

During their time together last October, he'd told her about the way things used to be, what he'd planned for his life.

What he hadn't done was tell her where he thought his life was going now. Which was nowhere. But it must have been pretty obvious to her.

True, Grace was entrusting Mica with their son. Though his insecurities wailed inside him, he was determined to be a good father, to do the honorable thing. But the fact that she only seemed to see Mica as a convenient childcare provider hurt. A lot.

He tossed the phone onto his desk, next to his computer. For weeks, even months, he'd been working on designs to retrofit the old tractor, but in the cold light of day, his ideas always seemed as inoperable as his arm. And

Mica had found himself tumbling into a tunnel of depression.

Since the accident, and the brief interlude with Grace last October, nothing in his life had had purpose or meaning, except…

"Jules."

Mica leaned forward in his desk chair and rose to his feet. "Jules Barzonni." He paused and let the sound of his son's name roll around in his head. It was a good name. A sturdy and sound name. He liked it.

"The only problem is…"

He picked up his iPhone again and this time he tapped Grace's number.

She picked up on the second ring.

"Hello? Mica?"

"Grace," he said, feeling a bit off-balance after hearing her voice. Sweet and tentative. Melodic and haunting. A voice that, for over a year, he had wished he could forget. "I need to talk to you about our son."

"Our son?"

"Yes," he replied. "If I drove into town, could we talk?"

"I'm just about to give Jules his dinner. Then he needs a bath and—"

"Okay," he replied. "Tonight's not good."

"I've been on the phone and at the computer

all afternoon and evening. I haven't had time to get to the store. I don't have anything here to fix for dinner. So I'm not sure…"

"What's with you, Grace? You fly back here, specifically to hand Jules over to me, and then you shut me out? You make no sense."

"My fault," she said. "After the way we left things, I didn't know what to say or how to say it."

"So you pull the silent act on me again."

"I'm sorry."

"We need to talk, Grace."

"We do. But not tonight. I'm dead tired and to be honest, I have a mountain of work I simply have to get done in the morning. By sunrise, my team will be on the phone and I have to take care of some very pressing matters, and I—"

"Grace," he interrupted. "I get it. What about tomorrow night? I'll get some Chinese takeout. Okay?"

"Uh, sure. I guess."

"See you about six?"

Mica ended the call. He looked down at his battered jeans and scuffed boots. He remembered when he'd seen Grace at The Louise House when she'd first arrived back in Indian

Lake. He'd looked like crap. Dirty. Muddy boots. She hadn't liked it.

Before tomorrow night, he had work to do. Laundry. Boot polish.

Soap. Shower. That'll help. He rose from the chair and turned off the computer.

I hope.

IT HAD BEEN a long day at the computer for Grace.

She'd been surprised to find over forty emails from her team. She'd expected to put in some hours during her time off, but she'd thought they'd give her at least a day or two before flooding her inbox.

The first email she opened was from Etienne. He'd sent three photos of designs he'd executed per Grace's directive. She groaned at the too-yellow chartreuse silk dress and the sky blue plastic rain poncho she'd thought would be killer. "Well, I need to bury it," she mumbled as she typed a reply email to Etienne.

When Grace had left Paris, she'd sketched fourteen day-wear designs and two gowns. She needed every single one of these pieces to stand out so she could secure a place in a show. These first stabs were a disaster. She'd been too rushed trying to leave Paris, distracted by thoughts of Mica and caring for

Jules. Just hours ago, she'd doubted her decision to bring her son here, but now this proof of her subpar work renewed her confidence that she was doing the right thing. For Jules and her career.

She sent the email back to Etienne and told him to scrap both pieces. The fabric for the dress was wrong, and the poncho didn't sit right. It would be cumbersome to wear. She needed a different rainproof fabric. Perhaps a waterproof twill or a waterproof microfiber. She promised she would send new designs by the weekend.

Rene sent his detailed spreadsheets regarding their menswear sales. She'd left him in charge because his business acumen was akin to hers. As expected, he ended his email with affectionate concern about her and Jules's trip.

She emailed him back that all was well.

Grace opened her sketch pad, took her pencil and closed her eyes as she always did, allowing inspiration to come into her head. She made the first strokes and then her hand began flying across the paper. She imagined a muddy brown caplet with blood-red lining over a pencil-thin brown wool skirt and brown boots—cowboy boots, like the ones Mica always wore…

Jules started to cry. He'd dozed off in his baby carrier and she'd let him rest. She needed the break to get her work done.

Or some of it.

She set aside her sketch pad and lifted Jules out of his carrier. "Oh, sweetie. Guess what? Your daddy will be here—" she checked her watch "—in ten minutes. And I still have to give you a bath and get your PJs on."

Jules swatted her face with his tiny palm and giggled. She nabbed his hand and kissed it. "You're my fella. You know that? Not so tall, but dark and very, very handsome."

She went to the refrigerator and pulled out a bottle of formula and a half-used jar of pureed baby food. She heated both in the microwave.

"So, how about carrots and if you're lucky, some applesauce for dinner?" she said, cooing to Jules.

She settled him back in his carrier, put a bib around his neck and had just given him the first few spoonfuls of pureed carrots when her doorbell dinged.

"I'm guessing that's your daddy."

Jules smiled and toyed with his bib.

"I'll be right back."

Taking a deep breath, she opened the door.

She couldn't help it. She had to brace herself against the onslaught of Mica's presence.

He wore clean jeans, a plaid shirt and a sheepskin-lined leather jacket, which was dusted with snow. He carried two paper sacks in his right arm.

"I didn't know what you liked, so I got a bunch," he said with a smile that could melt glaciers.

"Come in," she said.

He wiped his black boots on the mat. "I remembered. No dirt on the boots. I wouldn't want you to have to scrub floors on my account."

"I appreciate that," she replied, marveling at the fact that he remembered something she'd said to him fourteen months ago. It had been a mean remark. "Mica, I'm sorry for being so harsh back then. I was just..."

"Angry?" he asked.

"Yes. I was. I thought...well, you know. I thought a lot of things and they were wrong."

"I remember," he said, walking down the hall that led to the kitchen.

Jules was making all sorts of noises as he heard them approach. When Grace and Mica entered the kitchen, he started twisting and rocking and nearly pitched himself and the carrier over the edge of the table.

"Whoa! Hold on there, buddy!" Mica shoved the bags onto the counter and shot over to Jules, catching him before he tumbled to the floor.

"What the heck?" Grace said, rushing over to them.

"I've got him," Mica said. "Shouldn't he be in a high chair? He looks too big for this thing."

"He is. But I haven't been able to borrow or rent a high chair from anyone here yet."

"You should have told me. I could have arranged it."

"You? Mica, two days ago you would barely even—"

He spun around to face her, his blue eyes flashing so intensely that Grace had a hard time remembering where she was or what she was doing here.

"Grace. You come here, out of the blue, to tell me I have a son. That you want me to take care of him. Fine. But then you have to include me."

Grace sighed. "You're right. I'm so used to doing everything on my own, I didn't think…

And a week ago, Jules was fine in this carrier. He just got excited when he saw you, is all."

"Yeah." Mica's face softened, along with his tone. "He did. Didn't he?"

"He likes people."

"I'm hoping he likes *me*."

"Me, too. I want him to get to know you. For you to learn to be a real dad to him."

"Put 'er there, buddy," Mica said, holding out his hand for Jules to grasp. Jules pulled Mica's hand to his mouth.

"Did you wash your hands?"

"Not since I left the house."

"Then take off your coat and go over to the sink and wash up. Then he can suckle your finger all you want. I'll get us some plates for the food."

"Good. I'm starving. Hey, can he eat any of this stuff yet?"

Grace rolled her eyes. "Of course not."

"Not even the rice?"

"He could choke. But he does have six teeth. Maybe if I cut up some of the steamed broccoli, he might try a smidge."

"I gotta see this," Mica said eagerly.

Grace took out two plates and silverware and opened the steaming boxes of shrimp fried rice and kung pao chicken.

She filled two glasses with water from the tap. "Sorry I don't have any wine or tea. I haven't been to the store since I landed. All I have is food for Jules. Mrs. Beabots gave me some leftovers…" She stopped. She was rambling.

She frowned as she placed paper napkins from the brown bag on the table. In Paris, she always prepared pretty meals for company. But she was only in Indian Lake for a short time. Accoutrements for dining were not on her priority list. She hadn't planned to serve dinner to anyone. She should have realized that Mica might be a guest. Or more than that.

There was a great deal she hadn't thought through and she wished now she had.

She cut up some broccoli, speared the tiniest piece with her fork and held it out to Jules. He leaned forward, put it in his mouth. In less than two seconds, his face soured and he spit the broccoli onto his bib.

"I take it that was a no-go," Mica said.

"I should have started with something he's used to. I puree most of his food at home. He's had carrots and green beans, but broccoli is new to him."

Mica smiled. "Kinda cute, though, the way he knows what he likes and doesn't like."

"Yeah," she agreed tentatively.

With her fork hovering over her golden chicken, she asked, "Why are you here, Mica?"

"Well," he said wiping his fingers on a paper napkin, "I think we should move on since you're not here for very long."

"Move on?"

"Yes." He looked at her with earnest eyes. "We need to get married."

Grace's heart banged once in her chest and stopped as if it had no reason to beat again. "Married." Shockingly, she realized this was what she'd always wanted to hear from Mica. This was her teenage dream come true. Mica was asking her to marry him. She should be on top of the world.

But she felt cold, as if she'd just settled quite permanently in her grave. Something was wrong. Every ancient instinct a human could call upon in a moment of crisis had gone on alert. She should run. Seek shelter. The world was not beginning, but ending.

She knew better than to allow her ears to hear the rest of what he was saying.

"I want Jules to know his roots. His heritage. I want him to know all of my family and be a real part of our family. He's a Barzonni. I want this for my son."

Mica hadn't said that he wanted her or cared about her. He hadn't even said he loved Jules. He was performing a responsibility that was expected of him because he was a Barzonni.

A pang speared her heart.

She had only one choice and she took it.

"No, Mica. I won't marry you."

CHAPTER SEVEN

MICA WAS SPEECHLESS as Grace rose from her chair, clearly bent on escorting him from her apartment. He couldn't possibly have heard her right. She was turning him down? Was she out of her mind? What kind of game was she playing?

He bolted to his feet and grabbed her arm. "Wait a minute."

"No, you wait a minute. I came to Indian Lake to get your help with our son. Granted, I didn't go about any of this the right way. I should have told you about him when I discovered I was pregnant. I didn't want to burden you because you were going through all kinds of—of…personal things. I thought I was sparing you from more trauma. I screwed up. I made a mistake. I see that now. But I'm not going to marry you. I only need your help for a while."

"No way, Grace. He's my son. Period. I

won't walk away from him the way you walked away from me."

"What are you talking about?"

"You left here last October and I haven't heard from you since. You'll be here a week and then take off again. For some vague amount of time. And then when your work settles down, or you change your mind about leaving Jules with me—I'm guessing you'll want him back. Then you'll leave me a third time, and who knows if I'll ever hear from you again. No way. He's mine. Ours. Forever. That's what I believe in. Forever."

"This is ridiculous. You don't love me, Mica."

His words caught in his throat. He'd been ready for another argument. He hadn't figured on introspection. "What? Who said anything about love?"

"I did."

"Why?" He stepped closer to her, feeling a magnetic force drawing him in. When he was near Grace, he felt bewitched. But love? He'd never been in love. Though her rejection last year had hurt him deeply, and he wanted to hold her now and kiss away her concerns, he didn't believe he loved her. If they loved each other, none of this would be happening, would it? Loving someone meant trusting them, and he wasn't sure he could trust her after she'd kept Jules a secret for so long.

"Mica, when I marry a man—if I ever do—it will be because I love him and he loves me in return. I won't settle for less."

Her eyes blazed righteousness and resolution. Mica thought of simply trying to appease her, for Jules's sake, but she'd see right through him. He would be honest with her, even if she hadn't always been with him.

"Then I won't help you," he said. "Pack him up and go back to Paris."

"You can't mean that."

"I do," he replied firmly, wondering if she could sense his anxiety. If she left now, he might never see Jules again. He could fight international courts and spend a fortune he didn't have to gain custody…and he'd make a lifelong enemy of the woman who'd intrigued him ever since that summer day in the pool. Despite her betrayal, there was good in her. He believed that she'd come to Indian Lake because she wanted to do the right thing—by him and by Jules. Mica hoped she'd make the right decision now.

"Mica, do you have any idea what's at stake for me right now? This week?"

"I—"

"You can't because you still don't understand the world I live in. Fashion Week starts in mid-January. Two of my designs were on the runway in October and they sold. My name is just a whisper right now, but with my fall designs, the big houses are looking at me. I didn't want to put it off any longer, but this trip is horrible timing. My team is going nuts even though I'm trying to stay in touch as much as possible. I need to work all day and night until the show. I'm taking a stab at some ready-to-wear designs as well. They don't show until February, but they're just as important. Jules deserves my full attention and I can't give it to him. I want him to know you. I want you to know him and love him as well. I know it may not look that way to you, but I want the best for our son. I need help, Mica, not ultimatums."

Well, didn't he feel like a heel. And envious. Grace was driven by passion for her work. He could only imagine the stimulation and excitement that would create. She had what he wanted desperately for himself. He'd been wrong to think she was self-centered. He was the selfish one. At the same time, it was deeply important to him that Jules know all that it meant to be a Barzonni. Perhaps it was pride, but it was more than that. Mica revered his father for all he had sacrificed for his family. He was only beginning to understand what his mother had forfeited when she chose to keep her promise to Angelo and marry him.

It hit Mica that his parents had entered into a marriage that was less than romantic and idyllic for the sake of the life they intended to build in America. His father had escaped poverty in the streets of Sicily and his mother had chosen to devote her life to her sons and the farm. Family and all its heraldry, lineage and expectations rattled through Mica's bones like anchor chains. He could no more allow Grace to raise their child alone than fly to the moon. He was Jules's father. He would do all he could for his boy for the rest of his life. Jules was a Barzonni and that meant a lot of things to Mica.

Like his parents, Mica believed in family and that a family should stay together at all costs. Though their life together might have been less than ideal, Angelo and Gina gave everything so that their sons would inherit the farm, and know what it was to earn the pride in the land they tilled and sowed. Mica wanted to give Jules the best he could and that meant he needed to marry Grace.

It was his honor and his duty to his son.

All he had to do was convince Grace that marriage was the right thing to do.

"Grace, you're right. I don't know much of anything about your career, but I'm willing to learn. What I'm trying to say is that I should be a part of your life. Jules's life. We should share in everything."

She stared at him like he'd lost his mind. She blinked. "Really?"

"How can we possibly be the best parents for our son if we aren't involved in each other's lives?"

"You're right, of course," she said tentatively.

"Not only do I need to learn how to take care of Jules, but I also need—I mean, want—to know about you. Your work. Who are these people you work with? And what is Fashion Week and why is it more important than any other week?"

"Oh, Mica." She laughed. "It's not a week, but a showcase. Every fashion critic from every magazine around the world will be there for one purpose. To judge my work."

His mouth rounded. "Oh. That's...that's— holy cow. Big."

"Very big," she said.

He couldn't take his eyes off her. She was

doing it again. Giving him that open, caring gaze that went straight to a place deep inside him.

"Now you," she said spearing another piece of chicken. "Tell me about your work."

"What work? I haven't…"

"Don't give me that, Mica. I know you. That head of yours is full of all kinds of ideas. I can hear them whirring in there," she teased.

He shook his head. For the past year, nearly every idea he'd had had turned to dust before he could translate it to his computer.

"It's been a struggle, but I have been working on voice-activated farm machinery. I want to create a system that can be activated even from a cell phone."

"Like an app?"

"Similar." Mica was uncomfortable talking about his failures when Grace was clearly on the cusp of success. Listening to Grace opened his eyes. He hadn't worked the long hours that Grace did. He'd puttered at his designs and hadn't attacked his work head-on. He could do better. Much better.

Grace had always seemed to instinctively know what he needed. Like she had last October. Despite all she had going on in her career, being pulled in several directions at once, when she looked at him, she made him feel like the only person in her universe.

His head told him to be wary. She was the woman who'd deceived him. But Mica's heart told him otherwise.

It was enough that his anger was deflating. He'd take that.

Grace didn't know it, but she was changing his world with or without Jules.

Jules had been toying with a snow pea, not quite sure if it should go in his mouth or be sent flying across the room. He chose the latter.

Then he rubbed his eyes. Frowned. Rubbed his ears and started fussing. The fidgeting and scowling turned into sobs, which escalated into high-pitched cries.

Mica glanced from Jules to Grace. "Is he okay?"

"Oh, sweetheart," Grace said, rising from her chair. She went to Jules, unhooked the belt on the carrier chair and lifted him out. She put him over her shoulder but Jules just screamed louder.

Mica rose. "Here, let me try."

"You sure?" she asked.

He shrugged and took Jules in his strong arm. Jules let out a bellow. Mica looked pleadingly at Grace, who held both arms out. "Looks like I've lost my touch."

"I'll get his bottle ready. That always settles him down."

"Yeah. He's probably hungry, huh? Is it just green food he doesn't like?"

Grace went to the fridge, took out a prepared bottle and put it in the microwave. "He likes green beans and peas. I thought he'd like the snow pea. Apparently not. The chicken was too spicy for him."

"I should've thought of that," Mica replied, noticing that Jules's cries were getting louder as he tried to wiggle out of Grace's arms.

The microwave dinged and she withdrew the bottle, but when she moved it toward Jules's mouth, he pushed it away and cried louder.

"What's going on?" Mica asked, concerned.

"I'm guessing he's teething again."

Mica snapped his fingers. "I remember Gabe's baby went through this." He reached in his back pocket for his iPhone. "I'll call Gabe."

"No, that's okay…" Grace protested, but then Jules let out a bloodcurdling scream. "Actually, I'll take any advice he can give us."

Mica nodded as Gabe answered. "Hey, Gabe. We have, er, well…" Mica began. He hadn't told anyone in the family about Jules yet, though it was his bet that his mother had texted, emailed and smoke-signaled the entire Barzonni tribe. "I need help with Jules."

"Uh-huh. Jules. The son you forgot to mention to me, Liz, Nate, Maddie, Rafe and Olivia? That Jules?"

"Knock it off. There hasn't been time."

"Mom found time."

"I'm serious, Gabe."

Jules screamed again.

"Hear that?" Mica asked. "Grace says he's teething. What did you do when Zeke was teething?"

"Me?" Gabe answered. "Merlot, mostly."

Mica's jaw dropped. "For the kid?"

"What? No, for me. We put teething gel on Zeke's gums."

"Hold on." Mica put his hand over the phone. "You got any teething gel?" he asked Grace.

"I don't believe in it. I read a thing on the internet. It's not good. I believe in natural, organic—"

Mica nodded. "I get it." He went back to the call. "Gabe. She doesn't have any. She wants organic. What can I use instead?"

"Chardonnay's not bad," Gabe quipped. "Or whiskey. Just rub a tiny bit on his gums. It won't hurt him."

"She hasn't got any wine. No food here, either. She just flew in yesterday…"

"Say no more. I can be there in twenty minutes. This is an emergency."

"Okay. Thanks." Mica hung up.

Grace shifted a sobbing Jules to her left shoulder. "What did he say?"

"He's coming over. He said wine was okay."

"Not for my baby!" she squealed. "No alcohol, Mica."

"Okay. But he's our baby," he amended.

"I know." Grace leaned her cheek against Jules's head. "Oh, no."

Mica sensed her alarm. "What is it?"

"I'm not sure." She pressed the back of her hand to Jules's forehead. "He feels warm."

"Really? He was fine a few minutes ago."

"I have a digital thermometer in his diaper bag." She nodded toward the quilted bag on the counter. Jules kept screaming.

Mica went to the bag and found the thermometer. He handed it to Grace. She put the thermometer on Jules's forehead. "It's ninety-nine six."

"Is that bad?"

"It's not too high, but it's still a fever. And he keeps rubbing his ears." Her eyes were round with worry. "Do you know a pediatrician we could call?"

He shook his head. "No, and half the offices are closed for the holidays. Aside from the ER, there's no one…" He held up his palm. "Hold on."

Mica hit Nate's number. He waited while it rang.

"Now who are you calling?" Grace asked.

"Nate. He's a doctor."

"A cardiac surgeon, Mica. Not a pediatrician."

Mica shrugged. "He can diagnose, can't he? You need help. I'm here to get it for you." He paused as Nate picked up. "Nate! I need a favor. I'm over here at Mrs. Beabots's upstairs apartment with Grace. And, oh, so Mom told you guys? Fine. So, Jules is sick, we think. He's got a temperature and he won't stop screaming. We thought it was teething at first, so I called Gabe. He's bringing some wine for the baby… No. I mean, to put on his gums." Grace shot him a look. "Hey! Gabe's a vintner! I think he just wants to meet Jules, though. Anyway, Jules's temperature is nearly one hundred, so I don't think it's his gums…Oh, great. Thanks, Nate." He hung up.

Grace stood and started walking the floor with Jules.

"Nate's coming over. Maddie, too."

"Mica, is your whole family going to be here?"

He snapped his fingers. "Right. I should've asked Mom in the first place." He started to take out his phone.

Grace placed her hand on his. "It's okay. I think we'll have enough Barzonnis here to handle the problem. I'm beginning to think he has an ear infection. From the flight. He was good on the plane until we started descending. Then he screamed the entire time. I felt so sorry for the businessman next to me."

Mica wasn't used to hearing a baby scream like Jules. The kid clearly had a strong pair of lungs. He'd probably grow up to be an auctioneer.

Ten minutes later, Nate arrived with a canvas tote in hand. Maddie was grinning from ear to ear as she entered the apartment. "Grace! I'm dying to meet Jules!" she said, hugging her. Mica stood in the hallway with Jules in his arm.

Nate peered at the baby. "Wow, he does look like you. Hollers and bellyaches like you, too."

"Shut up. And thanks for coming."

There was a second knock on the door. As Grace greeted Gabe, Liz and toddler Zeke, Mica took Jules into the living room and placed him on one of Mrs. Beabots's Victorian sofas.

Nate took out his stethoscope, listened to the baby's chest and then used an otoscope to look inside Jules's ears. He felt his glands and looked inside the baby's throat.

Gagging on the tongue depressor quieted Jules down. He stared in confusion from Nate to Mica and then to Gabe.

Then he burst into tears again.

"I'm so sorry," Grace apologized as she picked him up.

"So," Gabe said, "what is it? Should we put some of this chardonnay on his gums?" Gabe lifted the bottle. "It's one of our best."

"Oh, Gabe, quit fooling around," Liz teased. She turned to Mica. "He brought the wine for you and Grace. We just wanted to meet the baby."

Mica exhaled. "That's exactly what I told Grace."

Nate put away his instruments. "He's got an ear infection and his throat is inflamed." He took out his cell phone. "I'll call the pharmacy and order some antibiotics. Mica, you can drive down and get it. It's only a couple blocks. Pick up some children's fever reducer, too. The liquid comes with a dropper and it tastes pretty good."

"You use it yourself?" Mica joked.

Nate looked at Mica, a slow smile coming to his face. "Good to see your sense of humor has resurfaced, Mica." He slapped his brother's shoulder. "Get the meds. Grace, make sure he eats. Some cereal, bread, pasta. Carbs, you know? So he doesn't get a tummy ache. He should improve by morning. I'll text Matt Ferguson, a pediatrician friend of mine. I'll give him the rundown and you can text him or call him over the next few days."

Maddie hooked her arm through Nate's. "Speaking of New Year's, you are coming out to Gina's party, right?"

"Uh…" Grace looked at Mica.

He swiped his face with his palm. "I forgot about the party."

"Mica!" Liz and Maddie said simultaneously.

"I've had a lot going on." He turned to Grace. "My mother has a huge New Year's Eve dinner every year. Crown roast of pork. All the trimmings. Champagne. Then afterward, we go out to the Lodges for dancing and the countdown to midnight. Mom told me to invite you."

"We'll all be there, Grace," Liz said. "Jules should be much better by then. And Gina's got plenty of baby stuff. Even an extra high chair for Jules so he can sit next to you at the table. Say you'll come."

Grace swung her gaze to Mica and pinned him with an emotion that was nearly electric. The faces of his brothers and sisters-in-law swirled around him as if he was the center of a kaleidoscope. His world had been spinning since Grace returned. He'd been numb for months and now he felt everything. The only problem was—he hadn't had time to sort things out.

Time.

He was already counting down the days that remained until Grace left.

"Do you want me to come, Mica?" she asked hesitantly.

"I do," he replied, swallowing the lump in his throat. "You're family now."

She turned to Maddie and Liz. "I'd be honored."

CHAPTER EIGHT

"THIS IS A DISASTER," Grace said, looking up from her suitcase. Jules, who was dressed in a black wool jacket and matching pants with gold braid that she'd designed and made herself, scooted over to her feet, then sat back on his bottom.

Now that he was better and his fever had broken, Jules was back to being his usual sweet self. She was amazed at how much Jules's first illness had frightened her. For his whole life, he had practically lived in her hectic artistic workrooms, being cuddled and cooed over by some of the top models in Paris. He'd always seemed unperturbed by all the hustle and bustle, and other than colic when he was three months old, he'd never even had a fever.

When Mica had called in half his family to help, she'd thought he was going overboard. She'd been wrong. Jules was the picture of health. The only trouble was that now she had to attend Gina Barzonni's formal New Year's

Eve dinner, and Grace, an up-and-coming Paris designer, hadn't brought a thing to wear.

She lifted a midnight-blue-and-black woven poncho interlaced with silver threads. She could pair it with a wool skirt, but she'd stand out like a sore thumb amid the velvets and satins at Gina's party.

Jules clapped his hands and blew out a long raspberry.

"Even you're a critic, huh?" Grace chuckled and put the poncho on the bed, then picked up Jules. "Well, if Mica can call in his troops, I'll have to call in mine."

"You've come to the right place." Mrs. Beabots beamed. "Several of the girls come to me during the holidays. They just don't make lovely dresses like they used to, and they certainly don't sell them in Indian Lake," she continued. "Gina's party is always elegant and we do love getting dressed up for it—and the dancing at the Lodges."

"I can't thank you enough," Grace said, giving Jules his pacifier. He smiled and threw his little arms around her neck, burying his head against her shoulder.

"I'm happy he's feeling better. There's nothing worse than trying to help a child who can't speak," Mrs. Beabots said as she went toward her bedroom. "Babies and helpless animals. I'm a pushover for both. But don't tell anybody."

"I'll never say a word." Grace chuckled.

The tinny, antique sound of the doorbell rang out.

"That will be Sarah and Isabelle."

"Isabelle's coming, too? I can't wait to see her!"

"She's a renowned artist now. She paints the loveliest fairies and water sprites," Mrs. Beabots said. "For my money, the girl has nailed her naturescapes. I love what she's doing now with oils. I bought one for the dining room. It's a woman reclining in a forest glen with tiny fairies peeking out from under the fallen leaves."

"It sounds lovely."

"It is." She went to the front door and greeted her guests.

Fairies? Grace stared after Mrs. Beabots wondering what kind of silliness she was talking about.

Mrs. Beabots returned with Sarah and a pretty, elfin-faced woman with hair that hung nearly to her waist. Grace remembered her well.

Isabelle instantly put her arms around Grace and Jules. "I'm so happy to see you again. And your beautiful baby. I want to hear all about Paris!" Isabelle blurted out. "Do you like it there?"

"No. I adore it," Grace said effusively. "It's heaven."

Isabelle unwound the gray-and-black scarf around her neck and took off her matching tweed jacket. "I just got married this past summer—Scott and I didn't go on a honeymoon, but we've talked about Paris so much. I've downloaded dozens of virtual tours on my phone," she said, gushing.

"That's great," Grace said, remembering her run-in with Isabelle's brother on the train last October. "Congratulations on your marriage." Why did her old friend's news give her such a pang of sadness? Grace hoped it didn't show. Jules laid his cheek against hers, taking her out of her thoughts.

"It's so nice to see the three of you together," Mrs. Beabots said. "All artists in your own right. You have a lot in common."

"Well, today we all have something else in common, Mrs. Beabots," Sarah said. "Gina's party is tonight and I, for one, haven't shopped since Charlotte was born."

Grace took in the wrinkled black skirt and stretchy, rust-colored top Sarah wore.

Mrs. Beabots pointed at Sarah's outfit. "Isn't that the same top you wore when you were pregnant?"

"It is," Sarah replied glumly. "I was bored with it then and I'm still bored now."

Mrs. Beabots said, "There was something to be said for the maternity clothes of fifty years ago. Those trapeze blouses and capes had a certain swing and elegance. I remember one that a friend of mine wore in Paris. It was black with a sequined silver collar and cuffs. She was a blonde like you, Sarah, and she looked like a queen."

Grace hung on Mrs. Beabots's every word. She envisioned the way she would encrust the collar with black seed pearls, jet beads and silver sequins. She'd pair it with black-and-white harlequin pants and black leather ballet flats. Mrs. Beabots was right. No wonder she and her team were having problems. The offerings for the average woman were the same styles, same colors, year in and year out. Unless one lived in Paris or New York or London or could afford haute couture, everyday fashion was bereft of innovation.

"All of this is to say," Isabelle added, "that none of us has anything to wear to Gina's party. And Maddie and Liz told us we should wear something special because Gina hired a professional photographer this year. I don't understand. What's the big deal?"

Mrs. Beabots smiled. "Oh, I know this one. Gina and Sam are going to announce their engagement. Their wedding will be at the end of January."

"So soon?" Grace gulped. Again, she didn't know why other people's weddings were of any particular concern to her. Except for the fact that she kept hearing Mica's voice as he asked her to marry him.

Marriage. In all her life, even her daydreams about Mica when she was a teen, she hadn't actually gone so far as to consider marriage. Grace wasn't sure she was the marrying kind. She'd lived her life alone, pursuing her own goals. Making decisions. She was an independent woman.

Then Jules had arrived and suddenly Grace's life wasn't just about her.

She was a mother now. Raising a child on her own, she could now admit, wasn't as simple and straightforward as she'd thought it might be. But becoming a wife—a partner? She wasn't sure she wanted to take on that role.

"What are you going to wear, Grace?" Isabelle asked, her eyes filled with admiration.

"That's why I'm here. I hadn't planned on a formal affair. I do have a crimson off-the-shoulder blouse from my fall line that might be right, but I need a skirt to go with it."

"Oh!" Mrs. Beabots exclaimed. "I have just the thing." She motioned for the women to follow her.

Once in the bedroom, Mrs. Beabots flung open two white, paneled doors revealing a walk-in closet almost as big as Grace's entire Paris apartment.

"What is this?" Grace gasped.

Sarah and Isabelle shot her knowing smiles.

Mrs. Beabots waved her hand toward the interior. "This, my dears, is where I keep my treasures."

Grace felt as if she was walking into a fashion designer's museum. The clothes were arranged by color, with all the blouses on one side of the room alongside the dresses, long coats and jackets. On the opposite wall were skirts and trousers. Grace realized that she was looking through clear plastic garment bags holding Christian Dior skirts that possibly could date back to 1947, when Dior's "New Look" put Paris couture back on the map after World War II. She saw Yves Saint Laurent jackets and slacks. A Molyneux black evening gown. Suits by Courrèges. Grace knew them all. She'd studied fashion history nearly all her life. When she was ten, she dreamed of wearing gold lamé gowns. Now she designed clothing and hoped that one day, her pieces would end up in a history book. It was her passage to immortality. Grace believed that deep inside her, she possessed enough creativity to be that good—the best in her field.

And nothing was ever going to stop her.

Somehow, Mrs. Beabots's closet represented the dream that Grace had cobbled together for herself from long years of yearning, a million and half hours of work, associations she'd made and lost, sacrifices...

Yes. She'd given up a lot to be in Paris. Time she could have spent with Aunt Louise. The one person who loved her above all others.

Grace was astonished at the number of days and years her dream had taken from her life, yet she still wasn't where she wanted to be. Had it been worth it? Had she made the right decision?

Jules wiggled in her arms. What else was she sacrificing in order to succeed?

Grace walked over to a large plastic bag holding a skirt constructed of yards of pink chiffon. A thick white satin sash was sewn onto the waist. "This is Dior, isn't it?"

"Yes, dear. It is. You have a good eye and it will be perfect with your crimson blouse."

"Oh, I couldn't. This is priceless."

"Perhaps. But I'd rather have the memory of seeing you in it at Gina's party than visit it in this closet. My delight is in having you girls experience a tiny portion of what my life was like when I was young and living in Paris."

Grace put Jules on the carpet so he could move around and she could inspect the clothing more closely. "This was circa 1950, I believe. Where did you get it?"

"Oh, I bought it from a girl I knew in Paris. She'd been a model for Dior and he gifted her with the skirt. It's too long for me, but when she sold it, she needed money. At the time, I thought I was paying too much. Now, of course…"

"It's worth a fortune," Grace said.

"A small one." Mrs. Beabots smiled as she took a black suede jacket with gold piping on the lapels off the hanger. "Here, Isabelle, try this on."

While Isabelle stuck her arms through the sleeves, Grace wandered over to a set of drawers with clear plastic dust covers. She peered at the silks. "These are Hermès."

"And Dior, Chanel, Yves Saint Laurent and a few others. I always like a splash of color. Pick one out for Isabelle, to go with her jacket."

Isabelle shook her head. "Those scarves are worth over three hundred dollars each. What if I lose it?"

"What do you think that jacket is worth?" Grace chuckled. "I'm guessing a couple thousand."

Mrs. Beabots smiled mischievously. "This is the last time I bring a know-it-all into my closet."

"Oh, Mrs. Beabots." Sarah laughed. "You're having a blast with us and we love it. We all know your treasures are, well, treasures."

"We do?" Isabelle asked as she touched the jacket sleeve. "I can't wear this."

"Sure you can," Grace said. "And you'll do it with your head held high. Trust me, you'll feel excruciatingly marvelous all night long. Nothing changes a person's perspective like the clothes she wears."

Sarah dropped the gold earrings she was holding back into their velvet tray. "Why is that? Are we so shallow that a sweater can alter our mood?"

Grace shook her head. "I don't think it's shallow. Sarah, you're a designer—you understand the power of color, shape and texture. I imagine you do, too, Isabelle, because of your painting. Well, it's the same with fashion. A red lipstick reflects my attitude on a particular night in a different way than a beachy coral does during the day. Haven't you ever had an outfit or a piece of clothing that made you feel special, more like yourself? That's what I'm talking about."

"I guess so," Isabelle answered. "I just hardly ever have time to do more than paint, take care of our kids and spend time with Scott. I never have an afternoon to go from shop to shop trying to put an outfit together. I like dresses, because it's all in one. Some shoes and earrings and I'm done. Of course, I look at you and I think, with a bit more effort, I could do this. Grace, believe me, I get what you're saying."

Grace heard the appreciation in Isabelle's voice and suddenly felt a spark of enthusiasm hit her creative cells. She'd been recharged, as if her battery had run low.

It had been a long time since she'd actually talked to women outside the fashion-and-design industry. Her friends were her design-team members. She had coffee with models and fabric artists. Her life in Paris revolved around fashion. Her peers should have ignited her talent, but lately, they had not. It wasn't their fault. The problem had been within Grace. She'd been so overloaded with Jules, she feared she'd lost her imagination.

Grace realized that she'd buried her creativity under a mountain of deadlines, expectations and her own egocentric need to succeed.

It was no wonder her sketches didn't materialize into the visions in her head. Due to financial strains, she'd chosen to work with a new silk weaver from Lyon whose fabric was subpar. It had been a bad choice and a waste of valuable time because the fabric was simply not right. To make matters worse, the English wool she'd ordered was dense and the weave too loose for the jackets she'd designed.

She looked at the riot of color in Mrs. Beabots's closet. These vintage clothes were the best the big houses could turn out at the time. They didn't settle for second best. They didn't use remnant merino wool or cottons that couldn't hold their dye. They demanded the best from themselves.

Grace stood in front of Isabelle and flattened the collar until it sat perfectly. "This jacket was meant to be worn with a simple and comfortable sheath dress, or a plain skirt and sweater. We'll find something and you will feel and be amazing."

"I have just the sheath," Mrs. Beabots said, handing Isabelle a sleeveless black silk number. Isabelle went behind a Chinese screen and when she emerged, Grace studied the outfit, tilting her head from left to right. "You should wear half your hair up and away from your face, the rest tumbling down your back. Then we'll stud your hair with rhinestones that will glitter in the lamplight. Let your hair be your accessory. Then we need long earrings."

"Shoulder dusters!" Mrs. Beabots said. "I love them!" She turned to a velvet-lined drawer and pulled out a pair of long gold bars studded with rhinestones. At least Grace thought they were rhinestones. In this closet, they could be diamonds.

"Put these on, dear," Mrs. Beabots encouraged.

Isabelle turned toward one of the three full-length mirrors. "That's me?"

"Wait until I put those rhinestones in your hair," Grace said.

Sarah beamed as she stood behind Isabelle. "You look incredible. You're…transformed."

Grace stood back from the group as they

continued admiring her selections. Her mind was ricocheting with ideas. Her new designs needed to be comfortable and utilitarian for those women who went from offices or an artist's easel to a kid's school play and then to a dinner or a friend's party. She would take the mainstays in every woman's closet and give them a touch of glamour. Not glitz, just subtle glamour like the gold piping on the Yves Saint Laurent jacket.

She needed workable fabric. She knew just where to find the perfect fabrics for these designs.

"This is it!" Sarah squealed, holding up a long, off-the-shoulder dress in black crepe. It was classic and elegant. "I've seen this before and always admired it. It's Chanel, I think. I have black heels and new gold-and-rhinestone earrings I got for Christmas from the kids."

"Perfect!" Mrs. Beabots said.

"Thank you so much, Mrs. Beabots. But now I have to scoot." Sarah hugged the three of them in turn. "I can't wait to see you in that Dior skirt at Gina's party," Sarah told Grace as she left. "You'll be gorgeous."

"I'd better go as well," Isabelle said.

Grace picked up Jules and followed Mrs. Beabots out of the closet. She closed the doors reverently, feeling as if she'd walked out of a dream and back to reality. Her mind whirred with a tornado of design ideas. All Grace wanted to do was sit down with her sketchbook and get to work.

Yet she had to focus on the fact that in a few hours, she'd be at the Barzonni villa with Mica. Surprisingly, her heart swelled with anticipation. Half the reason she wanted to look stunning tonight was to see his reaction. She wanted to surprise him. Entice him. Push him.

Did he have feelings for her?

They hadn't resolved a thing and time was running out. She had no idea what her next move would be, but she couldn't let him talk her into marriage.

Maybe the Dior skirt wasn't such a good idea after all.

"Grace, dear. Don't you want to try that skirt on?"

"It's very generous of you, Mrs. Beabots, but perhaps I shouldn't wear something quite so…eye-catching."

"Nonsense. What on earth would you wear instead?"

Grace let out a breath. "A suit of armor."

CHAPTER NINE

THE SUN CAST LONG, crisscross shadows of bare-armed trees over the snow-dusted Barzonni fields. Inside the villa, no family member was exempt from party preparations. Both Nate and Gabe had arrived early with supplies, food, flowers and cases of Gabe's wine.

Rafe, Olivia and Julia, Olivia's mother, worked alongside Gina in the kitchen.

Mica and Nate put the leaves in the dining table, then spread out the long Irish linen cloth. Nate brought a stack of china plates.

"I can't believe how this party grows every year," Mica said.

"And it's going to keep growing. Don't forget, we're setting a kids' table in the den as well."

"Kids' table," Mica mused. "I remember when there were only four kids at that table. This year we have Luke and Sarah's three, Scott and Isabelle's two, Danny Sullivan and two Barzonnis."

Nate paused. "Two Barzonnis?"

"Yeah. Zeke and Jules," Mica replied.

"Uh-huh."

Mica curled his fingers around a group of sterling knives. "What's that supposed to mean?"

"I'm just wondering if you'll be making a similar announcement to Mom and Sam's tonight."

"No." Mica ground out the word, gripping the knives so tightly he thought he could snap one of them in half. He continued setting the table.

"So, you haven't popped the question? I recommend the old get-down-on-one-knee style. It worked for me." Nate chuckled, then looked at Mica. "What?"

"I did ask her. She turned me down."

Nate straightened and put his hands on his hips. "For real? She's the mother of your baby. She has to marry you."

"She doesn't see it that way."

"Okay. This I hadn't figured. I mean, Maddie says that Grace had a crush on you when we were kids. Quite obviously, her feelings were the same last autumn. You must not have asked her right." Nate slapped his forehead. "You didn't have a ring. Is that it?"

Mica tossed the knives on the table. They jangled and slashed each other like broadswords. "No, Nate. I didn't have a ring. And no, it has nothing to do with my style. She doesn't want to marry me. Plain and simple."

Nate's expression was concerned. "Is it… the arm?"

"She says not. But I can't be sure."

"Aw, man. I just didn't think Grace was like that." He scratched his head. "No, I can't believe that. It's got to be something else."

It was something else all right, but Mica especially didn't want to tell his successful and blissfully happy brother that Grace wanted a man who loved her. Mica didn't know what love was and he certainly wasn't going to lie to Grace. She deserved better than that.

Mica had been struggling for over a year to adjust to his new reality. He liked to think he'd done a decent job of accepting his limitations, but the truth was, he had a long way to go. Life was tough and then it got tougher— that was his new mantra. There wasn't much to make him happy anymore, and when Grace had turned him down, she'd underlined his losses with a blunt instrument.

When Grace hadn't contacted him after her month in Indian Lake, he'd understood she wanted more for herself than a life here. It had hurt, but he'd been okay with it. His life was a tangle of opportunities unrealized, crushed expectations and nonexistent hopes. And he'd done little to pull himself together. He couldn't perform his old duties on the farm. So, he'd turned to his design work. But nothing had panned out. It took determination and focus to go back to the computer, but too often he allowed himself to wallow in the muck of self-pity.

I am responsible for my lack of accomplishment.

He knew it and his family knew it, though they gave him a wide berth—too wide. But to be fair, he'd also been avoiding them lately. He saw the pity in their eyes. He saw their frustration.

Now he was a father. Meeting Jules had lit a fire inside Mica, giving him the first nudge out of his depression that he'd felt in months. Jules gave him hope for the future, but Mica still had no idea where his life was going next week, let alone next year. He wanted more than anything to do right by Jules, and to Mica, that meant marrying Grace. But part of him understood why she'd said no. She deserved a guy who had a thriving career, focus and ambition. Why should Mica expect her to settle for less?

But what if I could be that guy? What would I have to do?

He'd have to show her that not only was he capable and dependable, but also that Jules belonged on the farm, where he would grow up with aunts, uncles, cousins, a very doting grandmother and soon, a new grandfather. It would take a lot of sacrifice on both their parts, but he was asking no more than his own parents had done for the welfare of their family.

"Don't worry," Mica said to Nate. "I've still got time to convince Grace that she *and* Jules belong here as part of our family."

Nate took a step closer to Mica. "Is that what you've been saying to her?"

"Partly. Mostly. Yeah."

"No wonder she turned you down."

"What? Why?"

"You're telling her that her only option is to leave Paris and live with you on the farm. Oh, I bet that really swept her off her feet." Nate nodded and pursed his lips. "Yeah. Every woman wants to know that all her hard work, ingenuity and brilliance doesn't matter a whit. She was just daydreaming to think she could be a name in the fashion world." Nate slapped

Mica's back. "If I'd said something like that to Maddie? She would have kicked me out the door. Hard."

Nate walked away, shaking his head.

Mica scooped up the knives and continued setting the table, muttering to himself.

He knew that feeling and he despised it. It had become his bedfellow ever since the accident. How could he not feel inadequate, when he could no longer do most of the farm work he'd built his adult life upon? Everything he'd been striving toward had been taken away from him. True, the farm would probably be fine in the end, but Mica would not get the same satisfaction, the same drive, out of its success if he was unable to work the land.

And now he had Jules to think of, too. He believed in making his son a true Barzonni, in raising him here, but now Mica realized he'd need to do more than just learn to take care of a baby. He had to provide for Jules, set a good example. Mica still hadn't fully forgiven Grace for keeping their son a secret, but maybe her bringing Jules here was the shock Mica needed to make him take stock of his life. Change his thinking. For over a year, he'd been stuck. Now he needed to move forward.

But how?

GRACE ARRIVED AT the party with Aunt Louise, Mrs. Beabots and the Bosworth family.

As they pulled in to the farm, Grace noticed the barn roof was decorated in lights shaped like fireworks, flashing on and off. Below was a small replica of New York's Times Square "ball" that would drop at midnight.

"Is there anything Gina doesn't think of for her parties?" Grace asked.

"Nope!" everyone in the van shouted. Jules clapped his hands.

She leaned down to Jules and tickled him. "You are Barzonni through and through."

Jules giggled.

Grace was the last in their group to enter the house. Gina was hugging Mrs. Beabots, who was complimenting the hostess on the decorations. The children raced to the den to watch a movie and play with their friends. Over the heads of Luke and Sarah, Grace spotted every Barzonni family member and was especially struck at how radiant and happy they all looked. Hugs and kisses and laughter filled the spacious rooms and Grace felt as if she might burst into tears. Her father had died young. Her mother died just as Grace graduated from high school. She didn't have brothers or sisters and had never had this kind of holiday gathering in her life. It was amazing to her that Gina could put all this together and then share it with such generous abandon with her family and friends.

The men were dressed in tuxedos, which Grace hadn't expected. The women were a sea of gold, silver, black velvet and deep sapphire dresses and long skirts. No one had skimped on accessories or jewels.

It was a happy night, she thought the minute her eyes came to rest on Mica.

He was staring at her with deep blue eyes that bored a path straight to her soul. That gaze kept her riveted to the spot as he walked up to her. He took her hand in his and kissed it.

"Welcome to your first New Year's Eve extravaganza, à la Gina," he quipped. Then he leaned over and kissed Jules on the cheek. "Hello, son. How're you feeling?"

Grace felt the edges of her heart melt as Jules grinned at Mica and thrust his arms toward his father. "He's a lot better today. I think he wants you to hold him."

"Be proud to," he said, wrapping his arm around the baby as he took his perch on Mica's shoulder. "We're putting the coats in the den closet. I'll walk over with you."

"Fine," Grace said, unbuttoning the top button on the long, white wool coat she'd brought from Paris. She slipped off the coat and opened the den closet.

"Wow," Mica gasped. "That's some...did you make that? I mean, design it?"

Grace hung up her coat and turned toward him, smoothing the folds of the pink chiffon. "I made the top, but the skirt is Dior. Mrs. Beabots's Dior skirt, I might add."

"And that means?"

"It's vintage, Mica, and irreplaceable. I better not spill anything on it. I'm tempted not to eat a thing, to be honest."

"No worries. We'll stick with white wine and champagne, and at dinner I'll throw a bath towel over your lap."

"I'll take it," she said, lifting a finger to Jules's hand. "Thank goodness he's all but cured. He turns six months tomorrow, and I wouldn't want him to be sick for it."

"Six months." Mica looked at Jules, wonder in his eyes.

Mica shifted his gaze back to Grace. "You look beautiful. Beyond beautiful," he whispered. "Are you trying to impress me?"

Grace's stomach fluttered like it had years ago in the swimming pool. Then it sank. Mica didn't love her. Her mouth went dry. To diffuse her sad thoughts, she glanced around the room. Timmy and Annie were putting a DVD in the player while Danny settled in at the kids' table. Little Zeke was playing with a musical toy. "I thought I already had," she said.

Jules slapped Mica's cheek. "Da!"

Mica gasped. "Did he just say something?"

"He makes those sounds all the time."

"No, Grace. Clearly, he's trying to say 'Dad.'"

She rolled her eyes. "Oh, Mica. Babies don't talk at six months."

"That's what you think. Mom says Nate walked and talked in full sentences at eight months."

"I find that hard to believe."

"You need proof?" Mica jerked his head toward the living room. "Come on. I'll find Mom."

Grace chuckled as she followed Mica. They were waylaid by every couple present. Everyone wanted to hold Jules, congratulate Mica and hug Grace.

She was overwhelmed by the caring and love she felt from old friends and new ones. She met Katia and Austin McCreary, who arrived just as two waiters dressed all in black walked through the room serving flutes of bubbling champagne. Katia was one of the most beautiful women Grace had ever met, impressing her with her Michael Kors black crepe gown. It had enormous rhinestone epaulettes at the gathered shoulders, a round, rhinestone-studded buckle at the waist and a slit skirt. Grace raised an eyebrow. Apparently, some of Mrs. Beabots's friends understood and followed fashion. Grace had the feeling she and Katia would share a lot of common interests.

Before she could say much more than hello, though, Sam Crenshaw tapped his champagne glass to get everyone's attention.

"Good evening. Before we toast the coming new year, Gina and I have an announcement to make."

Gina, dressed in an aquamarine wool floor-length sheath and glittery sandals, moved closer to Sam as he put his arm around her.

"Most, if not all of you, know that Gina has accepted my marriage proposal."

Mica moved next to Grace and though he still held Jules in his right arm, he wouldn't meet her eyes as Sam spoke.

"There has been a change of plans," Sam said. "Mica? Where are you?"

"Over here," Mica replied with a nod.

"Ah. Well, your mother and I have decided that due to the new additions to the family—

by that I mean Grace and Jules—we are going to move the wedding from the end of January to tonight."

Gasps and excited whispers rippled through the crowd.

Grace felt Mica go rigid, as if he'd been turned to steel. She could swear he'd stopped breathing.

"Mica? Are you all right?"

He turned and handed Jules over, still not looking at her. He marched up to Sam, who had just leaned down to kiss Gina.

"We didn't discuss this," Mica said.

Gina pulled away from Sam's embrace and smiled at Mica. "Because Grace has to leave so soon and all our friends were here tonight, we thought, why wait? Grace is family now and we wanted her to be part of our happiness."

"This isn't happening," Mica mumbled.

Everyone applauded and rushed forward to congratulate the happy couple. Mica and Grace stood like pillars in a swirling river.

Apprehension gripped Grace. She'd expected to get to know the Barzonnis better once she'd introduced them to Jules, but without Mica's love—without even some small sense that he cared about her—it didn't feel right. Although Jules was related to them, she wasn't. She hadn't chosen to marry into this family, the way Maddie, Liz and Olivia had. She'd only just rejected Mica's proposal yesterday. Deep down, she wished she could have accepted it, wished he'd given her a reason to, and that stung. Tears filled her eyes.

Mica's attention was riveted on his mother and Sam. Grace could only wonder at the thoughts in his head. He'd been hit with a lot of change lately. First, his accident. Then Jules. Now his mother marrying for the second time.

She opened her mouth to say something to him, then closed it again. What was there to say? Grace turned away, her skirts swishing elegantly around her legs. She wished she felt the joy of wearing the Dior skirt, but instead, the only thing she felt was the heaviness in her heart.

CHAPTER TEN

MICA FOUND GRACE in the kitchen feeding Jules a bottle.

The place was a beehive of activity as the Indian Lake Deli catering staff that Gina hired was preparing the salad plates with baby spinach, Asian pear halves, pomegranate seeds and goat cheese. Olivia's mother, Julia, was inspecting the crown roast of pork and a turkey that would be served.

Julia nodded toward Mica when he came in and was about to speak to him when one of the waitstaff asked her a question about the scalloped potatoes.

Mica looked over at Grace, who hadn't seen him. Her eyes were on her baby.

When Mica walked up, Jules reached out a hand toward him. Mica offered his forefinger and Jules wrapped his little fingers around it, smiling as he continued to suck on the nipple.

"Are you mad at me?" Mica asked quietly, taking a tentative seat next to Grace at the table.

"No," she said with a flicker of a smile. "I guess I got a bit emotional out there. And I had to feed Jules." She paused for a moment and looked at him. "Mica, we have some serious decisions to make and as lovely as this party is, I really shouldn't be here."

"Where should you be?"

"In front of my computer helping my team. Better yet, I should be back in Paris. They're winging too much without me. The tiniest detail makes all the difference. They know it and I know it."

"I'm beginning to see that, too," he replied, gazing at her holding their son. His chest swelled with pride and an unfamiliar yearning came over him. Even this morning he had found himself counting the hours until the party, when he'd see Grace and Jules. He'd tried to think of excuses to call her. When he did text her, she responded hours later, saying that she'd been with Mrs. Beabots. Then she was answering emails. Then she had to bathe Jules. She was always busy. He wasn't.

And that bothered him, too.

Grace was incredibly driven and focused, and he had a hard time forcing himself to turn on the computer. His design ideas weren't gelling, which reinforced his feelings of failure and inadequacy.

Grace would only marry a man who was worthy of her. He knew he was no prize. He had little to be proud of in his own life.

Except for this little boy, who was stealing his heart and soul by the second.

"Maybe we could figure out a work schedule for you over the next few days," he offered.

"What do you mean?"

"Like I could take care of Jules all day so that you can work. My mom has a crib here, though I see that Zeke is already sleeping in it tonight. We've got a high chair and I could rent or borrow anything else you want for the rest of the week."

Gratitude glistened in her blue eyes and settled on her soft lips. "Mica, that would be… wonderful. I've come up with some killer ideas just today that I can't wait to sketch. I want to see what fabrics we've got in the workshop and what we could order."

"So, this is good?" he ventured.

"Yes. Very."

Jules had finished the bottle. Grace lifted him to her shoulder, threw a napkin over her blouse and patted his back. She continued rubbing his back until he burped. Once. Twice.

Gina came into the kitchen and looked around. "Oh! Grace. There you are! My photographer is here and I want photographs of all the women." She held out her hand. "Mica. You take over with Jules while Grace comes with me."

"Uh, sure," he said.

Just as Grace was about to hand over Jules, the baby filled his diaper. "Oh, dear. Sorry, Gina, I have to change him first."

Gina clucked her tongue. "For heaven's sake. Mica can change him. Mica, use the laundry-room counter. Zeke is sleeping and I don't want to wake him by taking Jules to my room. Okay?"

Grace looked concerned.

Mica touched her arm. "I've got this."

He took Jules, and Grace reached into the big bag at her feet. "This is the last diaper. I forgot to buy more this afternoon. I'll have to stop at the drugstore on the way home." She hesitated, still holding the diaper. "You do know how to work these things, right?"

"Sure. Pull tab. Just like a beer."

"Oh, Mica." Grace groaned and rose, tucking the diaper under his arm. "There are baby wipes and diaper cream in the bag as well. Seriously, come get me if you need—"

"Grace. I got this," he replied firmly. She helped hook the bag over his shoulder, then he carried Jules to the laundry room.

Mica grabbed a soft bath towel from the dryer and spread it on the counter. He laid down Jules and peeled off the little wool pants Grace had made.

"Your mom sure can sew, can't she? These are quality trousers, old man."

Jules squealed and shoved his fists in his mouth.

Mica pulled the tabs on the disposable diaper and took a step back. "Whoa! All that was in that little tummy of yours?"

Mica folded the diaper up and tossed it in the trash. "I'll take that out right away."

Jules had started squirming and laughing so much that he kept scooting the towel closer to the edge of the counter. Mica still needed to use the baby wipes. In order to reach the diaper bag while holding on to Jules, Mica took his numb hand out of the tuxedo jacket pocket where he'd tucked it and set it on Jules's belly. He knew he had no strength to actually hold the baby in place, but he hoped that the pressure and weight of his arm would keep Jules safe long enough for him to grab the baby wipes.

Jules yelped and laughed.

Mica bent down and as he did, Jules kicked. Terrified the baby would fall, Mica focused on exerting his shoulder muscles, praying he'd strengthened them enough in physio to stabilize his arm for a few more seconds.

Jules remained on the counter, safe and sound.

"See that, buddy? We make a good team."

Mica finished cleaning him up, then spread the protective diaper cream on the baby's soft skin. He unfolded the clean diaper and shoved it under Jules's bottom.

"Just a pull and..."

The diaper tab came away in his hand. "Nuts."

He fastened the other side, but after trying to tuck the diaper into Jules's pants, he saw it wasn't going to work.

"I need tape," Mica said, putting his left hand back on Jules's tummy as he opened the overhead cabinet, where his mother kept glue, tape and other useful things.

"Hey! This is perfect. Clear Gorilla Tape. That will hold it on."

Mica tore off a piece of tape using the dispenser cutter. The piece was longer than he'd wanted, but as far as Mica was concerned, the more the better.

He sealed the diaper, then tickled Jules's side.

The baby grabbed Mica's hand and laughed.

Slowly, Mica put Jules's pants back on. He threw the baby wipes away and put the towel in the washer.

They returned to the kitchen just as Grace was coming back in.

"Photo shoot over?" Mica grinned.

"It is," she replied and reached for Jules, who lifted his arms and let out a bloodcurdling scream.

Two of the waiters stopped what they were doing and stared at them.

Jules screamed some more, tears rolling down his face.

"What's going on?" Grace asked. "Is he sick again?"

Mica shook his head. "He was fine while I was changing him," he said meekly. "Though I did have a bit of a problem…"

Grace rushed into the laundry room and Mica followed. He pulled out another bath towel from the dryer. "Here, lay him on this. It's still warm…and soft."

Grace whisked off Jules's pants. "What is this tape?"

"The tab came off. I improvised."

Grace seemed to relax a smidge. "Oh. Well, it looks like some of the tape came off and got stuck to his skin."

Guilt made Mica's stomach churn. He should never have volunteered for a task he had never performed. Jules's cries ripped into him.

"Oh, Jules! I'm really sorry. I thought it would stay put."

"It's okay. Get me the diaper bag and the diaper cream. Then a cotton swab."

Mica followed her instructions. She put the cream on the swab and carefully slid it under the Gorilla Tape, easing Jules's tender skin away from the strong adhesive. "There, now, sweetie, it's all better."

"I'm so sorry, Jules," Mica said, smoothing the baby's hair and touching the tears on his cheeks. "I didn't mean to hurt you."

He looked at Grace, whose fear was abating. "I'm really sorry. I just don't know that much about babies. I helped Gabe a couple times with Zeke, but…"

"It's okay, Mica. I'm new to this myself. Poor Jules has to put up with two parents who are still in on-the-job training."

"I suppose most parents are like us, huh," Mica said.

His stomach felt like lead.

He'd thought he was doing so well, but he clearly couldn't be counted on to so much as change Jules's diaper without a mishap.

Would he ever be of any worth or help as a father? He had a great deal to learn and fast. He'd trudged through a fog of family responsibility since he'd graduated college. His inertia, his lack of drive, had underpinnings that went further back than his accident.

Mica had settled.

Meanwhile, Grace had kept her standards high. She wanted a man who loved her. She wanted a successful career that brought her acclaim. She owned her ambition. Mica had a vague memory of dreams like that. When he was in college he'd thought his inventions could change the world.

But he'd given up.

He'd settled for his father's dreams.

The accident was Mica's first wake-up call. Jules was a shock and an awakening.

He knew for sure now that if he was going to be a real father to his son, he needed to make something of himself. Biding his time and ambling around the farm weren't doing Mica any good and his inaction sure wasn't building a future for Jules.

His responsibility to his child was paramount. He would learn how to care for Jules and how to do it properly. He could see it was going to take time.

Grace, however, wasn't giving him much time. Nor was she considering all the pitfalls of her strategy. Bouncing Jules around from continent to continent might solve Grace's career dilemma for the moment, but in the end, her solution would only cause heartache.

And Mica would do everything in his power to prevent that—for Jules and for himself.

CHAPTER ELEVEN

MICA SIPPED A glass of Gabe's chardonnay a half hour later as he surreptitiously watched Grace, with Jules perched on her hip, chat with Katia and Austin McCreary. Austin chucked Jules under the chin, while Grace told some story that caused Katia's eyes to grow wide before she frowned in concern, then gave Grace a big hug and a smile.

Grace's iPhone pinged, and she excused herself. As she greeted the person on the other end, she managed to kiss Jules's cheek and nod at Maddie and Nate. Mica could tell from the shake of her head and her concentrated expression that this was yet another call from Paris.

Work.

Her design team needed her again. By his count, this was the third call this evening.

Shame pinched the edges of his conscience. He remembered how he'd ridiculed her when they were kids, telling her she had no idea what hard work was. His ego and pride at being a farm boy and a Barzonni had clouded his thinking.

He realized now there was nothing silly about her. She handled Jules and her overseas calls deftly. Her friendly manner was infused with caring and genuine affection for everyone present. She was open and happy and concerned about others. Even when they were kids, she'd been forthcoming about her opinions and goals. He just hadn't listened. She was as ambitious as the rest of his brothers. Even his father.

It was Mica who lacked drive.

What does she need me for? Frankly, Mica knew what Grace needed. She'd told him so. If circumstances were different, he thought, he would have fallen in love with Grace already. But after the way she'd kept Jules from him, he couldn't trust her. He could feel just about everything else for her—admiration, respect, attraction—but without trust, there could be no love.

Gina went over to Grace and insisted on holding Jules. Surprisingly, Mica's son gladly went to his grandmother. He snuggled into her shoulder as if he'd known her his whole life.

Still on the phone, Grace sidled over to a wing chair near the roaring fire and dug around in Jules's diaper bag. She withdrew her iPad and began swiping and tapping as she talked.

A few moments later, Grace put the iPad away and ended the call.

She went back over to Jules and thrust her hands out to him. Grinning, the baby nearly leaped into Grace's arms. Sam came up, put his arm around Gina's waist and whispered something in her ear. She nodded, excused herself and followed Sam to the kitchen.

Grace was then joined by her Aunt Louise, Cate Sullivan, Trent Davis and Sarah. Grace's smile was luminous and inviting as she fell into easy conversation with them.

Mica had always marveled at how the talent for easy conversation and making friends had passed him by. His mother had worried about him when he was young, and he preferred the solitude of his room or the mechanical shed to being with people. His father had accused him of brooding. Mica wasn't quite sure why he seemed to better understand the workings of tractors and machinery than he did people.

People were a mystery to him.

Except for Grace.

He'd made fun of her and mocked her. Teased her. He'd been arrogant, thinking that his life, his way of doing things, was better than hers. He'd been young and self-centered. And he'd been wrong. Grace had always worked diligently toward her goals. She still did.

He felt a slap on the back. It was Rafe. He wore a white dinner jacket, tuxedo slacks and black dress cowboy boots. Rafe was munching on one of Olivia's delicious macarons.

"What's up, bro?" Rafe asked, not looking at Mica but keeping his eyes on Olivia as she took Jules from Grace's arms.

"Not much."

"Yeah?" Rafe popped the last of the cookie into his mouth. "You gonna make this wedding happen before Grace goes back to Europe?"

"Of course I am," Mica replied, sounding more confident than he felt.

"Nate says you botched it," Rafe said bluntly. "No ring, huh?"

"Will you guys knock it off about a ring?"

Rafe grimaced. "Uh-oh. This isn't good."

Mica's eyes tracked slowly back to Grace. Suddenly, she looked like the most competent woman in the world. And beautiful, he thought fleetingly. It should be easy to trust her, to move forward and forget she'd kept Jules from him all these months. He could be a father now, so why should it matter so much? But the pain of being left out, ignored and made to feel immaterial in his own son's life banged around in his head. And his heart.

That was the devil of it. His head and heart kept crossing signals. One minute he wanted her out of his life, for her to leave Jules with him not just for a few months, but forever. The next, he saw visions of holding her next to him every night for the rest of his life, as they watched Jules grow together.

If only Mica could change her mind about the importance of love in their relationship. If they got married now, maybe he could come to trust her eventually. In the grand scheme of their lives, it wasn't all that much to sacrifice for Jules's sake. His mother had done it.

Jules had to come first. Mica would do whatever it took to secure a good life for his son.

Rafe was still munching his cookie. "She really isn't going to marry you, is she?"

"I don't think so." The words tasted sour.

"Dang," Rafe commented. "I'd guessed that's why she was back here."

"You guessed wrong."

"We all did, huh?"

"Yeah…" Mica looked down at his glass.

Rafe slid his arm around Mica's shoulders and squeezed. "Carpe diem, bro."

"Huh?"

"Take charge another way. He's your kid."

"She wants to leave him with me for several months. Then she'll come back for him."

Rafe's eyes rounded. "So, what does that make you? Temp Daddy?"

Mica lifted his head, suddenly filled with strength. "Absolutely not. Never. I'm his father now and always." Mica straightened his shoulders.

"Prove it." Rafe nodded toward Grace. "To her."

GRACE WATCHED MICA across the room by stealing glances at him as she talked to Mrs. Beabots and Isabelle. When she shifted Jules from her right to left shoulder, she saw Rafe and Mica talking. She didn't know what Rafe had said to Mica but Mica's demeanor had changed. He walked toward her, his intense blue eyes riveted on her face. That was one of the things she'd always loved about Mica. He wasn't the kind of person whose attention flitted from person to person like a hummingbird. He focused on one person at a time, as if there was no one else in the world.

She remembered that. And so many other things.

Like the feel of his lips on hers. The way he held her to his chest with so much strength he didn't need two arms. But she wasn't here to tell him those things.

She didn't dare.

"Mind if I hold my son?" he asked.

"Of course not," she replied, handing Jules to him. Jules smiled at Mica and the pacifier in his mouth dropped out. Grace had tied a ribbon to the pacifier and clipped it to Jules's shirt, so it didn't fall far.

"Hey, buddy. How're you doin'? Forgive your dad for the tape incident?"

Jules whacked Mica's cheek and giggled.

Mica blinked in surprise, then chuckled. "Does this mean we're even?"

"I'm guessing."

Mrs. Beabots smiled up at Mica. "I just had an idea. Why don't you come over for dinner tomorrow night, Mica?"

"Mrs. Beabots, no," Grace protested. "You've done too much already."

"Nonsense. I'll make something special. Mica should spend time with you and Jules."

Grace's phone pinged. She looked down at the caller ID. "It's Etienne. Again."

"And he is?" Mica asked with an edge to his voice. Was that...jealousy? His face was too placid, perhaps too carefully controlled, for Grace to tell what he was thinking. Or feeling.

"My team leader. We had a deadline moved up."

"On New Year's?" he scoffed.

"There are no holidays in haute couture," she grumbled and moved off to the side to take the call.

Within minutes, Grace heard the tinkle of a knife against a crystal wineglass and Sam's voice calling everyone back to the living room.

"Sorry, Etienne. But the wedding..." she said haltingly.

"You want us to design a wedding dress?" Etienne asked.

"No. No. I'm at a wedding. I'll have to call you back tomorrow."

"Grace! *Tu es une exaspération!*" He hung up.

Grace put her phone away, feeling guilty. Her evening out would cause her team to fall another eight hours behind. Another workday lost. Coming to America might have been the worst move she'd made yet.

No, she admonished herself. Weeks and months from now, she'd be glad she told Mica about Jules and asked for his help.

The crowd gathered in the living room. The massive fireplace was built of rock and stone, with an opening so large, Grace thought she could walk into it without stooping. The wood mantel was covered with fresh cedar and pine boughs and studded with silver beads, balls, white lights and white satin ribbons.

Judge Harry Miller, a tall, salt-and-pepper-haired man, held a bible and stood between Gina and Sam. Gina clutched a bouquet of white and red roses, while Sam, dressed in a black tuxedo, looked dashing and quite possibly more radiant than the bride as he reached out to take her hand.

Grace hadn't moved or breathed since she'd taken her place next to Mica, who still held Jules. The room fell silent as Judge Miller began the ceremony, but Grace hardly noticed anyone...except Mica.

Grace shivered when their shoulders touched, and the way Jules snuggled down in the crook of Mica's neck melted her heart. But Mica stared straight ahead, watching the interplay between his mother and Sam with an intensity she could almost touch.

Suddenly, it struck her that this happy moment for Gina might not be so joyful for Mica. Mica had been close with his father and often spoke reverently of Angelo. Mica loved his father, but it was more than that. He idolized him.

Tonight, his mother was marrying another man. Liz had told Grace the story about Gina and Sam and that their love for each other went back more than thirty years, to when Gina had first moved to Indian Lake. She'd barely been out of her teens and had promised Angelo she would come to America once he had established himself. Before she'd married him and moved to the farm, Gina had lived in town. And there she'd met Sam Crenshaw.

They'd gone to the movies and had sodas together and Sam had lost his heart, according to Maddie.

But Gina was a woman of honor and though she'd told Sam she loved him, she had been unwilling to go back on her promise to Angelo.

Then, two years ago, Angelo had had a heart attack and died one afternoon when he and Rafe were putting Rowan through his paces on the training track the two of them had built with their own hands.

With their own hands.

That was a Barzonni claim to fame. Everything on this farm had been built, sawed, painted, plowed and seeded by a Barzonni. Mica shared in that history.

Grace tilted her head to the left and watched

Mica's reaction as Gina put a ring on Sam's finger.

Had Mica just winced? Or was he reacting to Jules?

The judge continued reciting the vows.

Gina's "I do" was loud and clear and overflowed with happiness.

As Sam put a ring on Gina's finger, Grace could swear Mica's face had paled. In the flickering firelight, she was certain she detected a mist in his eyes.

Her heart went out to him. She'd been so enthralled and immersed in her own concerns, her business and her baby that she hadn't made room for all the emotions that Mica was going through. She'd been prepared for his shock and his anger. But this? What was all this?

This wedding had been sprung on all of them. Mica hadn't had a chance to process any of it. And talk about bad timing. Grace had shown up on his doorstep with his baby on the day Sam had proposed.

Did he feel his mother was dishonoring his father? Or did he feel that his mother had been cheated of real love all her life, and that this was Gina's last grasp at happiness?

Mica had always kept his emotions in check. Even last year, he hadn't been romantic or rhapsodic about their relationship. At the time, and in the months since, she'd chalked it up to the fact that their time together was so short. She'd always intended to return to Paris. Like she did now. But maybe she'd mistaken his need to protect himself for a lack of care.

It was possible all she was feeling was guilt, but the truth was, she'd loved him since she was fifteen. Coming back to Indian Lake, learning about the accident and losing herself in his mournful and confused blue eyes had confirmed it. Or so she thought. But this flood of compassion and warmth for Mica, of caring for him as much as she cared about Jules or herself, was new. And she didn't know what to make of it.

She no more belonged in Indian Lake than she did on Mars. But right now, Mica needed a friend. He was hurting and lost and she wanted to ease his pain.

Grace slid her arm around Mica's waist and leaned into him. She wished she knew exactly what he was feeling so she could say the right thing. Mica was extraordinarily silent about nearly everything.

In some ways, this moment was no different. He didn't speak or even look at her. But he didn't move away, didn't flinch when she rested her head on his shoulder.

The gesture was so slight, but coming from Mica, it was meaningful. With each hour she spent with him, she was beginning to understand him better.

She simply wanted him to know that she cared about him—and wanted to help, even if he didn't want her.

CHAPTER TWELVE

MICA WAS IN the process of programming a microcontroller on a voice-activated circuit board when his iPhone rang. He ignored the phone and plugged the input supply into a 12-volt battery. Though the microphone that came with the unit was adequate, he wondered if using a more highly sensitive piece would be better.

With the plethora of commands needed to operate a tractor, his invention would require a highly sensitive microphone that shut out all other machinery sounds and featured voice-recognition software that could understand a variety of accents and dialects. And Mica was not a coding expert. He needed a partner or corporation that could provide the software he needed to create a final product. He was using a voice-recognition app for his proto-type, but until he could find a coding expert, Mica was stuck. Still, it felt good to be back in the workshop, bringing his ideas to life. His conversation with Rafe at the New Year's party had lit a fire under Mica, and he was grateful for that spark.

The iPhone quit ringing. Then it beeped. Someone had left a voice mail.

Mica carried the unit over to the tractor he'd parked inside the mechanics shed. Earlier, he'd raised the hood on the engine, propped it up with a sturdy rod and placed a very bright work light inside. Painstakingly, he'd pried off the dashboard and exposed the wires and dials inside the tractor's operator cabin—such as it was. This was a 1982 Allis-Chalmers 8050 and Mica's favorite. He called it the Red Angel. Painted glossy, tomato red, this old tractor had an enclosed cabin that allowed farmers to drive in the windiest of spring planting weather or through October's icy rains.

Mica had recently realized the enclosed cabin offered even more advantages, especially for his accessible designs.

Voice activation would help people with mobility issues, but what about those with asthma or other breathing difficulties who still wanted to work the fields? Mica added an air-filtration system to his mental list of features for his invention.

He hooked the output supply connector to the ignition wires, trying not to get frustrated that it took him more than double the time it used to when he'd had the use of both hands. He was determined.

The phone rang again and he ignored it; if Rafe or his mother wanted him, they knew where to find him.

Mica plugged in the microphone. He'd set up the system to require two commands within a certain time frame in order to activate the unit.

"Ignition on," he said. After a second he added, "Ignition stay."

The LED light number lit up, indicating the presence of his voice. For another second, nothing happened.

Then the tractor roared to life.

"Eureka!" He shot his good arm up in the air, grinned widely and did a little jig, his boots smacking against the cement floor.

"I did it!"

He stopped and his face fell as he stared at the tractor. His victory was small. Crude and rudimentary. In the scheme of things, getting the tractor to start was inconsequential. Mica was eager to move to the next phase, when he could command all the gears, brakes, speed and steering. He also wanted to install hand-grips on the vertical walls on either side of the entrances about three feet above the running boards. He envisioned drop-down steps that would make it easier for a person with limited leg movement to climb into the cabin. One of the things that he'd noticed about farm equipment was that a person with any kind of hip, knee or even back issue often needed a hydrolift to get into the vehicle. Mica had come up with ideas to change that.

Programming and turning on the tractor was the first thing he'd accomplished on his own since the accident. But he still had a long way to go. "For now, I need to take this baby out for a test drive."

Mica hit the garage-door button. As the door moved upward, Mica sucked in his breath.

"What in the world?"

He stared out at a gorgeous snowfall. Fat, white flakes the size of feathers floated to the ground. Mica had lost track of time since he'd come to the shed shortly after breakfast. He's been so deeply focused on his work that he hadn't thought about the time. He glanced at his watch. It was nearly two o'clock.

"Beautiful." He smiled. "So beautiful."

A series of rings interrupted his thoughts again. Mica strode over to the worktable. "What can be so important that—" He lifted his phone and read the caller ID.

Grace? He tapped the screen and took the call. "Grace."

"Oh, you're there," she said. She sounded a little out of breath, as if she'd been running. "Mica. I'm so glad. I know you told Mrs. Beabots you'd come for dinner tonight, but I need a really big favor."

"A favor?" He couldn't stop the surge of irritation that rose inside him. She had kept Jules from him for six months, then shown up unannounced, expecting Mica to take over on a moment's notice. What bigger favor could there be? As much as his love for his baby boy was growing, he didn't appreciate the way Grace was playing on his emotions. Since she'd arrived in Indian Lake, he'd felt like he was in a pinball machine, his emotions being batted all over the place. No wonder he liked working on machines. Much less angst.

He ran his tongue over his lips, then glanced at his tractor as he considered giving her an excuse.

"Mica, I need you," she said in that soft, breathy voice he remembered from those haunting nights when he'd held her so close he could smell her French perfume… "Please. It's about Jules."

That did it. "What is it? Is he okay?"

"Yes. Well, er, he's a bit cranky. It's my team in Paris. We have a Skype conference this afternoon, and Mrs. Beabots is making a fabulous soup for us tonight. I can't possibly interrupt her and ask her to watch Jules. It wouldn't be fair—she's done so much. And I'm—"

"You sound frazzled."

"I'm at my wits' end, Mica. I was up all night with Jules. I think being sick and then the party and the wedding...it was too much for him."

"You want me to come over and take care of him while you conduct business. That about it?"

He could hear her intake of breath. It hit him that she had been afraid to call him. That she was truly worried he would turn her down. Part of him wanted to. But she'd come here to help him learn how to be Jules's father. And now when she was presenting him with an opportunity to bond with his son, he was tempted to turn it down out of spite.

As aloof as he could sometimes be, Mica didn't consider himself to be self-centered. Maybe he was.

For so long, keeping his life simple and uncomplicated, avoiding relationships and all their drama had seemed like a wise choice.

He kept busy with the farm and his machines. Then, the accident had made withdrawal seem like his only option. The upheaval that Grace had brought with Jules had changed everything. Already, he'd needed to call his brothers for help. He'd sought their advice. He'd found value in their family friends' interest in Jules. They cared about Grace and the baby. It was even possible they cared about him. And that had been the greatest revelation of all.

Mica wanted to be the kind of guy who people liked and wanted to be friends with. He wanted Grace to be his friend. Besides, if he couldn't even get along with her, how could he expect her to marry him?

"How soon?"

"How soon can you get here?"

"I need to clean up. I've been in the shed all morning and I'm kinda…" He looked down at his old, grease-covered jeans and his faded Purdue sweatshirt. "I'm a mess. Give me an hour."

"See you later, Mica."

He hung up and went back to the tractor and said, "Ignition off. Ignition stay."

The tractor turned off.

Grace had come here expecting Mica to take over his share of the parenting. Since last night, he'd been hoping she would call soon. Or he was going to call her. He needed to spend time with Jules and learn as much as he could about his son and his care.

Yet he realized his need to work all morning had come from the understanding that he was no longer a selfish, singular man in this world. He had obligations and responsibilities now. He had Jules, and he didn't want his son to grow up and be any less proud of him than Mica had been of his father.

If he was to examine his dreams the way he dissected a tractor engine, Mica would see that his goals hadn't changed since he'd gone to college. He'd always wanted to create a better way to farm. A better harvester. A more finely tuned combine. Conveyors that more accurately planted tomato plants. He had wanted to improve farm life through machinery.

But now he saw the needs of others in a different light and that illumination gave rise to his new inventions.

Jules had given him the motivation he'd been lacking to take those ideas to the next level. Given Mica new hope and a new vision. He would do anything for his son.

GRACE WATCHED OUT the upstairs window as Mica drove his truck into the driveway below.

The snow was falling in fluffy flakes, and on any other day, she'd be tempted to take Jules outside, even for a few minutes so he could feel snowflakes on his little face and look at her through snow-covered eyelashes.

She would have liked to put him on a wooden sled and pull him down the sidewalk, but she couldn't. She had to work.

Grace knew she wasn't alone in feeling guilt as a working mother, but it seemed to be weighing heavier on her these days. She should have taken Jules to see the Christmas lights around the Eiffel Tower. She should have walked down the stunning Champs-Élysées with him even if he was too young to remember it in the future. She had read in a parenting magazine once that babies actually did benefit from delightful, beautiful things. Their minds were enhanced by classical music, and babies who were exposed to art early on were better able to think and process their world.

Being an artist, Grace believed this. Her mother had often told her that she'd taken Grace to museums before she was christened. Of course, Grace's mother never missed a gallery opening or a new art exhibit in Chicago. Grace couldn't remember a time when art, beautiful clothes, colorful flowers and stunning architecture didn't fill her with a sense of awe. Grace hoped to instill that kind of passion and appreciation in her son.

He was only six months old and already she wanted so much for him. All mothers probably thought their baby was the most intelligent, most beautiful and gifted child on the planet, but Grace knew Jules was different. When Mica told her that Rafe had walked and talked at eight months, she believed him. Jules was trying to say words. Jules was smart and intuitive and her friends in Paris saw it.

With how much her work had ramped up even in the past few days, Grace was feeling worse and worse about not giving Jules the attention he needed. She just hoped that bringing him here, leaving him with Mica, was the solution. That Mica and his family and all their friends in Indian Lake would continue to nurture her exceptional son.

The knock on the apartment door shattered her thoughts and caused a dozing Jules to jump awake. He let out a bellowing cry.

"Oh, sweetie." She lifted him out of his carrier. "Maybe Daddy and I should go shopping for you," she said.

"Da," Jules said and touched her cheek as she walked to the door.

Mica was wearing his camel-colored leather jacket with sheepskin lining. He had a soft brown scarf around his neck and his jeans were washed denim. Snow covered his raven-black hair.

"It's really coming down out there." He smiled as he brushed snow off his head, some of it falling on Jules's face.

Jules scrunched his nose and then his eyes widened. He smiled broadly and reached for Mica.

Grace's emotions swung from guilt to love, admiration, concern, fear and finally love again. Jules acted as if he understood Mica was his father. Was that possible? And if it was, why would she be wary of it? Jules looked so much like Mica; no wonder she'd continued to pine for him the whole time they'd been apart.

She'd longed for Mica. But she'd also known she could never have him. Her life could never be his life. She knew it as she knew the stars would never fall from the sky.

But as Mica's blue eyes fell on her face, wonder and delight filling them, causing them to brim with tears, she thought that maybe, possibly, somehow, she could make Mica love her.

CHAPTER THIRTEEN

THE MOMENT MICA laid eyes on Jules and Grace, all thoughts of winter storms and drifting snow vanished. He felt a wave of warmth rush over him.

He unbuttoned his jacket.

"Mica, please come in. There's barely any heat in that stairwell," Grace said. "Let me take your coat."

"Jules…" Mica smiled at his baby son as he took off his scarf. He looked at Grace and paused. He didn't know how she could look more beautiful than she had last night, but she did. Her blond hair was pulled up in a knot at the back of her head, revealing her long, slender neck. She wore a pale pink sweater embellished with a satin ribbon that revealed a glimpse of shoulder. Oh, he wished things could be as simple with her as they had been a year ago…

Jules kept squirming out of Grace's embrace, reaching for Mica.

Mica blinked. Things could never be simple with him and Grace again.

"I think he wants you to hold him," Grace said as she took Mica's things.

Before Mica could reach for Jules, the baby leaped out of Grace's arms, threw his hands around Mica's neck and hung on like a monkey hugging a palm tree.

"Did you see that?" Grace asked.

"I did! I swear he's knows I'm his dad."

Grace's expression softened. "Jules, this is your daddy. Can you say 'Daddy'?" She placed her hand on Mica's cheek.

If he wasn't holding Jules, he would have pressed his hand over hers. It felt warm and soft and caring. He shivered.

"Da," Jules said.

Mica held his breath. "Did you hear that?"

"Uh-huh." She smiled at him, her eyes sparkling.

"Come on in," Grace said, and he followed her to the kitchen. She hung Mica's jacket on the back of a chair. "It's a bit wet from the snow. Maybe it will dry off here."

Mica chucked Jules under the chin. "Is it possible he's grown since last night?"

"Oh, he's been eating a lot since we got here. And as we saw with the carrier, he's in a bit of a growth spurt right now. He's been moving around a lot more, too."

Mica chuckled. "He's a sporty little guy. Maybe I should buy him a football."

"I think he's a bit young." Grace smiled up at him. "But knowing how smart Jules is, he'd probably memorize the entire playbook before he's a year old."

"Gabe would be ecstatic."

"And God forbid we don't please Gabe," she joked.

Mica noticed she was wearing some pointy-toed flats that were decorated with plastic jewels. The heels were clear plastic. He'd never seen anything like them.

"Nice shoes."

She peered down at her feet, then turned her left foot. "You like my shoes?"

"I do."

"Come on!"

"Seriously. They're cute. It's like you have your teen crown on your toes."

"Mica…" She narrowed her eyes.

He could tell she was ready for a fight, but he didn't want to fight with her. In fact, it was the last thing on his mind.

"Where did you get them? The shoes?" he asked.

"They're mine. I mean, I designed them."

His mouth fell open. "I knew you designed dresses, but those…involve leather and—"

"A very good cobbler," she added. "I have the best guy ever. He's young and looking to make his mark. His father was a cobbler for Louboutin."

He shook his head. "I don't know…"

"Christian Louboutin. Famous shoes, purses. His signature is the shiny red soles on his spike heel shoes."

"Ah!"

"You know them?"

"Uh, no." But he was darned sure going to look this guy up.

"I've got three new designs I came up with during my sleepless nights. I was inspired by Sarah and Maddie, actually. See?" She showed him a drawing of a putty-colored winter coat. "The shawl collar stands up and can protect against the cold. Sarah says the winter wind hurts her neck and chin. And this sweater has a scarf running through the boatneck. The jade green reminds me of Maddie's eyes."

"Those are really good," Mica said, inspecting the sketches.

Just then, Jules pressed his mouth to Mica's jaw and licked.

"What is he doing? Does he think I'm lunch?"

Grace walked up to Mica and put her hand on his numb arm in such a way that he could feel the pressure of her hand, if not the touch itself. He liked it.

"He's been doing that for about a month," she said. "It's a teething thing, I think."

"It really tickles. Feels funny."

"Yes, well, enjoy it. In a few months, he'll have all his teeth and never do it again. It's the little things you have to relish while they last," she said, her tone wistful.

Mica walked over to the Victorian sofa and sat with Jules.

"So…what are you working on this afternoon?"

She raised her eyebrows, seeming surprised at his interest. "It's this Skype conference. Etienne is getting it set up in Paris." She looked at her watch. "It's three o'clock here, which means it's ten there. It was the earliest Etienne could get the team together—but they're used to working late nights. They're going to show me some mock-ups."

That got Mica thinking. If Grace could conduct business over the internet, then maybe she wouldn't have to race back to Paris quite so soon. He'd have more time to convince her that marrying him was best for their baby.

Best for us.

Grace was chattering on about a jacket she'd designed, and Mica had to struggle to pay attention.

How could he believe marrying him would be good for *her*? *Just look at her.* She was animated, her eyes alight as she talked about her work. She rushed out of the room and came back with another pair of shoes. These were platform shoes with spiky heels that only an acrobat should be able to balance in, but Grace put them on with ease. Standing in her black, silky pants and that pink sweater, she looked like a million bucks. No—a gazillion bucks.

He was glad he was sitting down. Jules was climbing up and down his chest, nearly straddling his shoulders, but he didn't care. He couldn't take his eyes off Grace.

"It's so hard to come up with something innovative, but I think—no, I know—my forte is in the fabric. I remember when I was a little girl, my mother would take me to the fabric room in the basement of Marshall Field's in Chicago. She would make me touch all the wools, silks and knits. She taught me the difference between cotton and batiste. Handkerchief linen and damask. She'd tell me to lift the cloth to my cheek and feel its life. The weave. She told me to imagine the face of the weaver who made the linen from flax."

"Really? Your cheek?"

"Yes," she said, pointing to Jules, who was trying to kiss Mica on the cheek again. "Just like he's trying to find out about you through touch. Fabric is all about tactile sensations."

He was fascinated.

Mica had spent his life figuring out what made machines tick. Grace had spent her years not only learning about fashion, but also about people. Suddenly, he wanted to know all about her and find out all the things she knew. He wondered if one lifetime would be enough.

He was struck with the clear fact that marriage between them was the right thing. Even if it wasn't the best thing for Grace and him, they had to make this decision for Jules. Their son deserved the best they could give, and he deserved to have both of them in his life. Mica's parents had chosen the right path. They'd created a life for their sons filled with honor, respect and the knowledge that responsibility toward others were the true joys of life. Mica knew what it was like to be proud of his parents' achievements. The swell in his chest and the tingles of admiration every time he looked out over their plowed and growing fields filled him with awe and humility. Jules should have that. Jules should experience that kind of pride.

And love? He believed that his mother had loved his father in her way and that he had loved her back. Maybe theirs had not been a romantic love, but it had been something. Couldn't he have that something...with Grace?

He couldn't deny the attraction between them, and every time he was with Grace, he looked forward to being with her again. Was it Jules? Or was it more to do with her?

If he was honest, there already was something between them. Mica just didn't know what to call it.

The trouble was, he had less than a week left to figure it out.

Just then the laptop on the kitchen table pinged.

Grace jumped and her arms flew out to her sides like someone had just put ice cubes down her shirt. "That's them!"

"What do you want me to do? Take Jules to the other room?" The baby was now dozing on Mica's chest.

"No, this is the first time he's settled all day. Stay right there. Earlier, he wouldn't stop crying. If he does start fussing there's a bottle in the fridge and you can warm it in the microwave. Then you should take him into the bedroom. There are some diapers in there, too. But no Gorilla Tape." She chuckled lightly.

"Thanks." He smiled.

She smiled back at him. It was a friendly smile, laced with enough encouragement that Mica felt his heart swell. They were getting closer. That was more than a good thing.

She raced over to a kitchen chair and grabbed the diaper bag. "There are some toys in here. He's got a stuffed dinosaur he loves. He named it."

"Let me guess. Da?"

"No. Ba."

Mica looked at Jules. "Quite a linguist, aren't ya?"

The computer pinged again.

"Here we go!" Grace said. "Wish me luck."

Mica's good spirits plummeted. She wanted him to wish her luck. It seemed like such a simple request, but his engineer's brain mapped out all possible outcomes. If she succeeded, she'd go to Paris and never come back. If she failed, she might still go to Paris and never come back, and never have time for Jules because she'd be working twice as hard. Would she leave him here for good, or take him back with her? Either way, Jules would lose out. And really, did Grace need any luck at all? Mica could already see she was amazing. Didn't she see that?

True, he was no expert on haute couture. He didn't know this Louboutin guy at all. In her world, Mica was uneducated. But he thought he could recognize a shining talent when he saw it.

"Good luck." He smiled.

"Thanks," she said with a smile, then whirled around to the kitchen table.

Mica could see the laptop screen, and Grace apparently intended to do the meeting without headphones. He didn't want to pry, but with a snoozing Jules still pinning him in place, Mica found himself paying attention.

Etienne was the first person on the screen. He was in his twenties, thin, his dark hair gelled into spikes. He wore a purple shirt and a pink tie and had a cross earring in one ear.

Next was Jasminda. Grace had told him she was the youngest team member, at nineteen. Her hair was thick and blunt, framing her face like a theater curtain. She wore long earrings and a tight, low-cut T-shirt.

Rene Charles entered the meeting room last.

He was a dead ringer for Bradley Cooper, and upon seeing him, Mica sat up straighter on the sofa, though he did his best not to disturb Jules. Rene was tall, fit and wore a cable-knit sweater much like the one Mica was wearing. *"Bonsoir, chérie!"* Rene smiled. "How are you, gorgeous?"

"Exhausted," Grace replied.

Mica ground his jaw. Was Rene flirting with her? Just who was this guy to Grace?

"Bonsoir, Grace!" Etienne said. "Can you hear us?"

"Oui. Bien."

"Grace," Jasminda began, "because you just sent over your sketch for the winter gown, I wanted to show you the fabric I found in that shop in Montmartre."

Jasminda held up a shimmering white cloth. "It's from India."

"Are those sequins?" Grace asked.

"Yes, silver, pearl and white on white. It's amazing. It looks like fairy dust."

"But how will it fall? I want the skirt to kick out and scurry away from the legs as the wearer walks. It should look like drifting snow around her feet."

"Of course. I think this will work. I'll baste it together tomorrow and send you a video."

"Now, Grace," Rene began. He had what Mica would call a radio voice. "I'm going to show you some of the things we've come up with. It's easier this way, so we can get your immediate input. Also, I rigged up some photographer lights. I borrowed them from Guillaume."

"Oh, great," Grace said. "How is he?"

"In Tunis on an outdoor shoot. He couldn't lug all this stuff with him. That's why he's letting us use his equipment," Rene said.

Grace sighed in relief. "That's good. I wasn't sure we could afford the rental fees."

"Grace, *ma chérie*, how many times do I have to tell you not to worry. I'm here for you. Always."

"I know, Rene. You're so sweet."

"Bien." Rene approached the laptop and lifted it to pan around the room. As he did, Mica caught a close-up glimpse of Rene's slim, wide-shouldered physique. Mica had never considered the individuals on Grace's team. Nor had he guessed that there might be another guy who cared for her. *A handsome one,* he thought. *And the guy lives in Paris. He's already part of her world.*

"This is the first one, Grace." Rene turned the camera on a stop-sign-red leather jacket.

It had a short waist and wide lapels with gold zippers on the bell sleeves and up the front.

While Grace and her team commented on the styles and designs, Mica took note of the work space itself.

The place was practically barren. The floor was old and from what he could see when Rene showed a row of shoes, the floorboards were warped. There were clothes racks and make-shift screens. He saw cutting tables and sewing machines that looked as old as the one his mother had used when he was a kid. Though the professional lights should have made the place look better, he noticed that the walls had cracks and some plaster was missing around the doorframe.

Mica didn't know how he'd envisioned Grace's life in Paris, but this wasn't it. Somehow, he'd thought she worked in a chic place like one of those 1950s movie sets, with thick white carpet, white-and-gold paneled walls and an MGB roadster sitting outside her front door.

But this was a bit frightening.

She'd told him that she took Jules to work almost every day. Jules could move around on his own now, which meant he was all over that old and probably dirty floor. Maybe getting splinters or sewing pins in his soft skin.

City lights twinkled through two double-hung windows. There were no draperies, only old, rolled-up shades of some kind. He could only imagine how cold and drafty the place must be in winter. And Parisian winters were known to be brutal. Maybe not as icy and cold as Indian Lake, but they certainly weren't balmy.

Rene settled the computer back on the table. The three of them gathered around the screen to say their goodbyes.

Before they signed off, they all asked about Jules and his health.

"He's fine," Grace said. "Jasminda, how is your mother doing? I'm so worried about you taking care of her."

"She misses your hugs. We all do."

Then she spoke to Etienne about his sister, whose boyfriend had dumped her right before Christmas. Apparently, the girl had been a sobbing wreck and she was only sixteen.

"I know just how she feels," Grace said. "You tell her that I had my heart stomped on when I was the same age, and it's a pain she will have learn to live with. I want her to be strong and I—"

Grace stopped herself, as if she'd just remembered that Mica was in the room. While he sat in mute shock, she spun around to look at him. "Sorry. I didn't mean for you to hear that."

"It's all right," he said.

She lowered her head and turned around.

"Who's with you?" Rene asked.

"Mica. Jules's father."

"Is he?" Rene's face filled the screen. "I'd like to talk to him."

"Not now, Rene. Some other time," Grace replied firmly.

Rene tried to shove Etienne aside, but Etienne was having none of it.

"Grace, *chérie*," Etienne said. "I need you to concentrate on those sketches I emailed you this morning. I want to match the first one with that faux fur I found from the distributor in Singapore. *Bien?*"

"Oui," she replied. "I'm signing off now. I'll be back soon and we'll get this all together."

"We have to, Grace," Rene said. "We have so much riding—"

"I know, Rene. I know. *Bonne nuit.*"

"Bonne nuit," they said simultaneously, and the computer screen went black.

Grace sat in the chair for a moment and then got up. She was smiling. "It went better than I'd thought. They're all so marvelous."

Mica inhaled deeply, suddenly aware he'd

barely taken a breath in the past few minutes. He was guilty of assuming all kinds of things about Grace and none of them had been accurate.

He'd misjudged her, underappreciated her talent as a designer, her management skills, even her openheartedness toward others.

This view into Grace's Paris life had opened his eyes. She was passionate about her work in a way that he was only beginning to feel with his inventions. No wonder she refused to marry him. He was asking too much of her. She could no more leave her life in Paris than he could wish his left arm alive. If he demanded she move to Indian Lake, Grace would slowly become diminished. Her passion would die and she would blame him for it. In the beginning of his parents' life together, before their children were born, their commitment for each other was underscored by their passion to build the farm. They had a love for the land so deep in their souls that they were willing to sacrifice for it and for the family they wanted.

Mica's life was already much different because of Jules. He had a family. It would be easy for Mica to sacrifice for Jules, but Grace would have to abandon everything else that made her own life worth living.

Guilt and insecurity enveloped him. Did he have the right to ask so much of her? Grace had told him she wouldn't marry him. She'd told him she wanted to be with a man who loved her. But even if they did fall in love, he saw now, it wouldn't last. He could never give her what she wanted or needed. His life was here. Hers was in Paris. For a long time, Mica had thought Grace had an easy life. Now he realized she had worked incredibly hard for the successes she'd gained.

Yes, he'd been the one who'd broken her heart when she was a teenager. She'd told Etienne that she'd never gotten over the pain. Maybe that was why she refused to marry him. She knew better than to put her heart in harm's way again.

His list of apologies was getting longer by the minute. He only had one choice. And he should take it.

He rose slowly, setting Jules carefully on the sofa.

"Grace. I'm sorry."

"For what?" she asked, walking toward him.

"For hurting you back then—when we were kids. I didn't know and I should have." He touched her cheek, wondering if this was the same cheek she'd used to feel the fabrics all those years ago. Her first step toward her dream. "I never meant to hurt you last autumn, either. I was in so much pain. So much distress. And very confused. You were like oxygen to me. When I was with you, I thought maybe I just might live again. You gave me that, and I thank you."

Her eyes fell and when she lifted them back to him, they were filled with tears. She put her hand over his.

"And now, Mica?"

"And now…"

Not a word came to his head as he lowered his mouth to hers.

The feel of Grace's lips on his was almost more than he could stand. And when she put her arms around his neck, he thought he'd taken his last breath. His heart slammed against his chest and she'd have to be numb not to feel it. He slid his hand from her cheek and down to her waist. Then he pulled her closer. He pressed his hand against the small of her back and the force of her heart beating against his chest, nearly in rhythm with his, brought back every memory of those October nights over a year ago.

"Grace," he breathed.

She kissed him back with that same sweet

surrender he'd found dear and oh, so necessary. He could go on forever.

But she couldn't. Wouldn't.

She was leaving. Going back to Paris. Back to another life. Maybe even another man.

It was Mica who broke the kiss. He knew he had to for self-preservation. Kissing Grace would get him into more trouble than he'd bargained for and he didn't need distractions. Not now.

"Grace. Marry me," he said in a rush, hoping he hadn't sounded too pleading.

Her eyes held hope, longing. He knew his kiss had softened her. But was it enough?

"No."

"Grace. You know it's the right thing to do."

"For us?"

"For Jules," he replied honestly.

"That's what I thought you meant," she said and pushed away from him. "I already told you I can't." He didn't miss the bitter disappointment in her voice.

Mica didn't press. In too many ways, she was right. He needed to stay focused on his invention and on making himself into the kind of man she would never want to leave.

He had a lot of work ahead of him.

CHAPTER FOURTEEN

MICA HAD BLINDSIDED Grace with his apology. She hadn't expected his emotional delivery, and like an impetuous fool, Grace had walked into Mica's kiss with abandon. She'd wanted him to kiss her, but she shouldn't have. Locked in his embrace, she'd hoped for a slice of a moment that maybe he would feel the same things for her as she did for him.

She didn't want to crave another kiss, but she did. In that moment when their lips touched…she could swear he felt *something* for her. Maybe it wasn't love. But it was close.

The fact that he broke away from her so quickly, as if he'd stuck his finger in a light socket, jolted her back to reality. This was Mica. Married to his father's land. And that was the crux of it. Mica's roots went deep into the soil of Indian Lake. His family's arms would always hold him. She'd loved him for so long, wanted his love in return so long, that she'd never thought about what would happen if she ever heard him tell her that he loved her back.

Her life was in Paris. She'd built a career there, and she was responsible to all those who worked with her. She had dreams of her own she would never abandon.

Though their lives were an ocean apart, she never wanted this moment with him to end.

"I should go," he said. "I have to run an errand for my mother."

"No, you don't," Grace countered.

"How do you know?" He stepped back, dropping his arm and giving her a steely look.

"Because your mother just got married. I'll bet that kitchen is overflowing with leftovers. She doesn't need anything."

"The hardware store is open today. The kitchen drain is clogged and…" He fumbled with his words.

She glared at him. "I'm not buying it. But if it's me, just say so."

He shoved his right hand in his jeans pocket and slumped, staring at the floor for a moment.

Gathering courage?

"Okay, I confess. I liked kissing you—too much."

Oh. So that's it. She smiled, feeling vastly encouraged. "And that's a problem because…?"

He let out a frustrated breath. "Grace. We have about a hundred unresolved issues and instead of hashing them out, I kiss you and I lose my focus."

"I should think that would help clarify things for you."

"Apparently not." He glanced over at the sofa and gasped.

Grace spun around. "Jules!" she yelled and raced toward her baby.

Jules was wide-awake and sitting up. He had ripped the head off his toy dinosaur, and he was shoving the stuffing into his mouth.

Grace scooped Jules off the sofa, stuck her fingers in his mouth and retrieved the polyester. Mica was just as quick and yanked the headless T. rex from Jules's hand.

The minute the stuffing was out of his mouth, Jules let out a wail. Grace placed him over her shoulder and tried soothing him.

"It's okay now, sweetie. You scared Mommy. That's all."

"And Daddy," Mica said, stroking his back.

Grace swept her hand over Mica's and his thumb locked around her thumb. He moved closer to her and kissed the top of Jules's head. His eyes skimmed Jules's red face and as the love in Mica's gaze grew, she tuned out her baby's cries. All she heard now were the soothing words Mica showered on their son.

She felt his warm breath as he spoke. She felt as if she was inside a protective bubble, where only love and caring existed.

Though Mica clearly still held resentment toward Grace, any negative thoughts he might have had about the baby himself had been dispelled.

She'd always believed it, but for the first time, she could *see* that Mica would be a good father. Though he'd professed to prefer machines to people, he'd underestimated himself. With his son, he was caring and giving.

Mica's caresses and gentle words had quieted Jules, who lifted his head from Grace's shoulder and turned a tear-streaked face to them both.

"Oh, it breaks my heart to see him cry," she said, wiping Jules's tears with her fingertips.

"Here," Mica said, taking a handkerchief from his back pocket.

"Thanks." She wiped Jules's face and swept the handkerchief under his runny nose.

Jules smiled at her, turned in her arms and said, "Da." He put his little arms out to Mica.

Grace watched as Mica's face filled with a smile that she could only describe as coming from his heart. Her throat thickened with emotion and her eyes stung. "Here. He needs you."

"Come here, buddy." Mica scooped Jules up. Again, Jules clasped both hands around Mica's neck and leaped to his chest.

Grace cocked her head. "You know, it's like he knows you can only use one arm."

Mica's face lost its glow. "It's that obvious, even to a baby?"

Grace cringed. "Oh, no. I'm sorry, Mica. I—"

"It's okay." Mica gave her a half smile. "I noticed that, too." He looked at Jules, who had already scrambled over to Mica's left shoulder. "See? I wonder if he knows anything that we're talking about, or if he just thinks I'm his jungle gym. Anyway, I think babies are a lot smarter than we give them credit for. I think they know all kinds of things."

"So do I, Mica," she said, touching Jules's cheek. "My mother used to say that babies were still connected to heaven. She believed they were smarter than any adult. They just can't talk, is all."

"Na. Na," Jules said. The baby started wiggling around as if he was about to jump across Mica's chest again.

Grace's eyes widened. "It's almost like he's been trying to form words since we got here."

"Maybe we should be tutoring him or something."

"I'll let you do that," she said, suddenly uneasy. Tutoring. Lessons. Classes. Schooling. It all cost money. Money she didn't have and wouldn't have if she didn't spend her time wisely. She had a mountain of work to do for Etienne and the team. It would be great if Mica could take care of Jules for the rest of the day so she could spend her afternoon at the computer.

Mica placed his forehead to Jules's. "Say 'Mommy.'"

"Da." Jules giggled.

"Try 'Mama.'"

Then Mica leaned over and kissed Grace's cheek. "Mama," he repeated.

"Ma."

Grace knew Jules was just imitating sounds, but her knees went buttery and her heart expanded. Her days with Mica were numbered, and she would carry these moments with her for the rest of her life.

"See?" Mica said. "He's a quick study. I'd say he's going to be smarter than all my brothers put together. That Barzonni blood is the best." He chuckled, making Jules giggle along with him.

Grace felt an icy prickle scurry across her skin. In the next breath, Mica would be back to talking marriage. Without the first hint that he loved her.

Because he doesn't.

Frankly, she'd been surprised he'd gone two whole days without pushing the issue.

She had to give him points for coming to her rescue today. She'd been on Skype for over an hour going over all their designs. Of the thirty items her team had presented, she was only truly happy with five or six. She knew exactly what was wrong.

Fabrics.

Jasminda's talent was in evening and cocktail ensembles. When it came to sportswear and daywear, she was out of her element. Etienne was a good organizer and his eye for detail and accessories was unmatched, but he was a follower.

Rene was the one whose creativity most closely matched hers. Rene's forte was menswear; a soaring market across the globe, especially in western Europe and the United States. Grace needed Rene and Rene needed Grace's eye for color, fabric and design.

Rene was charming and brilliant, and he had been protective and caring toward her all through her pregnancy. They worked well together, and Grace had a feeling he would jump at the first sign of romantic interest from her. But so far, he'd left the ball in her court, honoring her dedication to her career and to Jules. She had sometimes wondered, if it wasn't for Mica, whether she could have a future with Rene.

But there was Mica. She wouldn't be who she was today without having known him. She'd had a flame for him since high school. And he was the father of her child.

As Grace watched Mica trying to teach Jules another word, which wasn't happening, she wondered if she'd ever be able to give up the Mica dream. Once she was back in Paris she would have to face the fact that Mica—at least the Mica of her dreams—was part of her past. They'd have to figure out a way to co-parent Jules, but she had a lot of life in front of her. Once she made it to the next step in her career, she just might decide to look around for a relationship.

Or not.

Up to this point, Grace had enjoyed being single. Determined to excel, she'd gotten satisfaction from her work. Jules had added a whole new dimension of love and fulfillment to her life. But after months of juggling both, something had to give. In some ways, Mica had a point about marriage: having a partner was practical. But Grace had always been happy enough on her own. If she was going to get married, it had to be for love. Nothing less.

Mica turned to her with a sour look on his face. "I think I need to try my skills at changing him again."

"Oh! Gotcha."

"Where are the diapers?"

"In the bedroom. I'll show you."

"It's okay. I can manage. I know you said you had a lot of work to do. I'll change him and then I'll fix that bottle you mentioned."

"Are you sure?"

"Uh-huh."

Jules grinned over Mica's shoulder as they walked away.

She waved to Jules.

"Ma. Ma."

Grace felt her heart squeeze and release. As they disappeared into the bedroom, she ran her fingers through her hair. No matter how hard she tried, she couldn't seem to let go of Mica. If anything, she was more in love with him now than she'd been last autumn. The revelation should have brought joy, but all she felt was an aching loneliness as she faced a future without him.

CHAPTER FIFTEEN

WHILE MICA FED JULES his bottle, Grace went to the enormous floor-to-ceiling window in the living room and looked out at the snowstorm. In the matter of a few hours every tree limb, rooftop and street had been covered in a foot of snow. Garbage cans looked like dwarfs lined up along the curb. It was difficult to distinguish the sidewalk from lawns and driveways. The church across the street looked like a castle out of a winter fairy tale.

The late afternoon sun was blotted out by heavy clouds and the streetlights cast silver shadows on the road below. The scene beyond the frosty windowpane reminded her of the fabric Jasminda had shown her during their Skype conference.

"That's it!"

Grace shot back to the kitchen table and grabbed her iPhone and sketch pad. She snapped a couple dozen shots of the snowfall, the street, the houses and the trees.

Then she sank to the floor and started sketching a line of winter sport clothes, dressy pants and blouses, and evening dresses and shoes. Instead of her usual brilliant colors, tropical hues and exotic florals, she chose black and white. Gray, charcoal, slate, pewter, midnight blue and Mediterranean blue—the color of Mica's eyes.

She knew an English cashmere manufacturer in Yorkshire who wove wool that draped like crepe. She would use their nearly gossamer wool to execute black, wide-legged, high-waisted party pants encrusted with jet beads. To pair with them, a white blouse with snowflake-pearl buttons, and the silk would come from Lyon, France.

Grace flipped the page and sketched skinny, snow-white pants with knee-high boots and a faux-fur-trimmed white-and-silver poncho.

Next, she drew a charcoal wool pencil skirt to be worn with a blue-black angora sweater with cap sleeves and a knee-length, gray-and-blue silk scarf from a fabric she'd found in Lake Como, Italy, on one of the few holidays she'd ever taken.

She had just started another drawing when she heard footsteps behind her.

"He's asleep."

"Huh?" She looked up and blinked, startled to see it was already getting dark. Grace had been so immersed in her creative dimension that she'd forgotten about Mica. Jules. The world. Her worries. It was times like this that frightened her just a bit. She was capable of retreating into her work for an entire day. She didn't want to admit it, but she feared she might fail to take care of Jules properly.

What if he needed her and she wasn't paying attention? What if he hurt himself, or he grew up feeling like she cared more about fashion design than about being his mom? What if? What if?

Grace knew she was getting ahead of herself, imagining tragedies that hadn't even happened. Did all mothers do that?

"I gave him his bottle, which he finished quickly. Then he fell asleep. I laid down with him and just watched." He smiled. "I knew you were busy, so I stayed with him."

"Where is he now?"

"Lying on the bed…" He gestured toward the bedroom.

"Oh. I have to put him in his carrier, otherwise he'll roll off. Without a crib here…" She rose stiffly from the floor. "I guess I lost track of time."

"No, you stay here. I'll take care of him," he said, offering his hand to steady her.

She took it.

A simple thing, wasn't it? Holding someone's hand. But not for Grace. His grip was firm, his strength apparent in that he nearly lifted her completely off the floor with one arm. And the feel of his palm against hers was electric.

His scent—a spicy soap with a hint of vanilla—lingered as Grace went back to the computer. She took photos of her sketches and emailed them to Etienne. Then she started an email detailing her ideas, the course of action they should take and which designs she wanted to concentrate on first.

She requested that Jasminda contact the cashmere manufacturer in Yorkshire the next day, once businesses were open after the holiday. If she could purchase that fabric, then they'd move forward. Grace told Etienne to use her credit card for the purchases. Her business account had run low the closer they got to Fashion Week. She was gambling a lot on her designs and she believed in her talent. She had to dip into her personal money to keep the business going. Again.

Mica came back to the kitchen. He put her

hands on her shoulders and peered at the computer screen.

"Whatcha doin'?"

"I—"

The lights went out. The computer shut down. The whir of the little space heater from the bedroom halted.

"What's going on?" Grace asked.

"Power's out." Mica went to the window. He turned back to her. "The whole block is down."

"What?" She shot up from her chair. "Does this happen often?"

"No." He took out his cell phone and punched out a number.

"What are you doing?" she asked.

"Calling the power company to make a report. And to see if there's any news about this outage."

She glanced over his shoulder to the window. The streetlights were out, but she could see that the snow hadn't abated at all. It was still coming down in waves of fat, white flakes.

"What's the address here?"

"Eleven twelve Maple Boulevard," she answered.

Mica gave the information to an automated-response voice mail. Then he used his phone to check the local weather alerts.

"This isn't good," he said.

"What? Why?"

"There's a state of emergency. They aren't letting people drive in this storm unless it's an emergency."

"You're kidding. They can do that?"

"Uh, yeah."

"I'm surprised your family didn't call to tell you."

"Actually…" He grimaced and held up his phone. "They did. I turned off my notifications when I went to change and feed Jules. I didn't want anything to wake him up."

"So, we're snowed in?"

"Seems like it," he replied, looking around. "Are there flashlights up here? We can use the app on our phones in a pinch, but we should try to avoid draining the battery. You got any spare blankets?"

"Not that I know of. As you can see, there's not much of anything up here. And we're expected downstairs for dinner—" she looked at her watch "—in fifteen minutes."

Mica rubbed his chin. "Doesn't Mrs. Beabots have a wood-burning fireplace in her library?"

"Yes. A big one."

He grabbed her hand and pulled her toward the bedroom. "Come on."

"What are we doing?"

"Getting Jules and every bit of his supplies—diapers, bottles, warm clothes. All the blankets you've got up here. Then we're going downstairs."

"Right. For dinner. But why all the stuff?"

"I need to make sure we survive the night. I don't like the idea of Mrs. Beabots alone down there, either. We might be stuck here for days."

"Days?" Fear bolted through her. "What are you saying?"

"The last time we had a power outage on the farm due to a snowstorm, it didn't come back for four days."

"Are you serious?" She glanced over at her computer. Her battery would barely last four hours. Let alone four days. "This is a disaster."

"It is," he said. "We have to keep Jules warm."

Grace dropped his hand and rushed past him into the bedroom, guilt descending on her like the wet, heavy snow outside. For a moment, she'd been more concerned about work than about her baby. "Of course we do."

MICA HELD JULES in his carrier and stood behind Grace as she knocked at Mrs. Beabots's back door. Grace held two blankets, the diaper bag and her laptop.

"Mrs. Beabots?" Grace turned the knob and pushed the door open. "It's Grace and Mica. Are you here?"

"I am." Mrs. Beabots came into the kitchen from the dining room holding a five-branch, silver candelabra with all the candles lit. The kitchen was bathed in light. She smiled as she put the candelabra on the island. "I'm so glad I believe in candles everywhere."

"So am I," Grace said. "I think we'll need them."

"Oh, Mica. Thank goodness you're here and not out driving in this storm. I thought I saw you drive in earlier. Now hurry in and shut the door. We don't want to lose any heat."

"I was worried about you, Mrs. Beabots," Mica said, lifting Jules's carrier to the island. Grace had placed a baby blanket over the top of the carrier to keep him warm. Mica lifted the edge to make sure his son was still sleeping.

"Oh, pish posh," Mrs. Beabots said. "I've been through many a power outage. I should have had a generator put in this old house years ago, but I didn't. What I did do was buy an extra cord of wood this fall. Lester MacDougal delivered and stacked it for me."

"You're reading my mind," Mica said. "I

was thinking I'd build us a roaring fire. We can crowd around it until the power comes on."

"Absolutely," Mrs. Beabots said. "The good thing is that my soup is ready to ladle out. And I made homemade bread to go with it. We'll have a fine feast for this evening."

"All right, then." Mica looked at Grace. "You get Jules settled in the library. I'll go bring in the wood."

Mrs. Beabots lifted the candelabra. "And I'll light more candles. Mica, there are fire starters, kindling and a butane lighter in the box next to the fireplace."

"Excellent," Mica replied and headed for the back door. He stopped and realized he only had one arm, not two, to bring in the wood.

He turned back. "Mrs. Beabots. Do you have a tote or a carrier I could use?"

"I do. In the library is a leather sling in a metal frame. It's easy to carry." She cast him an easy smile.

He appreciated her not making reference to his arm. And he liked the fact that she expected him to take care of all of them.

"Got it," he said, his chest puffing with pride.

He entered the stately library. Along the mantel and on the end tables, Mrs. Beabots had lit tall white tapers. The flickering light across the velvet chairs and Victorian settee made Mica feel as if he'd stepped back in time. This had to be how the house looked a century ago, minus a gas lamp or two. Mrs. Beabots's portrait over the fireplace caught his eye. For years he'd been invited to this house for holidays and special dinners with his family. He'd enjoyed the food and the company, but he now realized how unobservant he'd been.

Everything in this room, from the chicken-wire glass doors on the bookcases, to the Bergere chairs, the needlepoint footstools and the paintings of Paris street scenes, was French. The portrait was stunning. He remembered that Mrs. Beabots had mentioned once that this painting was from her days in Paris, too. Her stylish clothing was probably made by someone with Grace's talent.

And that person's design had been immortalized in this painting.

Riveted, Mica realized he knew so little about Grace. She had depths to her that he couldn't and hadn't begun to fathom.

Was Grace looking for fame? For her name to garner respect? Admiration?

And if she did, was there anything wrong with that?

What drove her to work so hard? What gave

her the motivation and the ability to block out the rest of the world and focus so intensely on her work? He would give anything to find that kind of concentration.

Maybe Grace had been right about him—he'd been so self-centered that his creativity couldn't break through. He was, quite possibly, his own worst enemy. Was he a self-saboteur? Or had he just not found his niche?

And where would Grace be now if it hadn't been for the time they'd spent together last October? If it hadn't been for their…mistake?

"No," he said aloud. He would not believe Jules was a mistake. No child was. Babies were miracles.

A draft made the candlelight flicker, and Mica shook himself out of his thoughts. He went to the flue to make certain it was open.

He found some newspaper and kindling and piled them on the grate, then grabbed the sling and headed back through the kitchen.

"Please be careful out there, Mica," Grace said as she pulled bowls out of the cabinet. "I can hear the wind picking up."

"Here's a flashlight," Mrs. Beabots said, handing him an LED lantern with a handle.

He thanked her and went out into the storm. Grace was right. The wind had kicked up and sank what felt like frigid needles into the back of his neck.

Mica pulled the tarp off the woodpile, propped up the lantern, then tightened the sheepskin collar of his jacket around his neck.

Tonight, there were three people inside who were counting on him to keep a fire blazing. The warmth from the fire would keep a little baby and an elderly woman alive. It was no small thing. He would keep his arm around Grace and hold her close all night.

Yes, he thought. He believed in miracles. Even ones that called themselves a snowstorm.

CHAPTER SIXTEEN

"How will I warm Jules's bottle?" Grace asked Mica as they finished the tasty cream-of-shrimp-and-leek soup that Mrs. Beabots had made. Grace sat on the floor near the fire and held Jules in her lap. Jules played with a rubber SpongeBob toy.

Though she'd grown up with Chicago's bitter winters, she didn't remember any power outages. Once in New York during college there'd been a brownout, but it had lasted one day. And she didn't have a baby who depended on her. Mica ripped a hunk of bread off the loaf and said, "I'll get a pan, put some water in it and heat the bottle over the fire."

"But the bottle is plastic. It will melt."

"Then we put the formula in the pan, heat it and then pour into that little sack when it's cooled down a bit. Doable." He munched his bread and winked at her.

Mrs. Beabots looked up from her bowl. "Would Jules like a bit of my soup? I don't know what you've introduced to him, but he's got a couple teeth, so…"

"Good idea!" Mica said before Grace could protest.

Mica dipped his spoon into the broth and held it out to Jules, who leaned forward and bit. Half the soup ran down his chin onto his bib, but he swallowed the other half.

Jules smacked his lips and stared at Mica as if considering the taste. Then he squirmed in Grace's arms and reached for Mica.

"I think he wants another try," Grace said.

Mica obliged and this time Jules got a piece of soft carrot. He swallowed, looked at Grace and smiled. He clapped his hands. "Da!"

"Great," Mica moaned. "He probably thinks I made this gourmet concoction and I can barely even microwave pizza."

Mrs. Beabots clucked her tongue. "If you're going to be a father, Mica, you're going to have to acquire a great many new skills."

"I'm seeing that," Mica said, sharing two more spoonfuls with Jules before finishing off his soup.

"Here," Grace said. "You take Jules. I'll go wash these dishes."

Grace placed Jules on Mica's lap and once again, Jules crawled up Mica's chest like a monkey. Jules picked up his pacifier, which was hooked to his navy blue sweater, and tried to shove it into Mica's mouth.

"Uh, no thanks, Jules," Mica said. "Maybe later."

Mica put the pacifier in Jules's mouth, but Jules thought it was a game and popped it out again. He giggled and tried to share with Mica.

Grace gathered the bowls and spoons. Only a few feet away from the fire, the chill in the rest of the house made her shiver. In the kitchen, the wind howled against the north- and west-facing windows and seemed to cut right through the glass. She had a mind to go back and get her jacket.

Instead, she put the stopper in the sink and used as little hot water as she needed to wash up.

She looked out the kitchen window and saw candles burning in Sarah's house next door. Suddenly, she remembered that Sarah had a new baby as well. She glanced up at the chimney and saw that Sarah and Luke had a fire going as well.

She had to admit there was something cozy about this situation. But if the storm kept up, there was no telling how snarled the Chicago airport would be. She remembered winter storms like this when it could take several days to get a flight out. She couldn't afford to be away from the atelier any longer than she'd planned.

Grace went to the island and pulled up Sarah's number on her phone. She glanced at her remaining battery. Twenty-seven percent. She hadn't recharged it all day. She wondered if Mica had much power left, either.

It was all so oddly silent, this cocoon of snow that surrounded them. There was no one out on the street, the plows had not appeared and she hadn't heard a single car pass.

It was as if there were no people left in the world except the four of them.

"Hello?"

"Sarah, it's Grace. I'm at Mrs. Beabots's kitchen window. How are you doing over there?"

"We're fine. Luke's got a fire going. The kids are putting a puzzle together and Charlotte has already fallen asleep."

"Do you know anything about what happening?" Grace asked anxiously.

"Luke has one of those military-issue radios that gives everything from the marine forecast on Lake Michigan to national weather. The good news is that the snow is supposed to end within the hour. He's pulled every string he can to find out when the power will come on, but there are several transformers out all over town. We just have to wait our turn."

"How long will that take?"

"I don't know."

"Mica said that their power went out for four days once. I can't lose four days," Grace said frantically.

"That must have been out at the farm. We've never lost it for more than two days here in town."

"Oh, that's good news. I'm glad I called. My phone is nearly out of juice and Mrs. Beabots's landline is dead, so I should go. I think Mica has power on his phone in case you guys need anything."

"Grace. Don't worry. We'll all be fine. We can always walk over to check on each other. Tell Mica I talked to Maddie and she said Nate got home from the hospital before the storm hit. I guess Gina was worried. I haven't talked to Gabe or Liz. Did Mica?"

"He said they had all left voice mails. He might have answered them."

"Double-check, okay? I just don't want Gina or anybody to worry."

"Do…they do that? Check up on him a lot?"

"Yeah. Ever since..." Sarah stopped. "Uh..."

"I thought that might be the case. I don't think I'll say anything. But if you want to pass the word that you and I talked, that wouldn't step on anyone's toes...or ego."

"Gotcha! Take care, Grace."

Grace hung up.

She chewed her bottom lip. No wonder Mica could be hypersensitive. His family had apparently been treating him with kid gloves since the accident. Though she knew they loved him and wanted the best for him, their coddling probably only exacerbated Mica's feelings of ineptness.

She rinsed the dishes and then put them in the wood rack to drain.

She thought she now understood how Mica might be feeling. Bit by bit, Rafe was taking over more of Mica's duties on the farm. As of last night, Gina had remarried, complicating Mica's sense of pride at being his father's heir. Even though Sam wouldn't run the farm, as Gina's husband, he was a figurehead. And of course, what Mica had found out about Gina's feelings for Sam and for Angelo had made him question his memory of his father.

And she'd shown up with Jules in the middle of all this.

As she dried her hands, Mica walked in, pulling on his jacket.

"Where are you going?" Grace asked.

He lifted the LED lantern. "I saw some bricks out by the woodpile. Mrs. Beabots is getting cold, even with the extra blanket I put around her shoulders. Then I'm getting more firewood. We'll need a lot to get us through the night."

"Why bricks?"

"I'm going to put them in the fire, warm them, wrap them in towels and then put them under her feet. I'll get one for you, too."

She smiled. "How Victorian of you."

"Thanks." He winked. "I'm feeling a bit like a pioneer."

"Can I help?" she asked and then stopped. This was just the kind of thing his family would do. They would assume he was helpless. That wasn't why Grace had offered, but Mica might not see it that way. She held up her palm before he could answer. "On second thought, I'd better change Jules. I want to put a second sweater on him, too." She pointed to the door. "You take care of the bricks and wood."

Before he could answer, she walked away.

In the library, Grace saw the fire had waned. Mrs. Beabots was holding Jules.

Jules sneezed.

"Oh, goodness," Mrs. Beabots said. "I think the house is truly getting a chill."

Grace reached for Jules and took him in her arms. "It is. And Jules is just getting over something. Listen, I don't want you going to the kitchen. And maybe you should use the bathroom now before it gets much colder. I talked to Sarah and she said they are fine next door, but there's no word on when the power will come back on. Several transformers are out."

Mrs. Beabots stood and pulled the blanket around her. "I'm going to get another pair of socks and my sheepskin slippers. Do you have anything like that, dear?"

"No."

Mrs. Beabots looked from her dainty feet to Grace's. "I have an extra pair, but I'm afraid they won't fit you."

"It's okay. Mica is going to warm some bricks in the fire for our feet. We'll be just fine."

"Smart boy, that one," Mrs. Beabots said.

"He really is." Grace beamed.

Mrs. Beabots walked up to her, touched her cheek and said, "He chose you, didn't he?"

Mrs. Beabots started to walk away, but before she'd left the room Grace asked, "Why do you keep saying that? Mica and I—we're an accident. Something that shouldn't have happened. Jules is—"

Mrs. Beabots whirled around, the blanket falling in a whoosh from her shoulders. "Don't say it, Grace Railton. Don't you dare say it. Jules is an angel. A gift to make things right."

"Make what right?"

"Why, you and Mica, of course. You were meant to be. Any fool can see that."

Grace stared at her. "You're wrong. We're an ocean apart, and not just because I live in Paris. You know how demanding the fashion world can be. How competitive and difficult. Mica lives here in this quiet, peaceful place that I wish I loved enough to give up my life in Paris for. But I can't. I won't. I've worked too hard. We are so different..." Grace felt the ache in her heart rip through her body. As much as their different lifestyles were an issue, she knew that wasn't truly what was causing her pain. She loved Mica and he would never love her back. He had a responsibility toward her and that was all.

"I think he'll come around," Mrs. Beabots said.

"No. He won't. He doesn't want me."

"He told you that?"

"Yes," Grace admitted, feeling her blood turn to ice water. "Oh, he asked me to marry him, but not because he loves me. He doesn't. He wants Jules to have both parents, for us to be a family, but only for practical reasons. Mica believes we should sacrifice for Jules's sake the way his parents sacrificed for him and his brothers."

Saying it aloud only made it worse. And terrifyingly real. She realized in that moment that she'd come to Indian Lake because she'd actually thought Mica would confess that he'd loved her since that first kiss in the pool. She wanted to say "yes," but she also could not live a lie.

"Then I've been mistaken," Mrs. Beabots said. "I'd thought better of him than that."

MICA LAY ON the floor with Jules on his belly, throw pillows propped on his left side in case Jules rolled off. Grace had curled next to him and put her head on his chest. With his right arm around Grace, she snuggled closer to him by the hour.

Mrs. Beabots slept on the Victorian sofa behind them, a warm brick at her feet with three blankets and a mink coat over her. She slept soundly.

The fire was nearly out and Mica knew he'd have to disturb both mother and child to throw a few more logs on. Just not yet.

This night had been an idyll he never could have imagined. Not since before the accident had he felt this needed, or that his presence and contributions were necessary to the lives of others. True, their circumstances were not as dire as they could be, but the old Victorian house, with its high ceilings and noninsulated windows, allowed the heat to dissipate in minutes.

It was well past four in the morning when he finally rose to stoke the fire. He checked the wall thermometer Mrs. Beabots had placed in the hall just outside the library. The house was forty-nine degrees. Bone-chilling, but not deadly, as long as he kept the library warm.

Mica continued to heat bricks and rewrap them for Mrs. Beabots and Grace. They stirred in their sleep. Only once did Grace awaken.

All she said was "Come to bed."

His heart cried out with an unfamiliar yearning.

He slid back under the blankets, pulled Jules onto his warm stomach and held Grace close.

She didn't say another word.

The accident had turned Mica's world upside

down, and he hadn't felt like himself since. But tonight, he reveled in a sense of belonging he hadn't even experienced as a child. The happiest days he could remember had always been tinged with the feeling that he was an outsider. But maybe he simply hadn't appreciated his parents and brothers as much as he could have back then.

Mica was by no means the misfit of the family. That title went to Nate, who had run away right after high-school graduation to join the navy so he could save up for medical school and pay for it all on his own, without their father footing the bill. Gabe was also headstrong and independent. He had left the farm to become a vintner and marry Liz Crenshaw. Rafe had stayed, yet even his first love was Thoroughbred racing. That and Olivia.

Then there was Mica. He'd only ever belonged to the land and to the machines and engines he repaired. He'd never traveled or extended himself beyond what he knew and loved. And he'd always drifted away from people.

Yet, here tonight, he was part of a family. He was filled with an emotion so strong, he could hardly swallow. Mrs. Beabots had been a friend nearly all his life, but right now, he thought of her as the grandmother he'd never known.

He regretted his knee-jerk reaction when Grace had first shoved his son into his arm. Everything about his baby brought a warmth to his heart he'd never felt before. He loved Jules, and Mica would spend the rest of his life telling and showing his son exactly that. And Grace…

Grace was both integral to this family and an obstacle to keeping it together. Mica didn't know how he would convince her, but if she wouldn't marry him, then there had to be another way for them to be together.

Mica would find it because he knew now he was no longer a drifter. He could be the father Jules needed.

He would make it permanent.

With or without Grace.

CHAPTER SEVENTEEN

LIKE THE RUMBLE and thunder of an avalanche, snowplows roared down Maple Boulevard in the early hours of the morning, jolting Grace from a deep sleep. Opening her eyes and slowly coming out of a hazy dream, she realized she had one arm draped over Mica's chest and one arm curled up beside him. Jules was sound asleep on Mica's stomach as if he'd slept with his daddy every night since he was born.

She blinked. Though the fire was still blazing, which meant Mica had woken through the night to stoke it, the Tiffany lamps were on.

"Power's back," she mumbled.

Mica stirred, but didn't open his eyes. His arm tightened around her shoulders, then he ran his hand down her back and pulled her closer. It was the natural position of a husband who'd slept beside his wife for years. What was going on here? She nudged her nose against his chest, inhaling an intoxicating, spicy scent that was pure Mica. One that she'd never forgotten and never would. Looking at Jules lying on Mica's stomach, she was once again struck with the similarities between them. Jules's long dark lashes fanned against his cheek exactly like Mica's. Their dark hair was the same texture and color. Jules's lips parted only slightly as he slept, though he breathed through his nose…like his father.

Family traits. Family resemblance. Grace felt as if she could barely keep her head above water in the Barzonni sea. In Paris, she had designed and customized the world she inhabited. In Indian Lake she was an outsider, despite the fact that her Aunt Louise had been here all her life and Grace herself had visited often during her teen years here. Grace felt as if she was clinging to her plans with her fingernails, like the survivor of a shipwreck. And what a wreck she'd made of this.

The idea that she could just leave Jules with Mica for two months, then whisk him back to Paris was nothing short of absurd. She'd worried about Jules more on this trip than she had when she was at work in her atelier. Granted, Jules was getting older. He crawled now and was trying table food. When he was smaller and less mobile, he was easier to keep an eye on. But it wasn't just that. Something in her had altered drastically.

Perhaps is it was the fact that on this trip, she'd had long stretches in which she only had to think about Jules. And Mica. She wasn't glued to her design table or computer, or listening to Etienne and Jasminda argue. She wasn't in conference with Rene or on another overseas call to England.

For the first time since Jules's birth, she'd performed the role of mother more than that of businesswoman, designer or couture team partner.

Was this the real Grace she was exploring? Or was it another of the many facets most women polish in their lives? Was she any different than Sarah or Liz, who balanced careers and kids? She didn't think so.

And, of course, there was Mica. For over a year in Paris, she'd actually thought she was past her feelings for him. She'd thought that bringing Jules here would be uncomplicated. She'd expected his anger and shock, yes, but she hadn't counted on her own emotions. Her reaction to him last autumn had been a combination of compassion for what he was going through and the remains of a teenage crush that could never be anything more. All through her pregnancy and Jules's first months, she'd tried to convince herself of that. But after only a few days in Indian Lake, it was obvious that she'd been in denial. Her love for Mica was full-blown and devastating.

Lying next to him now, with their baby son sleeping soundly on his stomach, was something out of a dream—one that Grace should certainly never trust.

Mica had never opened his heart to her. She wondered if he even knew his own heart.

She looked up at the high, stamped-tin ceiling. She would like to tell herself that she and Mica were practically strangers, but she'd just be making up excuses again. She was a victim of unrequited love and it was time she faced that cruel fact.

No matter what Grace did to reason herself out of loving Mica, it wouldn't work.

"Grace…" Mica shifted and kissed the top of her head. "I think he peed on me."

"Oh, no!" She scrambled to sit up, but he didn't loosen his hold on her. "Mica, let me up. I'll get the diaper bag."

"The power's on, right?"

"Yes."

"Could you bring me a warm washcloth, then? Let's not wake up Jules until we have to."

Grace nodded. "Absolutely. The water heater might not have kicked in, but I'll boil some. You don't have a change of clothes, though. I'm so sorry."

"It's okay. I'll wash up as best I can. How's Mrs. Beabots?"

"Asleep."

"Good. I'll stay here and you get the things." His smile was slow and sleepy. His dark hair was mussed and his dark stubble only made his blue eyes more intense. He'd never looked so handsome.

She didn't know what came over her, considering she'd just been stewing over how painful it was to be in love with him, but she kissed his cheek. Then she grazed his lips with hers.

"Don't," he said.

"What?"

"I haven't brushed my teeth." He gave a low laugh, then pulled her close and planted a kiss on her temple.

I'm so toast, she thought and drew away from him.

"Be back in a sec."

Grace rose carefully so as not to disturb Jules or Mrs. Beabots. She tiptoed to the kitchen and put a kettle on to boil. She looked out the window and saw that the streetlights were glow-ing. Now that she was up, she could hear the furnace had kicked on and the house would soon be warm again. She found a French press near the kitchen sink and there was ground coffee in a blue-and-white French porcelain canister on the island. She rummaged around and found two coffee mugs, a sugar bowl and some cream in the refrigerator.

Just as the kettle was about to whistle she took the pot off the stove and poured water into the French press. She placed the cups, sugar and cream on a silver tray she'd seen Mrs. Beabots use. She found a bar of soap near the sink and two washcloths in a drawer. She put the rest of the hot water in a cereal bowl and added it to the tray.

When she returned to the library, Mica had scooted into a sitting position and placed Jules on his baby blanket.

Grace whispered, "Here we are."

"Thanks," Mica said quietly.

Mica dipped the washcloths into the hot water and then soaped one up. He lifted his shirt and scrubbed his six-pack. Grace couldn't help but stare. Her eyes darted to his.

"Told you I kept working out."

"But…"

"My arm didn't hinder my sit-ups." He grinned mischievously.

"Apparently not."

Grace turned to Jules and unsnapped his sleeper, glancing back at Mica. He caught her eye.

"What?" he asked, rinsing the suds off with the second washcloth.

"Sorry." She smiled and took off Jules's diaper, then cleaned him up with a wipe. Jules stirred, rubbed his nose and looked at Grace. He smiled and then closed his eyes, content that he was safe and his mother was taking care of him.

Mica dabbed at his sweater. "I'll take care of this when I get home," he said.

"What about your jeans?"

"Safe."

"I didn't give Jules his bottle last night. I'm surprised he slept all night," she commented.

"Maybe he likes sleeping with his dad," Mica replied proudly.

"I'm sure he does." She dug in the diaper bag for a clean sleeper and a fresh sweater. She was surprised that Jules continued to doze through the change of clothing. "Now that the heat is on, we'll all start to warm up," she whispered to Mica.

Mica plunged the sieve on the French press, then poured coffee into the mugs for them both. He added a huge dollop of cream and a teaspoon of sugar to hers. He drank his black.

Grace sat cross-legged on the floor and placed a blanket in her lap and then Jules on top of the blanket and put another blanket over him. She took the mug from Mica. "How do you know how I like my coffee?"

"Isn't that how all the French take their coffee?"

"I wouldn't say—" She stopped as she took a sip, then she narrowed her eyes. "This is too perfect."

"Okay, I lied about the French thing," Mica said. "I made coffee for you once before." His voice was wistful and he didn't raise his eyes from his mug.

"I don't remember," she said.

"I do remember," he said in a low voice tinged with a distant, mournful tone of loss.

He drank the rest of his coffee in silence. He looked as if his mind was a million miles away.

Grace put down her mug. She couldn't take it. She had to know what he was thinking. "Mica—"

"Grace," he interrupted. "Now that the crisis is over and we aren't going to freeze to death, we need to talk about all…" He glanced down at Jules. "This."

"I agree."

"Good. Then let's do the right thing and get married."

Grace's mouth fell open, then she slammed it shut. This wasn't what she'd call "talking." This was Mica making his declaration—again. For some reason he thought that the decisions should all be made by him.

"You can't be this arrogant," she hissed, glancing over at Mrs. Beabots. "We should go to the other room to have this argument."

"Fine. But the problem is that we don't need to argue."

"Sure we do," she retorted. "There is no way I'm going to enter into a loveless marriage like your mother did. I'm not going to spend my life wasting my years and my—my choices, chances, on…" Her brain had gone black again. She hated when it did that. She was so overwhelmed with emotions, she couldn't think. She saw black. Felt black. "On…you," she sputtered. It was all she could manage. And the second it came out, she wished she could stuff it back in.

Grace's heart cried out in pain. Her anger was simply protecting her from hurt. She wanted Mica as her husband. She wanted to spend the rest of her life with him, but above all she wanted him to love her. Just last night, even this morning, she'd felt flickers of that love. She wanted to believe it was there. Last autumn there had been long nights and golden afternoons when she'd convinced herself that deep down, Mica loved her. But they had vanished that day when he'd said goodbye with a cold wave at the Indian Lake train station.

He shot to his feet and pointed at Jules.

"He's my son," he growled. "He'll inherit *my* family's farm one day, and I mean to make that happen. I'm not about to let you spoil that for him."

Carefully, she put Jules on top of the blanket she'd used to cover herself that night. As she stood, she could swear she saw Mrs. Beabots pop one eye open and then close it. The octogenarian had been playing possum this whole time.

"Oh, so now I'm the bad guy?" She picked up her mug and the French press.

She walked past Mica, who was standing like a pillar of indignation in the middle of the floor. "Well? Are you coming?"

"What?"

"To the kitchen, where we can talk." She marched out of the room.

Mica followed her and closed the kitchen door.

"Look, Grace…"

"No, you look, Mica Barzonni. I'm not going to marry you. Got that? Women have babies every day of the week and raise them without fathers all the time. This is a new century. Times are changing."

"Not for me, they're not. A child needs both parents, Grace. Both. The statistics show that kids are better adjusted with both parents in the house."

"Since when have you boned up on parenting?"

He leaned his right hand on the island and stuck his face close to hers. His eyes were glacier blue and hot with anger. Fire and ice. Grace realized there was nothing she could say to convince him.

"Since you finally got around to telling me about the existence of my own son!"

It took every ounce of her willpower not to cry. She did feel guilty, ashamed and embarrassed that she had kept the truth from him. He had her on that front. He was punishing her.

She deserved it. But she wasn't about to go on being punished forever.

"I told you that I'm sorry. I made a mistake. I should have told you. And I have told you now. That's in the past and we can't do anything about that. So, can we be adults about this?"

"Sure." He clenched his jaw. "So, will you tell me the truth now?"

"What truth?"

"About what's going on? Why you won't marry me. You know it's the best for Jules. And yet you refuse. So there has to be a real reason, and I think I know what it is."

Confusion pinged around Grace's brain. "What are you talking about?"

"This is all about that guy, isn't it?"

Stumped, she asked, "What guy?"

"Rene? You're refusing to marry me because he's waiting for you back there in Paris. I saw him during your conference. I heard him, too. You both—you're a lot more than just coworkers. That guy's in love with you."

"Rene?"

"Yeah."

How could Mica tell if Rene was in love with her? If she thought about it, she had to admit she'd seen some signs of love, from time to time, but they'd both worked so closely and were both so driven, they'd never seen if it could go anywhere. Plus, she'd chalked a lot of their closeness up to the intimacy and intensity of their working relationship.

Still, Grace had not seen this coming. How could Mica see romance between her and Rene when he'd obviously missed the fact that Grace was deeply, irrevocably in love with him? But telling Mica that wouldn't do either of them any good. He would probably use her feelings as leverage in his marriage campaign, even as he remained adamant that he didn't love her back. Grace would hope Mica wasn't that cruel, but she could see how much he loved Jules. How much he would do for that little boy. And that scared her.

Mica raked his hair. "So tell me, Grace. Did you and this guy cook this whole thing up about bringing Jules here to dump him on me so you can go back to him? Did you ever intend to come back for your son?"

Grace pulled back her hand to slap him but stopped just as her hand was about to make impact. She whirled away from him and went to the other side of the island. She needed distance. "That is the most insulting thing I've ever been accused of in my life. You can't possibly think that, Mica. And I want you to take it back. Right. Now."

He exhaled deeply. "Okay, fine. But if that's not true, then what? You want to leave Jules here with me for a couple months, just long enough for us to bond—which we've done already, in case you haven't noticed—then take him back to Paris? Boot me out of the picture for good?"

"No!" she barked. "None of that is true."

"I'm sorry." He put his shaking hand on the island and looked down. Then he lifted his face to hers. "I just don't understand you."

"We're even, then," she snapped. "You know, Mica, I think something about me really ticks you off. Not always, but you can be the biggest jerk to me. Why is that?"

Silence.

"I really want to know," she said. "Is it because I was a teen queen and you still harbor some resentment about that? You're right that I handled my pregnancy all wrong, but Mica, all I wanted from you was some help. That's all. I'm not 'dumping' Jules on you. I love Jules with all my heart. I would never, ever give him up. And I hadn't thought far enough ahead, but I don't plan to keep him from you. That wouldn't be fair. I'm not an evil person, Mica."

Her throat thickened and cut off the rest of her words. It was just as well. Words were useless now. They'd come to the end of their road.

And it was a dead end. No fork. No road less traveled. No turning back.

Grace felt utterly alone at the moment she needed to feel wanted and loved. She, of all people, knew life didn't work out the way she wanted.

"No," he said softly. "You're not a bad person. Neither am I." His face softened and he stood back from the island. "I hope."

"I never said you were. Mica, I can tell you that Rene is not my boyfriend or anything like that. We haven't been plotting against you. I admit that he loves Jules. And he does have feelings for me…"

Mica pointed at her. "See? I knew it!"

"But I'm not going to marry him."

Mica's intake of breath was audible. "You aren't?"

"Definitely not. In the first place, we've never even dated. In the second, he hasn't asked me."

"Yet," Mica added. "You haven't dated and he hasn't asked you *yet*."

"That's accurate. Yes," she admitted. Who was she to predict the future? Once she was back to Paris and after she got her company up and rolling, there was always the possibility that she could get over Mica. Move on. Have a life. A half life.

"Grace, we have to come to some kind of agreement. If marriage is out of the question, then could we work out a custody agreement?" he asked.

"Sure. I have no objection to that."

"You don't?"

"No," she replied sincerely. "I want you to be in Jules's life. I want you to know all the joys like I have with him." Even as Grace spoke, she felt her heart break again. She was hopelessly in love with him. If Mica would only tell her that he loved her, she would marry him and never look back on this pain.

"Then I think I have a solution for us."

Grace felt the hairs on the back of her neck prickle as if bad tidings had swept over her. "Oh?"

"I have an attorney friend here in town. He can draw up a custody agreement for us. We can have his name legally changed as well. A few papers—" he snapped his fingers "—and then it's done." He smiled winningly.

And Grace felt her heart sink.

CHAPTER EIGHTEEN

ONCE RAFE HAD hooked the snowplow onto the front of Mica's truck, Mica was able to plow the long drive, the path from the house to the barn and the path to the horse barn. After the four-day power outage years ago, they'd equipped the villa with a backup generator, so Gina, Sam, Rafe and Olivia had been warm and safe all night.

Mica remembered his childhood years when the family had been snowed in and without power. He and his brothers had been ecstatic about the time off school. But it had been no vacation for his parents. Gina had done everything she could to save the food that was spoiling in the freezer. She kept five backup tanks of propane gas to run two gas grills. He remembered his father cooking at the grill with snow swirling around him.

Mica hung up his jacket and took off his wet boots in the laundry room. Though the lights had gone out, the situation between him and

Grace had been illuminated. They'd come to a decision. A conclusion that should have made him happy. But he felt hollow inside, which he didn't understand.

He was on emotional overload. In less than a week, he'd been hit with his mother's engagement and marriage, learned about Jules and wrestled conflicting feelings about Grace.

He needed a distraction to quiet his mind.

Withdrawal and retreat into his design work had always been his salvation when emotions vied for center stage.

The power outage made him wonder what kind of problems and solutions other people in town had faced.

Electric wheelchairs and scooters could only run on their batteries for so long before needing to be recharged in an electrical wall socket. Backup batteries or generators would help them, but not for long periods of time. He thought of the many people who used oxygen tanks at home. Unless they had a fully charged battery to run the apparatus, they wouldn't have oxygen. He could only guess at the numbers who had suffered. Then there were people like Mrs. Beabots, who were relatively healthy but still vulnerable, and perhaps not physically able to build and maintain fires to keep warm.

He sat at the computer at his father's old desk and rubbed his chin thoughtfully. Energy sources were the province of physicists, though as an electrical engineer, Mica had always been fascinated with energy sources and their applications.

Mica had set up his PC with a thirty-two-inch screen and had hooked up two laptops beside it to handle his engineering software. In addition to his 2-D drawing program, he had MATLAB, which gave him high-level linguistic and numeric computation. A third program turned his drawings and calculations into 3-D models, and a fourth cut down his design time.

With three screens in front of him, he sat back in his chair feeling just a bit like a space-shuttle captain, exploring new galaxies.

"And I am."

While the computer booted up, Mica took stock of the office.

His father had never particularly cared for this room, he remembered. Angelo was a man of the earth, wanting always to be outside, riding a tractor or, better still, one of his Thoroughbreds. Gina did all her work in the den:

accounting, bookkeeping, the taxes, correspondence and ordering supplies.

None of Mica's brothers had spent much time in here, either. When Gabe was in middle school, Angelo had introduced him to the corporate buyers. It was obvious that both Gina and Angelo had expected Gabe to take over the family business one day. But Gabe had seen his life differently. From the time he went to college in California, his dream had been to become a vintner. Angelo hadn't accepted this at first, but Gina had encouraged him. Rafe had spent every spare moment with his horse, Rowan. Nate ran away from home before the ink was dry on his high-school diploma.

No, this walnut-paneled room, with its Persian rug, overstuffed leather chairs, brass lamps and shelves filled with every novel and biography Gina had ever read, had fallen to Mica. Now it was his domain.

Once his father had died and Mica's arm had bailed on him, he'd acquired another computer and then another. Between his father's death and the accident, he'd worked on his designs sporadically, stealing a few hours on the weekends and in the evening. After the accident, he'd been too depressed to focus on his work, though he'd had the time.

What he'd needed was motivation.

Jules had given him that and plenty of it.

He hadn't realized until this moment just how far along he'd come with his designs. He was one of those helter-skelter kinds of engineers who invented all the parts, but didn't put them together until the very end. Partly in fear that the dang thing would never work. Partly because then the design and the challenge would be over. He was much like the novelist who wrote the ending, then the beginning, then some scenes in the middle. And prayed for the transitions that would glue everything together.

Mica knew now that his design would work, and he also knew he'd taken it as far as he could. From this point, he needed a manufacturer who saw the potential and would provide a coding expert to create the software Mica envisioned.

Mica had drawn up a list of his top six contenders for a partner. His favorite was Peerless Farm Manufacturing, which was located in Florida. He'd taken a virtual tour of their facility and liked what he saw. It was a small firm, run by two men who had gone to college together and were former farmers. Their vision and mission statements were similar to Mica's goal.

Yes, today was the day. He would make the greatest leap he'd taken in years. Possibly ever.

He opened his inbox and hit Compose.

He uploaded his resume, a description of his project and two 3-D models of the unit.

His hand didn't even shake when he hit Send.

Everything was just as it should be, he thought.

"Good morning, Mica," Gina said, coming through the door with two cups of coffee. She handed a steaming mug to him. He took a sip. It was rich and black and he instantly recognized his mother's favorite Italian blend. She only brought it out for special occasions. But then, only two days ago had been New Year's Eve and her wedding.

Her wedding. She was a bride again. A newlywed.

A thick wave of nostalgia washed over Mica, and he saw his father's face, tanned from working in the sun all summer. His dad was wearing overalls and a white T-shirt, his biceps flexed as he pulled a tree stump out of the ground. Mica had been driving the tractor. Gabe and Rafe worked the chains.

The tree had been struck by lightning and

had fallen across a soybean field. Recent rains had made the work muddy and difficult. Though not even in their teens yet, all three boys did man's work. Angelo demanded it.

He barked orders and shouted at them. He whirled his arm over his head as a signal to Mica to keep pulling the tree off to the side of the field.

Mica did as he was instructed, driving carefully so as not to disturb even the first soybean plant. And he didn't.

Angelo had often said that of all the boys, Mica's driving was like a second sight. Rafe could rein a horse as if he'd been born in the saddle, but Mica and machines were like one brain.

It was the only compliment Mica had ever received from his father.

Mica inhaled the aromatic steam. "This is from your private stash," he told Gina.

"Sam loves it. He says I make the best coffee he's ever tasted."

"Don't tell that to Maddie," Mica joked, looking at his mother. Only this time he really looked.

She was incandescent. She appeared twenty years younger this morning, with her dark hair clipped messily to her head, tendrils cascading down her neck. She wore a white turtleneck, jeans and a pair of leopard moccasins he didn't remember seeing before. But then, Mica hadn't been all that observant lately. Possibly ever.

And that was a real fault.

He'd been missing out on a lot. He cocked his head. "You're happy."

Lifting her chin, she let out a laugh. "Impossibly happy." Then her face grew more serious. "I hope that doesn't upset you."

Her comment took him back. Back to the other life, where she lived with his father and the four sons she raised. He was seeing her not as just his mother, but as a woman. Mica hadn't liked to think of himself as narrow-minded. He was educated, on his way to becoming a great designer, but when it came to living… he was failing.

And he didn't like it anymore.

"I have a confession," he began.

"Oh?"

"That afternoon when I found you in the kitchen—when Sam proposed—I was angry. I admit it. I guess I thought you should go on mourning Dad forever. Stupidly, I thought that we—well, Rafe and I and the farm—would be enough for you."

"You didn't know…"

"About Sam? No, I didn't. But now I do and I guess what I'm trying to say is that I've come to see a lot of things differently. You deserve to be happy, Mom. You do. I like Sam. He's very kind, isn't he?"

She stared into her coffee and then back at him. "Yes. He always was. That's what attracted me to him so many years ago. But I had promised your father..."

Mica held up his palm. "I know." He pursed his lips. "I was wrong to judge you. Very wrong." He stood and went to her. "Forgive me?"

"Of course, darling," she replied with a catch to her voice. She pressed her head against his shoulder. "I've been so worried about you. You've retreated into yourself so much since the accident, I was afraid you'd build yet another shell around yourself and there'd never be another chance for me or anyone to be a part of your life."

"And now?"

"Well..." She broke away with a wide smile. "Now there's Grace and Jules. What more could you ask for?"

Mica's face fell as he watched hope and love shimmer in her eyes. "Mom. It's not like that."

Gina shook her head. "What do you mean?

Not like what? Jules is your son. He—he..."
she sputtered. "Mica, what are you saying?"

"Grace isn't here to marry me and become
another daughter-in-law to you."

"That's because you didn't do it right. Nate
and Rafe told me." She set her mug on the desk
and put her hands on her hips. "Tell me, Mica.
Just how did you bungle this?"

"It's not me. It's her. All she wants is for me
to take care of Jules for a few months so she
can get her career in shape. She's swamped
with deadlines and fashion shows and a whole
bunch of stuff I don't understand."

"I know that the fashion world is very demanding. I saw that in Italy when I was growing up. I had lots of friends who were models
and designers."

"You did?" He was genuinely surprised.

"They tried out their new clothes on me,"
she said offhandedly. "It was a lark."

Now he knew where she got her sense of
style.

She narrowed her eyes. "I don't get it. Anyone with eyes in their head can tell she loves
you."

"What?"

"You heard me. Her face lights up when
you walk in the room, and for my money, the

only reason she's not marrying you is because you haven't shown her that you love her back." She paused and peered at him. "You do, don't you?"

He raked his hands through his hair, feeling every ounce of the frustration that had plagued him since Grace arrived. "I'm desperately trying to do the right thing, like you and Dad did. Obviously, you accepted your responsibility and fulfilled the promise you made Dad. You married him even though you loved Sam."

"Mica, I need to explain some facts of my life to you. True, I don't regret marrying your father and raising you boys. It was a wonderful life. But I realized some things when I came very close to losing Sam."

"What are you talking about?"

"A couple years ago, before your father died, Sam had a heart attack. I was terrified that my one and only true love would be taken from me. It's the craziest thing. Even though Sam and I never crossed those…boundaries, for the sake of our families, we never stopped loving each other. I went to see Sam in the hospital. Our family and friends were there, but no one guessed exactly why I went. Why I wouldn't leave without knowing Sam was all right. I suspect Mrs. Beabots knew. She knows everything."

"I'm beginning to see that myself."

"Your father was still alive. I knew his health wasn't great, but I never dreamed he was less than a year from death himself. But I wanted Sam to know, if he died that night, that I loved him."

"So, Mom, you're saying that real love…it never dies."

"No, Mica. It doesn't."

"Hmm."

"My life with Angelo was a good life in many ways, and if I had to do it all over again, I would. But I do regret giving up Sam. I am amazed, especially now, how much I love him. But when I almost lost him, I knew I had one chance to live my dream. Yes, I kept my promise to your father. I never swayed from it, either. But in doing that, I betrayed myself."

"Mom…" Mica felt his heart break for her.

"Mica, you need to decide if you love Grace or not. If you do, you two can figure out everything else—raising Jules here, in Paris… you'll find a way. But if you don't love her… let her go."

Mica's breath caught in his chest. "Let her go?"

"Exactly." Gina grabbed her coffee and left.

CHAPTER NINETEEN

THE LOUISE HOUSE was in a tizzy as Louise inspected the melted ice cream and the whipped cream and milk that had spent the night in a warming fridge.

Grace put Jules in the high chair that Louise kept in the back of the shop. She put a bib on him and placed a small bowl of half-melted vanilla ice cream on the tray. She started to spoon the sweet, creamy concoction into his mouth.

"Oh, for pity's sake, Grace, give him the spoon and let him dig in. What's the worst that happens? He gets his face dirty? I have stacks of washcloths. I need you over here."

Louise was rattled and Grace didn't blame her. Few people came into the ice-cream shop in winter, especially since it was usually closed during the colder months when Louise went to Florida. Her aunt could ill afford a disaster like this.

"What can I do?" Grace asked.

"I don't know. Look at these barrels. They're

half-melted. Now that the power is on, yes, they'll freeze, but the ice cream will be riddled with crystals. The flavors will be off and my reputation will be ruined. *I'll* be ruined and no one will ever come here again." Louise's eyes darted from the front door to the empty tables and chairs with the festive aqua-and-white-cabana-stripe cushions she'd made.

Grace put her arms around her aunt. "It's going to be okay. I'll think of something."

Louise sniffed but refused to shed a tear. "You're right. We have to think."

Just then a snowplow trundled down the road, this time dumping sand and salt on the street. The sun was poking through the dense storm clouds that scuttled off to the east. Grace peered out the window. A stream of SUVs and cars followed the plow, and the street was bustling with business owners shoveling and digging out their vehicles.

"Look, Aunt Louise. People are getting out! I bet Mr. Jenkins is going to build up an appetite with that long sidewalk he's got." Grace smiled and then stopped. She tapped her cheek with her forefinger. Then she snapped her fingers.

She went over to the five-gallon barrel of

vanilla ice cream. "This one seems to be the worst."

"The strawberry isn't much better. Some of the smaller tubs are okay as they were bunched together in the newer cooler."

Grace beamed and took out her cell phone and started Googling. "Aunt Louise," she said without looking up. "Does everyone here still listen to the radio in emergencies?"

"Yes…why?"

"How was the milk when you checked on it?"

"Um, fine. If we use it today. Same with the cream."

"Good. Because we're going to use it. All of it, I hope. Here we go!"

She punched in the number she found and grinned as the call picked up. "WLOI FM. How may I direct your call?"

"I'd like to place an ad for immediate airing. What are your prices for two lines every fifteen minutes for the next three hours?"

The woman asked her to hold.

Louise frowned. "What are you doing?"

"Posting our milk-shake-and-malt sale. All day. Dollar milk shakes."

"Only a dollar?"

"We make them short and often. We get rid

of the melted ice cream and cram the place with customers. No one can beat our price. You might even sell some of your candy bars, brownies and cookies while we're at it."

"You're a genius, Grace!" Louise whooped. "I'll put out the Open sign."

Grace finished her call then put on her coat and gloves. "I'll shovel the walk, and then we need to call to enlist some help. I don't think it will take long to fill this place."

MICA'S IPHONE RANG as he walked out of the mechanical shed.

"Grace? I was just going to call you."

"Mica! Thank God. You have to help me. Us, I mean."

"Again? This is becoming a habit of yours, Grace."

"Please, Mica. Could you come to The Louise House ASAP? We're under siege," she said. "And ask your mom if she has some extra milk you can bring."

"For Jules?"

"No. For half of Indian Lake. Hurry." She hung up.

Mica stared at his phone. One thing about Grace? She wasn't boring.

When Mica reached the The Louise House,

he had to park a block away. Cars were lined up along both sides of the street and filled the parking lot in back. The sun was bright, and if it wasn't for the cold and the dazzling snow, he would have sworn it was high summer.

Carrying two gallons of milk, he rounded the sidewalk hedges, went up the front walk and entered. Malt-shop oldie songs played on the jukebox and each time someone came in or out, Mica heard laughter. And frenzy.

Grace's voice cut through the chatter.

"Chocolate malt! Heavy on the chocolate. Strawberry milk shake! Make it two!"

Mica edged past the long line of people waiting to place orders. He couldn't believe it. Every seat was taken. People were standing along the walls, drinking milk shakes and talking about the storm. By the time he made it to the front counter, he'd heard several stories about the power outage.

He'd bet none topped his night of warming bricks and stoking a fire. A sleeping baby son on his stomach...

His eyes shot to Grace, who shoved a wayward strand of glistening blond hair out of her face as she dipped a scooper into a vat of ice cream.

"Grace?"

"Mica! Thank heaven you're here. We need an extra hand. Take off your coat. You can run the milk-shake machine." She sounded like she'd been running the shop for fifty years.

"Here's the milk," he said to Louise, who was pouring a pink concoction into a paper cup.

"Just in time." Louise smiled.

"Grace? Where is our son?" Mica asked, his voice a mixture of accusation and concern.

"Holding court." Grace jerked her head toward the center of the shop. "Sarah's watching him. No worries."

Mica looked over and sure enough, Jules was sitting in a high chair, his face covered in ice cream and chocolate syrup. He was laughing and giggling, trying to shove his spoon into Annie's face as she smiled and teased him. Next to him was Sarah's baby, Charlotte, who was almost as big a mess as Jules.

"He's okay like that?" Mica asked.

"Yes, Mica." Grace rolled her eyes. "He's having the time of his life. Now, here, take this stainless-steel tumbler and put it under the stem of the mixer. Everything is in it. Then give it to Louise. She'll serve it up. We need you."

"I see that," he said, taking the cup from

Grace. Their fingers touched just long enough for him to feel the electricity between them that never failed.

No power outage there, he thought.

Within minutes, Mica had mixed up four shakes.

"We're out of chocolate syrup," Grace told Louise.

"No, there's another five-pound can in the storeroom. Would you get it, Mica? Middle shelf to the right. Next to the Carnation Malted Milk and the Ovaltine."

"Sure," Mica said and wove through the crowd. He couldn't believe it. Who were all these people? There were dozens of faces he'd never seen around town or at the usual parties. But then, Mica hadn't come to town all that much in the past few years. Maybe not all that much since high school. He'd kept to the farm—injury or no injury.

Was his mother right? He'd been a self-righteous brooder for a long time.

He went into the storeroom and found the chocolate. It was one of those industrial-sized cans that could keep a shop like this going for a week. Though at this rate, they'd need more by the end of the day. He scooped it up in his right arm and used his elbow to turn off the light as he exited. That storeroom would be a good place for him to install a motion-activated light.

Yeah, he should do that for Louise.

Once again, he felt needed.

As he walked back to the counter, he saw Scott Abbot and his two kids come in the front door. He lifted his chin to Scott. "Hey, buddy. How's it goin'?"

Scott waved, holding three-year-old Michael's hand as he walked over to Mica. "We heard the ad on the radio. After we shoveled snow and the kids made a snowman, I figured they deserved a treat. What a great idea. A buck a shake."

"Yeah. Great idea."

"I shoulda thought of something like that for the bookstore. Cocoa. Coffee. They'd all work. I missed out on this one, though. Was that Louise's idea?"

Mica glanced at Grace, who was chatting with Cate Sullivan and six-year-old Danny. "I'm thinking it was Grace."

"Yeah? Boy. I should hire her for my PR," Scott said. "Well, good to see you. Tell your mom that was a fantastic party the other night. Isabelle was bowled over, and for my event-planner artist wife, that's saying a lot."

Mica nodded. "I'll tell Mom," he replied and turned away. His smile melted.

Wife.

Scott had a wife.

All his brothers had wives. Gabe had a wife and a son.

Mica had a son now. But no wife.

The thought took his breath away. He had to think about inhaling. Think about calming the thoughts in his head.

He slid behind Louise and put the huge can of chocolate syrup on the back counter. He found a metal pump that he'd seen Louise use, stabbed the tin can and inserted the pump. He threw away the empty can of chocolate and placed the new can next to Grace. Cate and Danny had moved on, and now she was digging vanilla ice cream from a vat.

Though she looked tired and a little frazzled, she kept smiling while the customers talked to her. Mica wished he had the use of both arms so he could twirl her around and kiss her.

Instead, he leaned close to her ear, where he could smell her heady jasmine-and-rose perfume. "Grace. Chocolate syrup is ready to go."

She turned. Their noses nearly touched. Her eyes locked with his and when she smiled he felt the warmth all the way to his heart. She leaned forward and kissed his cheek. "You're the best, Mica. Thanks."

Mica was mesmerized. He'd been feeling the voltage between them since she'd come back to town. Since she'd told him about his son. But her voice, her expression, held such longing and earnestness...

He didn't know how she did it or if she was aware of what she was doing, but each time he was with her, something was different. Something changed.

Mica was beginning to realize that *he* was changing.

"You really think that, Grace?"

"I do, Mica." She turned back to the ice cream and filled another stainless-steel tumbler. "Lots of people do." She lifted her blue eyes to him. The undisguised trust in them made his heart twist. If they weren't in a roomful of hungry patrons, all in need of sugar, he'd pull her to him and kiss her until they were both breathless.

"Thanks" was all he could say, and that took some doing. His mouth had gone dry.

On the one hand, he knew they might never see eye to eye on how and where to raise Jules. Together or separately. And at the same time, when he was with her, he wanted to kiss her.

Didn't want their time together to end. Last night, with her curled by his side…

It was all so complicated. He and Grace. Why couldn't it be simple for them, like it was for his brothers and their wives?

Uh. On second thought, he remembered that Liz had confronted Gabe with a shotgun when they'd first met. When Nate had come back to town after eleven years away, Maddie had socked him in the belly. Maybe it was a Barzonni curse that all the men had to overcome some serious challenges to be with the women of their dreams.

His mother was right. He'd messed this up. But he could fix it. He was an engineer. He could make this work.

It was a matter of making the right connections. And voilà. Ignition.

He smiled to himself and put the tumbler on the Hamilton Beach mixer and turned it on. The machine churned the milk, ice cream and chocolate syrup.

He was thinking long into Jules's future, whereas Grace was only focused on the short-term. Her latest designs. Her next show. She needed to think of every aspect of Jules's life, now and later. Jules deserved to know his Barzonni family, to benefit from their love and support. If Mica and Grace continued to lead separate lives, Jules would lose out. Either he'd spend his childhood being passed back and forth across an ocean, or he'd be cut off from one parent and one world he could be a part of. Mica had to convince Grace that they needed to live together. Stability and a sense of family was best for Jules.

If only Mica could make Grace understand.

His thoughts skidded to a halt. How could he make Grace understand, when he couldn't figure out what was happening in his own heart? All afternoon, he'd worked alongside her and though the shop was filled with half the people he knew in town, he was focused on Grace. He'd watched her. Laughed with her. And he'd felt something bloom inside him. It went beyond friendship and caring.

Something was changing inside him. It was more than the love he had for Jules.

This feeling had the kind of power that could alter his plans and goals. It could remap his future.

And it was all about Grace.

CHAPTER TWENTY

IT WAS AFTER four o'clock when Grace taped a piece of paper on the ice-cream shop door that read Sold Out. She turned the lock.

"Has this ever happened before, Aunt Louise?" she asked. "Selling everything in the shop?"

Louise finished cleaning the mixer, wiped her hands and sat down at the table, where Mica held a sleeping Jules in his lap. Grace joined them.

"Never," Louise said, massaging the back of her neck. "I can't say I'd be able to handle this kind of crowd on a daily basis."

"It was too much excitement for Jules," Mica said, smoothing a lock of dark hair from Jules's forehead. "He's been out for a half hour. That was nice of Sarah to watch him while we worked the counter."

Grace watched Mica's adoring eyes roam Jules's face as he spoke. It was as if he couldn't get enough of his baby son. She was pleased and surprised that Mica would take so quickly to Jules. "Sarah was busy with Charlotte most of the time. It was Annie who played with Jules. She's such a special little girl. If I ever have a daughter, I hope she'll be like Annie." The words spilled out of her mouth and it took her a second to realize what she'd said.

She and Mica locked eyes. He remained silent.

For so long, she'd defined her future by her career, climbing the rungs of the fashion ladder. She didn't for a second regret having Jules, but he'd been unplanned, and more children were not part of the life Grace was building.

But as Mica held her gaze, his deep blue eyes delving into her psyche, Grace feared the unthinkable—that she didn't know her own heart at all.

Though Jules was the biggest surprise in her life, he was also the grandest blessing. She had loved him from the moment she'd realized she was pregnant until this second, watching his little chest contract and expand, his eyelids flutter as he dreamed. And the situation with Mica had nothing to do with that. Even if she and Mica had been married and had waited to get pregnant, she couldn't possibly love her baby any more than she did now.

"I hope she'll look like you," Mica said softly. "Blonde and blue-eyed."

The breath caught in Grace's lungs as she realized that the only children she wanted were Mica's babies. She didn't care if her daughter looked like her or not. She hoped she would look like Mica, actually. There was nothing more striking than the contrast of rich raven-black hair and midnight blue eyes...

Louise coughed.

Grace's thoughts fell from her head. "Sorry. I just meant that Annie is an exceptional girl."

"She sure is." Louise slapped her knee and rose. "She filled the dishwasher for me twice today. I think it's finished running."

"I'll help you unload it," Grace offered.

As she stood, Mica took her hand. "Grace, we need to get some stuff for Jules. After you help Louise clean up, I thought we could go to the Tractor Supply."

"You want to buy Jules his first tractor?" She laughed.

"No." He shook his head and chuckled. "They have a lot of baby equipment and we still need a bigger carrier for him. I want to check out the cribs, too. Even though Mom has one for Zeke, if Liz and Gabe come over, then I'm still going to need one for Jules."

"You're right. We should go to the Indian Lake Grocery as well. Now that the town appears to be back to normal and the roads are clear, maybe you should take Jules to your house so you both can get used to different surroundings. His schedule. You know?"

"Yeah," Mica replied. "I should do that."

He released Grace's hand just as her phone rang. She pulled it out of her pocket. "I better take this," she said and walked to the back of the shop.

"Hi, Rene. It's getting late there. Is everything okay?"

"We're fine. Working like mad, as you know. We heard about your snowstorm."

"You're kidding."

"Chicago airports were shut down. International flights were canceled. That always makes the news here," he said and paused. "How's Jules?"

"Fine. He made it through the storm and power outage like a trooper."

"No power? That's disastrous."

"Mica handled everything perfectly. We were all huddled by the fireplace until the power came back early this morning."

"We?"

Grace knew where this was going and she

wasn't about to join Rene on his journey. "My landlady has a huge fireplace in her library. All four of us stayed there all night."

"Oh."

"So, did you find that gray silk I wanted?"

"Yes. It's on its way from Milan. Grace, you're going to die. The manufacturer sent me a photo. I'll forward it to you after we get off."

"Great. And get me the pricing for a heavy, winter-white satin or *peau de soie*—either one."

"How heavy?"

"Antique-grade heavy. I'm sending you a sketch I did for a bridal hood that falls nearly to the floor. The hood comes down far enough to nearly cover the bride's face. It will have fabric-covered buttons down the middle, with satin rosettes between them."

"*Mon dieu*, but that's original. How did you come up with that?"

"I saw it in a dream. Winter Bride theme and Red Riding Hood got jumbled up. I think it will work."

"Of course it will," he said. "It came from you, didn't it? All brilliance comes from you, Grace."

"Thanks, Rene." She looked up and saw

Mica staring at her from across the shop. His lips were pursed and his eyes hard.

Was he…jealous?

She'd thought Mica's earlier accusations about Rene had just been about Jules, about what he saw as her selfish intentions. But if Mica was jealous…

No. She had to be careful not to misread him. Not to pin hopes on illusions.

She'd done that one too many times before with Mica. She couldn't risk her heart again. She'd spent too much time and energy sewing and mending it, only to have it torn apart. She was a patchwork mess inside and for Jules's sake, she had to keep her focus.

"*Bonsoir*, Grace. I'll send that photo," Rene said.

"Ciao."

She walked back toward Louise, who was still putting dishes away. "Aunt Louise, I'll take over. You sit and rest."

"Don't mind if I do, sweetie."

Grace could still feel Mica's eyes on her as she bent to grab the last ice-cream scoops and tumblers from the dishwasher.

"I CAN'T GET over it," Grace said, watching Jules fuss and squirm in his carrier. "It's like he's grown up and out in the short time we've been here. He's all squished in there and his little parka is making him miserable."

"That is why," Mica said as he lifted a larger carrier off the shelf at the Tractor Supply store, "we need something bigger and better."

It had been Mica's idea to go shopping. His happy mood had been contagious and Jules had giggled during the drive to the store. Grace couldn't deny it. She cherished every minute with Mica. And their time together was growing short.

"Check it out," he said, breaking into her thoughts.

Grace wrinkled her nose at the navy-and-orange design. "That's a football on there."

"Footballs are good." He grinned.

"Mica, no," she said. "Isn't there something without an NFL logo? Put it back."

"Why? Look at all these features. Double seat belts. A padded head thingy here…" He lifted an orange velour pad. "This lining is waterproof but soft. And the handle is easy to grip."

"My friends in Paris will think I've been drinking the American Kool-Aid."

"Well you are American, aren't you? Come on!" He unbelted Jules from the old carrier.

Jules stopped fussing and clapped his hands as Mica lifted him with his one strong arm. "Da." Mica kissed Jules's forehead and put him in the new seat.

Grace's chest filled with warmth and love for both her baby and Mica. It was the strangest thing, but arguing with Mica over which carrier to buy was an excuse for her to be with him. Tease him. And watch his eyes light up every time they rested on Jules.

She was in the middle of a farm wholesale store and her happiness was overflowing. Jules wiggled against the headrest as if trying it out. He looked up at the large handle and then reached for it, letting his little hand rest on the side.

"He looks like he's in a sports car," Mica said proudly.

Grace looked down the aisle at all the baby equipment and clothing—winter jackets, sweatpants, sweaters, hats and little boots. Each item was stamped with a different football team logo. "Maybe we should try Baby Town. Find something more generic."

"Gabe says the stuff here is first-class. Rugged. And priced right," Mica said, sounding like a commercial.

"And as I remember from New Year's Eve,

Zeke wore a parka and a knit cap with a football logo on them."

"Yeah. So?" Mica rose from his crouch, lifting Jules in the carrier.

"Mica, I don't want my son—sorry, our son—indoctrinated with all this football mania. I understand Gabe going this route—he was all-state in high school."

"All-American in college," Mica added. "He could have gone pro."

"Yes. Fine. But that's not what I want for Jules."

Mica scowled. This time there was no fire in his eyes. Only ice. "Just what do you want, Grace? For our son?"

"Choices. Lots of them. I want a good education. I want him to travel and learn about other cultures and their art and history. I want to show him the homes of great artists like Monet. In Paris there are free lectures and symposiums. The ballet, symphony, opera and theater. At the same time, I want him to climb a mountain if he wants, or scuba dive off the Great Barrier Reef. And if he decides he wants to play football, he can do that. The point is, I want *him* to decide. I want him to have long-lasting friendships and know real joy in his life…" She trailed off, suddenly emotional. "I want him to have everything."

Mica sighed. "I want those things for him, too," he said slowly.

Grace supposed she'd had a head start on thinking about Jules's future because she'd been imagining it since the day she'd bought the pregnancy test. Soon, she'd have to think about a bigger apartment for them. The space she had now in the 16th Arrondissement was affordable, but tiny. Once she was back in Paris, she'd look for something that would give Jules room to play.

Jules blew a raspberry and giggled. "Da."

Mica beamed back at Jules. He turned to Grace. "What I don't get is why this baby seat is such a big deal."

Jules was cooing and stuffing his fists in his mouth. He was happy.

Grace's head was filled with Jules's yet-to-be-lived adventures. Visiting the Taj Mahal. Versailles. Venice. She had hundreds of plans for him, but they all took money and nothing would happen if she didn't become the success she knew she could be. And for that, she needed Mica on her side.

Smiling, she replied, "It isn't a big deal. We'll get the carrier."

AFTER THEY CHECKED out at the Tractor Supply, they went to the Indian Lake Grocery and stocked up on disposable diapers, baby food, zwieback toast and a new teething ring.

Mica drove Grace back to Mrs. Beabots's house. He was happy to have Jules all to himself for the night, but as prepared as he was, he was nervous.

"Are you sure you're going to be all right?" she asked.

"Sure," Mica said. "Think of it as a boys' night." He chuckled, hoping to convince himself and her of a confidence he didn't quite feel yet. "I've got all these supplies and you gave me his schedule. Bath at eight. Use plenty of baby lotion. Bottle at eight thirty. Then put him to bed. Should I read to him?"

"I always do. I put a Winnie the Pooh book in the diaper bag."

"Too bad. I was thinking more along the lines of an old Robert B. Parker mystery."

She glared at him. "Mica…"

"Just kidding. I'll save the mystery for myself."

Grace got out of the truck and then leaned back in to kiss Jules on the cheek. "You'll text me if you need me?"

"I will," he said in his most assuring tone.

"We'll be fine, Grace. This is what you came here for, isn't it?"

"Yes. Yes, it is."

"Then stop worrying."

Grace shut the door and stood in the drive waving as Mica backed out, his headlights shining on her until he reached the street.

"Well, here we are, buddy," Mica said over his shoulder to Jules.

Jules blew a raspberry, then clapped his hands.

"You like this, too? So do I."

Mica headed south down Maple Boulevard. He felt pride coursing through him as he drove cautiously toward the family farm.

He was alone with his son. The reality of it still rattled around in his head, banging up against the incongruity of his romanceless relationship with Grace.

He tried to tell himself that he barely knew her, but he couldn't ignore everything that had happened in the past few days. He was getting to know her better than he knew anyone.

"It's gonna be a great night, just you and me. We could watch my recording of Sunday's Bears' game together. Crack a cold one. Uh, for me, at least. I make a tasty microwave pizza. Or we could order in. They charge an extra three bucks to deliver to the farm, but Rafe does it all the time. He says Olivia is too tired to cook after working at the deli all day. Though, now that I think about it, she often brings food home for him. Not pizza, though."

Mica drove a few more miles in silence.

"My mother always made us great pizza. Maybe we could enlist her to whip one up for us. Does your mom like pizza? Funny. I never asked her."

Mica glanced in the rearview mirror as a truck passed him.

He checked his speed. Ordinarily, this was about the spot where he'd hit the gas and tear up some asphalt.

Not anymore. He had precious cargo on board.

He had his son.

Mica inhaled deeply. "I'm a father.

"And fathers have serious obligations and responsibilities to their children. Grace was right about what she wants for you, buddy. She's got it all together. Smart."

The night sky had cleared and this far from town, the stars glittered in clusters across the ebony dome above him.

It was the kind of night that poets wrote

about and sailors watched until dawn. It was the kind of night that should be shared.

As Mica neared the gates to the farm, he realized that even though his baby son was in the truck with him, an emptiness had overtaken him ever since he'd left Grace at Mrs. Beabots's house.

For the first time in his life, Mica felt lonely.

CHAPTER TWENTY-ONE

Stubborn fool. Mica could think of some other names to call himself, but for the moment, that would do, he thought as he wrestled with the folded crib. Sam had offered to help him get it up the stairs to his apartment above the garage, but no. He'd wanted to prove that he could do it himself.

Jules was in the kitchen; Gina had insisted he stay with her while she made little shell pasta that he could pick up with his fingers.

Mica refused to let himself backslide into the negative, self-defeating territory he'd occupied since his accident. The sides of the crib banged against the stone wall and hit the railing, but he didn't care if the thing was scraped and battered. He was going to do this.

He opened the door and hauled the crib into his living room, then propped it against the empty wall. He spread the sides out, latched the bottom boards together and closed the rest of the latches.

"Now for the mattress."

As Mica headed toward the door, the thermostat caught his eye. He liked to keep the apartment cool, but babies needed warmth. He turned up the heat and stepped back outside. And almost ran into Sam, who was climbing the stairs with the crib mattress. "Here, you take this," Sam said. "I'll go back and get the linens. Your mother washed everything in Ivory Snow. She called Grace to make sure Jules didn't have any skin allergies."

"Allergies?" Mica replied. "I never thought to ask—I mean, I did ask about foods…" Mica grabbed the mattress by the side handle.

Sam shrugged. "My son, Mark, had all kinds of skin allergies. It amazed me that he wanted to be a vintner. Everything bothered him. Sun, bugs, fertilizers."

"But it didn't stop him. You both built that great vineyard."

"Nothing stopped Mark. He wanted things so passionately," Sam mused.

"I'm sorry you lost him," Mica said, remembering Sam's son and his wife—Liz's parents— had died in a car accident. "I vaguely remember that funeral. Mom took me and my brothers."

"Yes. She did." Sam looked at Mica. "You

know, even that accident was a display of Mark's passion."

"How's that?"

"They were coming back from a wine seminar. I'm sure their heads were full of plans and dreams…" Sam's shoulders slumped.

"You still miss him."

"Every day, son. Every day." Sam turned. "Well, I'll get those sheets for you." He descended the stairs briskly, as if trying to escape their conversation and his memories.

"Passion…" Mica repeated as he took the mattress inside and placed it in the crib.

He stood back. Passion. That's what he admired so much in Grace. She was more than merely ambitious; she was filled with passion to make her designs the best they could be. She wanted the best for Jules, too. Though Mica could tell she adored her life in Paris, she'd come to Indian Lake because she'd needed help. Not just anybody's help. His help.

Was he just not seeing everything he should? His mother had said that Grace lit up when she was with him. Mica had noticed that in The Louise House earlier, but that was just how Grace always was, wasn't it? He hadn't noticed any change.

Grace's life in Paris had to be enormously

fulfilling with enough challenges to test her talent and skills. Her teammates obviously respected her. And it wouldn't take much for that Rene guy to stake his claim.

So, why exactly did Grace need to come across the ocean? Was it simply guilt that she hadn't told Mica about Jules?

Or was it something else?

Was Grace in love with him? Did her feelings go deeper than what they'd shared over a year ago? And if she was in love with him, why hadn't she said so?

A knock on the door interrupted his thoughts. "Here you go," Sam said, coming in. He held out a stack of sheets, soft baby towels, baby blankets and washcloths.

"Thanks, Sam," Mica said.

"Your mother is making pasta and salad. It should be ready in ten minutes. I'm broiling garlic and parmesan bread for us. See you in a few."

"Great." Mica smiled wanly, his head still swirling with unanswered questions.

Mica made up the crib and smoothed out a velvety soft baby blanket. He took the towels to the bathroom and placed them on the counter.

The rooms were warming up nicely, but he still felt the strange hollowness that overtook him sometimes, like when he was tilling the soil on his tractor on one of the tracks far from the villa. There, he would sit, with nothing but sky and bare earth for as far as he could see. At those times he would think about the choice he'd made to come back to the farm and work alongside his father and brother.

He hadn't leaped headlong into engineering the way Grace had jumped into fashion design. He'd puttered and sputtered and tinkered, but he hadn't plunged.

Choices. Grace's greatest gift to Jules would be a closetful of choices. She would be not only a good mother, but also an excellent mentor.

The more he thought about it, the more he wondered if there was anything he could offer his son that Grace could not. Other than a name.

And what did that name stand for? Passion. His father had enough passion for forty men. Nothing but death had stopped him from building his dream.

Angelo had wanted to get off the streets in Sicily. He had wanted a better life and he'd wanted Gina. But he hadn't known how to love his wife or his sons.

Mica could see that now.

He'd never had much of a bond with his father. And if he was brutally honest with himself, he wasn't that close with his brothers.

"Which is all my fault."

Mica had used isolation to protect himself from being hurt emotionally.

Grace had chipped away at his carefully constructed defense mechanisms. She'd forced him to think about other people. Other places. Other ways to live.

She'd been the earthquake he'd needed.

She'd shown him the importance of passion.

He ran his hand down his numb arm. His disability hadn't held him back, he saw now. He'd used it as an excuse to drop off the grid, stop challenging himself.

It was amazing to him that he'd cobbled together his invention at all. If he'd had Grace's passion he would have finished it and sent it off a year ago.

He credited her with the way he'd confidently emailed his prototype design to Peerless. She'd forced him to look more closely at himself. What he admired most was that she didn't treat him any differently than she did anyone else—unless Gina was right about her lighting up when he was around. Grace didn't expect any less of him just because he couldn't use one arm. In fact, he thought she was pushy at times. But maybe he needed that.

"I need it a lot," he grumbled.

He reached in his back pocket and took out his iPhone.

Courage might have been a stranger to Mica over the past year, but if he didn't go looking, he'd never find it again.

He pulled up Grace's number and sent her a text.

I miss you.

GRACE MUNCHED ON a protein bar and sipped hot chamomile tea as Etienne, Rene and Jasminda filled her in on the latest Fashion Week plans via Skype.

This conversation was less design-oriented and more focused on business. Rene had taken the helm and was steering their nervous crew through choppy waters.

"Grace, what are the chances of you coming back early. Say, tomorrow?"

Grace choked on her cinnamon-flavored oats. She reached for the tea and took a gulp. "Tomorrow? I can't fly tomorrow. I'll be home in a few days. Isn't that soon enough?"

"In a word, *non*." Rene grimaced. "I've been

in meetings at The Eloise House of Fashion all day."

"Eloise? They're talking to you?" She lowered her cup and leaned into the screen. Eloise was a young house, but lately it had been making waves in the fashion world. Big waves.

"To us, Grace. They want to talk to you."

"What? How do they know about me?"

"I sent over three of your spring ensembles when I heard they were hunting for new designers. They called and asked for more. I rushed over with some of the new pieces you sketched the other day. Jasminda threw them together practically overnight."

Grace dropped the protein bar. "This isn't happening."

"It is. They want to see you in their offices the day after tomorrow."

Her breath caught in her throat—Grace was speechless. "Can we stall?"

Rene rolled his eyes. "Stall? This is our first break. Granted, it's not as big as being courted by a big house, but it's a step. An important one, Grace."

"Rene. I can't…"

"The *directrice* wants to see you before Fashion Week. I think they'll buy for this year's show. That's why the tight window. I don't want to pass this up."

Jasminda was nearly vibrating with excitement. "You have to come back, Grace. This is for all of us."

"I know. I know," she replied, dropping her forehead to her palm. "I have to think. First, I'll find out if I can get a flight out. Do they know I'm overseas?"

"Yes," Rene answered. "I wish I'd lied."

"Why?"

"Because Eloise's assistant made a smarmy remark that you're not taking Fashion Week seriously."

Grace clenched her teeth. "Oh. That's not good."

"I told her it was a family matter. Life-and-death stuff."

"And that's not lying."

Rene grinned. "Technically, Jules is life. So…"

Grace had to laugh. "Okay. I get it. Thank you for that. It buys me a bit of time. I guess cutting my time here short by a few days isn't going to make that much difference."

Etienne slapped the table, making the screen shake. "*C'est magnifique!* I knew you'd come through, Grace. If they would take on your new designs for this show, especially your evening wear, we'd make a significant presence."

"Etienne," she interrupted. "Slow down. Let's not get ahead of ourselves. We've done well selling bits and pieces to all the houses."

"But Grace, a steady position at Eloise—" Jasminda said.

"That's right, Grace. You're the one who first told us Eloise was the new star in couture. Sure, they're new, but also fresh," Etienne said. "If I were you, I'd be on a plane tonight!"

Grace spread her palms and held them up. Since the night of the power outage, she'd had felt Mica warming to her. She was afraid to hope that he would come to love her, but something was happening. Something wonderful. If she left now, those sprouts of affection blooming between them would freeze.

But this was her career. It was her creation and the life she'd built. And her team depended on her. "I surrender. Okay? I'm in. I'll wrap things up here as best I can."

"Grace…" Rene leaned into the screen as Etienne and Jasminda did a happy dance in the background. "I know all this is tough on you, but everything I've said—remember that you said it first. You've got one of the best heads for business I've ever seen. But this trip was about your heart, wasn't it?"

"Yes." Her excitement drained away and disappointment and sadness took its place.

"And it wasn't what you thought?"

"No. Not really."

"Then come home. Come back here to the people who love you," he said. "We're going to be great, Grace. Your vision has always been marvelous."

"Thank you, Rene. Ciao."

"Bonne nuit."

The screen went black.

How odd, she thought. She'd dreamed of a coup like this since she was in design school and she'd worked hard to achieve it. Yet she didn't feel like celebrating.

Instead, she felt numb. Maybe it was shock. Or disbelief. She was finally on her way to rubbing shoulders with today's great designers.

"And how wonderful that would be," she said aloud, hearing a hint of delight in her voice. It still wasn't the joy she would have expected.

As she searched for flights, she thought about Jules spending the night with Mica.

This was the first night she'd ever spent away from her baby. Though the Skype conference had been a distraction, she'd felt adrift without Jules to care for. She'd skipped dinner except for the protein bar and tea. No appetite.

Earlier she'd wandered down to visit with Mrs. Beabots but found she wasn't home. When she'd gone back upstairs and glanced out the window, she'd seen Sarah and Luke, Timmy, Annie and Mrs. Beabots all bowing their heads in prayer before eating their dinner.

Grace felt a sense of loss for her and for Jules. Her world in Paris was frenetic, exciting, artistic and creative.

The world Mica offered was stable and defined by tradition and family.

Strangely, though Mica had been pressuring her to stay here and raise Jules in Indian Lake, he didn't seem happy.

Granted, the accident had something to do with that, but she guessed it wasn't all of it. He had a huge family, rich with traditions, more friends than he could count, and yet... he wasn't happy.

She pulled up the flights to Paris and sat back.

But he is happy with Jules...

Chills raced across her entire body, making her scalp tingle and raising the tiny hairs on the back of her neck. "Are you happy around me, Mica?"

Was it possible that she'd finally broken through his shell and pried open the vault around his heart? Was that what she'd actually hoped to accomplish on this trip?

Rene had seen right through her. Supposedly, this trip was about schedules and getting help with Jules. But it was actually about emotion.

True, she'd needed to tell Mica the truth. Living with gnawing guilt had started to affect her work.

There were lots of practical reasons for this trip, but underlying them all was her desire to find out once and for all if Mica had any feelings for her.

Well, you have the answer to that question, don't you, Grace?

She tapped in the confirmation number of her Paris flight and hit a button to reschedule.

This meeting at Eloise was crucial for her team.

Grace finished the transaction and turned off the computer.

She picked up her phone and realized the battery had gone completely dead. She plugged it into the wall and went to the bathroom to get ready for bed.

She washed her face and then smeared it with night cream. With her toothbrush stuck in her mouth, she went to the bedroom to check on Jules.

She was halfway there when she remembered that Jules was at Mica's. She stood stock-still in the empty apartment.

"I can't do this."

She went back to the bathroom and rinsed out her mouth. She stared at her reflection in the mirror.

How could she have thought she could leave Jules half a world away? He'd only been gone a couple hours and she missed him so much she ached.

She closed her eyes, placed her hands on the sink and groaned. Then she lifted her head. "How are you going to explain this to Mica?"

CHAPTER TWENTY-TWO

ALL NIGHT, GRACE TOSSED, turned, paced and finally sat at the table fiddling with her drawings. No ideas came to her. All she could think of was how much she missed Jules.

From the day Jules was born, they'd been inseparable. Her arms had grown accustomed to his weight. Her heart needed his nearness and her head would not quiet down from worry until she clutched him close.

What if Jules had slipped in the tub, gulped too much water and Mica couldn't pick him up fast enough? What if Jules choked on his food? He'd been doing that with his zwieback toast, but he loved it so much, she indulged him. Jules was crawling everywhere now. What if Mica didn't watch him close enough and he hurt himself? What if he rolled off the bed? What if he suddenly came down with a fever again?

Grace forced herself to wait until six before dressing and heading out the door to drive

Aunt Louise's car to Mica's farm. The cold wind bit through her thin wool coat with a vengeance.

What if the Barzonnis had encountered another power outage? There was no telling what these high winds could do across those open fields.

She started the engine, and while it warmed a bit, she texted Mica that she was on her way.

She didn't expect an answer. Surely Mica was sound asleep.

She backed out into the dark street, thankful for the streetlamp so close to the driveway.

Just as she reached the end of Maple Boulevard, her phone pinged.

"Mica?"

At the stop sign she glanced at his text.

Jules will be glad to see you.

"What does that mean?"

Now she was really worried. She wanted to text him back, but two cars pulled up behind her.

"Seriously? It's six in the morning!" She went through the stop sign and turned south. Both cars turned north toward town.

The highway had been plowed and was

bone-dry. It was as if the blizzard had never happened. Yet it was a night she would remember forever. Mica had been her hero, taking care of her, Jules and Mrs. Beabots. He'd had all the answers and hadn't flinched at the situation. Mica had been brought up on a farm and he'd obviously absorbed skills and knowledge she'd never had the opportunity to see him put into action.

Her cell pinged again.

On this part of the two-lane, divided highway, she was the only car. She glanced at the message.

I miss you.

"What?"

It was the first time Mica had ever voiced any feeling for her. As intimate as they'd been, she'd always felt that she didn't hold his heart. Not even a fraction of it.

"Last year, I would have been satisfied with a crumb. I would have tried to build on that. But now? With Jules—?" *It's all or nothing.* She loved Mica. She wanted him. She always had.

She turned into the farm gates and drove up the drive.

"Hi, Grace!" Mica called from the top of the stairs to his apartment as she got out of the car. "We're up here."

He looked handsome, freshly showered and shaved, his dark hair still a bit wet. His blue eyes gleamed at her. After climbing the stairs, she came to stand by him and he kissed her cheek.

"Good morning," he said brightly and then kissed her other cheek.

This time he nuzzled her neck briefly, but it was enough to set her heart pounding and send a rash of chills straight down her back and up to the top of her scalp.

She was ash. Cooked on the spot.

She closed her eyes as a flash of romantic possibilities crossed her mind. Mica in Paris. The three of them in Venice. Mica holding Jules as she roamed the silk factories in Lyon.

"You okay?"

"Huh?"

"You're holding your breath."

She exhaled. "I was."

His smile was happy and just a bit impish. "That's a good sign." He put his fingers under her chin and lifted her face closer to him.

"A sign?"

"That you won't mind a good-morning kiss," he said.

Before Grace could protest, not that she wanted to or thought she should, he kissed her. It was the Mica kind of kiss that had brought her to her knees one too many times. But there was something vastly different. His lips were soft and caressed her with a need to linger, as if he didn't want the kiss to end.

She couldn't help melting into him and filling her head with the scent of his lemon shampoo. She kissed him back like he was the only man in the world for her.

He held her with so much strength, she would have sworn he was using two arms, not one.

She didn't want this kiss to end. But she forced herself to pull away. "We should check on Jules."

"Yes," Mica said. He stepped inside. "I couldn't wait for you to get here. Jules is walking!"

"What?" Grace forgot the kiss. "That's impossible."

"No, really. He did. We're going to show you." Mica stepped around her and went to Jules, who was on two feet, gripping the mesh walls of his playpen. He was dressed in a sweater she'd designed, red with a black collar, black corduroy pants and little black-and-white oxford baby shoes she'd found at an infant designer's show on the Left Bank in Paris. She was impressed that Mica had put the outfit together just as she would have, rather than simply throwing something on.

Hmm. That's a sign, too. Isn't it?

Jules squealed with delight when he saw Grace. He let go of the walls, threw up his hands and promptly fell back on his bum.

He stared at them both and let out a cry.

"Oh, Jules." Grace went to the playpen and picked him up. Jules quieted immediately. She kissed the top of his head and got a whiff of... lemon? "He smells exactly like you."

"I know. We took a shower together this morning. He loved it."

"You what? How could you do that? What if he slipped?"

Mica puffed up his chest and grinned. "I put him in a sling around my neck. It was a father-son bonding thing. He washed my hair. I washed his."

Grace had to chuckle. "And I forgot his baby shampoo."

"Didn't need it. He liked my soap, too. Don't worry, I put that baby lotion on him so his skin doesn't dry out. You can't be too careful, you know. Winter and this dry indoor heat. I have a humidifier, though."

Grace stared at Mica, agape. "Seems you've thought of everything."

"Tried to."

Mica walked over and took Jules in his arm. Jules practically jumped on Mica. "Now, watch this."

Mica put Jules on the floor. "Okay, buddy. Let's show Mommy how you can walk."

Mica held Jules's left hand with his right. Jules steadied himself, then lifted his right leg, took a step. Then he lifted his left leg and took another step.

"Way to go, Jules! Super-baby! Right, Mommy?"

"Oh, Mica." She laughed, feeling a warm glow inside. At that moment, Mica's pride was effervescent—and she loved him all the more for the joy he found with Jules. "He started doing that just before we left Paris."

"Oh. I thought it was special for me."

"Afraid not." Without warning, her eyes flooded with tears. She nearly missed Jules's third and final step, before he twisted to the left and fell at Mica's feet. Still laughing, Jules crawled lightning-fast over to Grace, grabbed a fistful of her pants to pull himself up and, quite wobbly, hugged her leg.

Grace slid her hands under his arms and lifted him. She kissed his cheek and Jules clapped his hands.

"Grace, you're crying," Mica said, reaching over and wiping her cheek.

"I am."

"Why?"

"No one has called me Mommy before. It— it…"

"You don't like it?"

She shook her head. "The opposite. It sounds so…lovely." She kissed Jules's cheek again. "But you've always been my super-baby."

"He is special. It's that Barzonni gene pool. Brains. Good looks." He chuckled.

Grace caught his mirth. "You are so full of it."

"No! It's true! Can't I be the proud dad?"

Grace felt her heart melt. She could feel her love radiating toward Mica, and as she watched his deep blue eyes soften and an affectionate smile fill his face, she knew he felt it, too.

"Of course you should be proud," she said. "I know I am. He's a remarkable baby."

Mica touched Jules's cheek, his eyes never

leaving Grace's face. "He's you. You're the remarkable one."

"Mica—"

He leaned over and kissed Jules's cheek, then quickly raised his head and captured her lips once again. It was a brief kiss but packed with enough emotion to knock Grace off balance.

As he pulled away, he said, "This is how all mornings should start out, don't you think?"

"I, uh…"

"I thought you'd agree."

"I didn't. I do. I mean…"

"I'm making us breakfast." He changed the subject.

"I thought you didn't cook," she said, still thinking about this imagined morning filled with kisses.

"Oh, I've got some surprises up my sleeve." Chuckling, he motioned toward his galley kitchen. "Now come right over here and sit at the counter. Jules already christened his new high chair last night."

"What did you have for dinner?"

"Pizza. He loved it."

"Jules? Had pizza?" she asked, hoping her horror didn't show. It would be just like a guy to think a baby could have pizza. She hoped he hadn't let him sip a cola, too.

"I gave him a couple bites of the cheese. Not too much. I only wanted to see his expression when he tasted it. Mom gave me some macaroni and cheese. He likes those little pieces that he can pick up. No Italian sausage. She said it was too spicy for him."

"She's so right." She put her hand over her mouth to stifle her smile. Thank goodness for Gina's expert child-rearing.

Mica pulled a bowl of cut-up strawberries out of the refrigerator. "I cleaned these last night. Here's some cream. I didn't put sugar on them. I thought Jules should get used to natural flavors."

He spooned a small amount of berries onto a plastic child's plate and then put the plate on the tray in front of Jules. Jules picked up a strawberry piece and rather than smashing it, as Grace expected, he put the strawberry in his mouth and swallowed it whole. He clapped and smiled. "Ba!"

"He likes it!" Mica said.

Mica turned to the counter and opened a carton of eggs. "I'm doing scrambled. That okay?"

"Sure. But Mica, seriously, I can help."

"You are helping," he said, looking at her over his shoulder. "You're here."

The shroud of gloom that descended upon her was so real, she thought she could feel its fabric. She was leaving even sooner than expected. She'd been right that something had changed between her and Mica. Every moment with him today was bliss.

Everything in the kitchen slowed as Grace thought about the announcement she was going to have to make to Mica. He tore off pieces of paper towel and put strips of bacon on the towel, covered it and put it in the microwave. He scrambled eggs in a frying pan on the stove. English muffins popped out of the toaster. She heard him talking to her, but his words sounded as if they were being spoken underwater.

He was happy this morning. Genuinely happy. All because Jules had stayed overnight. He'd kissed her as if he loved her.

Sun splashed through the kitchen window, flooding the apartment with warmth and all the hope that came with a new day. She'd never seen Mica like this. Smiling at her, stopping every so often to kiss the top of Jules's head. Jules reached up to give Mica a piece of strawberry, which Mica then gobbled down while making faces at Jules.

It was the picture of domestic bliss.

Shockingly, Grace realized this was what she'd dreamed of in her other life, as that young girl who'd given her heart to Mica.

Even last year, when she'd fallen for Mica so intensely, she had wanted this in the deepest caverns of her heart. She hadn't let herself indulge in that fantasy because her career was too important. The stakes were too high. She hadn't wanted to get distracted.

But today, she was living her dream.

Perhaps that was why time seemed to slow down. It was her moment to relish this absolute happiness. The joy Mica and Jules shared seemed like a miracle. Jules had always been a friendly baby, but this was extraordinary. Grace could never have orchestrated this kind of instant kinship. Such things were out of her power.

Mica set a plate in front of her, then poured coffee. Offered her cream and sugar. Then he sat next to her with his own breakfast.

"Tell me what you think. I put chopped chives in the eggs. I forgot to ask you. Mom grows the chives in the winter, so I can vouch for their freshness."

Grace tasted the eggs. "Delightful." She lowered her fork as she swallowed over the massive lump of emotion. Her chest burned and her heart swelled. She wiped her hands on the paper napkin.

"Oh, Mica," she muttered.

"What?"

"I think I liked you better when you were being a jerk to me." She fought back her tears but it was useless.

"Grace, what's going on?"

"You're being so, well, wonderful."

"I can actually do that, Grace. When I'm not being a jerk." He lowered his voice. "I'm sorry for all that."

She laid her hand on his knee and looked into his eyes—eyes that had and would haunt her every day and night of her life. "Now I'm going to be the jerk."

"Grace…" His voice was apprehensive. She could almost hear the shields go up around his heart. The heart that had been so open to her and Jules only a second ago. The heart she was about to break.

"I have to go back to Paris."

He gave her a funny look. "I know that."

"No, something's come up. We have to leave tonight."

"Tonight?"

"Yes. I changed our flight."

"Did you say 'our' flight?"

"Yes. I was wrong to ask you to take care of Jules for me. This trip here has shown me that I can't stand to be without him for even one night. I thought I'd go crazy last night without him." She dropped her face to her hands and allowed a sob to escape. She had to toughen up. Mica would be furious. He might even slap her with a lawsuit, send lawyers after her, to stop her from taking Jules away. He could do all kinds of things. He could break her heart over and over again.

"So, you're taking Jules back with you?"

"Yes."

"I don't understand. You don't have anyone to help you."

"I called Aunt Louise last night after talking to Etienne and Rene. When I told her the situation, she said she would close the ice-cream shop for a month so she can help me. That gives us time to find a nanny or an au pair."

"And you don't need me?"

Need him? Did he just ask that? She'd never needed him more in her entire life.

His eyes held such longing, she felt a sapling of hope bloom inside her.

"I do need you, Mica," she blurted.

He stared at her for a long moment. "Apparently not." He dropped his gaze and tossed his napkin over his cold food.

She stood. "You stubborn Barzonni. What do I have to do or say to get through to you? I love you, Mica." He turned back to her, startled. "I do. That has never been the issue. This time here has only sealed my fate. I'll never love anyone like I love you. But that's not enough, is it, Mica? Go ahead, say it. I'm not enough for you."

"That's not it, Grace."

"Then tell me what it is," she groaned. "And it better not be about your arm."

"It is and it isn't. When you got here and told me about Jules, I was angry and hurt. I felt betrayed. Maybe I still do feel that way—a little. But I also saw your side of things. It's been slow in coming, but I've figured out some things for myself and about my career. And much of that is because of you. You're passionate and motivated. No obstacle is going to stop you. When I'm with you, I feel like I can take on anything. I feel a power I haven't felt since, well, college. You give me purpose, Grace. And more than that. When I'm with you, I'm happy. And that's very rare for me.

When Jules and I were here alone last night, this place felt so empty. I missed you, Grace. I really missed you."

She was stunned. "You—missed me?" Was that possible? She'd counted the days, the weeks, she'd hoped upon hope to hear him say that.

"Yes." He reached for her hand. "I thought that over the next few days… I had plans…"

"What plans?"

"Just to be with you. Tell you that…" His voice caught in his throat as if this was the most difficult thing he'd ever said.

Was he changing his mind? Did he even know his feelings for her?

Grace felt the pressure of his fingers as they tightened around hers. His eyes were filled with earnest intensity. She could almost touch the love coming from him. He was in love with her but he wouldn't say it.

"Tell me what?" she urged, holding her breath.

He glanced away and when he met her eyes again, his were guarded. "You've made this decision to go back to Paris and take Jules with you."

"I don't have much choice," she replied.

"You sure about that?"

She hesitated. The choice she made right now would affect all their lives. Only a moment before, her decision to leave for Paris, to accept her duty to her team, had been the only option. She hadn't dared to dream Mica might declare his feelings for her.

But now?

She'd betrayed him—again.

She loved this man more than anything. But her actions told a different story. Leaving now would crush him. She'd hurt him deeply by keeping Jules from him for months. Now she was taking Mica's son away again. She was a force of destruction. Yet she'd never felt as small and insignificant as she did now.

The dark shadow that fell over Mica's face mirrored the black feeling in her own heart.

In the short time she'd been back in Indian Lake, she'd witnessed Mica's transformation from despair to distrust, to affection and finally to love for his baby son. And he'd finally allowed her to see that he cared about her as well. And in one moment, with one decision, she'd ruined it all.

She was leaving him behind.

She didn't blame him for holding his tongue.

He took a deep breath. "Look, Grace, I want the best for Jules, for you, for...us," he said, his voice infused with emotion. Grace could only stare at him. Her heart skipped a beat.

Was it possible? Could her dream come true? She didn't dare speak and break the moment.

His eyes smoldered with yearning and hope. "I don't understand," she said, struggling not to cry.

"I have some things I have to prove to myself. Kinda like you had to prove to yourself that you could tackle Paris and the design world. I can't and I won't walk in your shadow, Grace."

"Mica. What are you saying?"

"You do need to go back, Grace. You have the world you've built for yourself back there. You'll figure it out. You always have." His words were like hammer blows. Hard enough to break her heart.

"What about Jules?"

"You and I will have to work that out. I'm sure we're not the first parents who have had to figure out visitations and work schedules."

"Mica, I'm so sorry it worked out like this. I really do want you to know Jules…"

"Oh, don't get me wrong, Grace," he said bitingly. "I'm not abandoning my only son. I'm letting you go back to take care of your show. Trust me, I'll be on the phone every day so that Jules can hear my voice."

Grace knew she deserved his derision. If anything, she wanted to hold him and tell him again that she loved him. But she didn't think she could stand up to another rejection, either.

He kissed Jules goodbye and then lifted his face to her. It was only a flash, but for a moment she almost thought Mica was going to kiss her.

Wishful thinking, she thought as he turned quickly toward the door.

"Goodbye, Grace."

She lifted her hand to wave and dropped it as he whisked out the door without a backward glance.

He was right. It was time they parted.

CHAPTER TWENTY-THREE

GRACE WAS PACKED by one o'clock and sitting in Mrs. Beabots's front parlor with Mrs. Beabots, Aunt Louise and Jules, waiting for Mica to pick her up.

"This is ridiculous—Mica's driving all the way into town just to take you six blocks to the train station?" Louise bit into a lemon scone.

"Now, Louise," Mrs. Beabots said. "Mica wants to see Grace before she leaves."

"He wants to see Jules, you mean," Grace said, taking a piece of scone and handing it to Jules, who promptly put it in his mouth and reached for another piece. She had no appetite at all. The hollow feeling inside her had grown like a vast tunnel. In all her life, she'd never wanted to stay in Indian Lake so badly.

Because she'd needed to leave for Paris earlier than planned and take Jules with her, she'd broken Mica's heart again.

What kind of person kept a baby from his father for sixth months and then yanked him away just when the two had bonded? She had no excuses for herself. Only blame.

Mica's anger and disappointment in her were justified. She was angry with herself. Maybe she'd been wrong to tell him that she loved him. Maybe she'd pushed him too much.

Oh, Grace! Maybe. Maybe. When it comes to being a fool in love, you win the prize.

Still, she couldn't help wondering what decision she would have made if he'd admitted that he loved her.

But he hadn't said it.

Her heart felt like a stone in her chest.

Grace didn't miss the look Mrs. Beabots and Aunt Louise exchanged. She pointed an accusing finger at them. "No. Stop thinking that, both of you. He doesn't want me."

"I'll bet my bottom dollar he never said that to you," Mrs. Beabots protested.

"Well, no. Not in those words. But he didn't tell me he loves me. Even after I told him that I love him. He's as silent as a tomb."

Mrs. Beabots nodded. "Raymond was like that. Strong, silent type. Frankly, dear, they're more mush than the average man. You can trust me on that one."

"I wouldn't know," Louise said.

Mrs. Beabots stood as Mica's truck came up

her drive. "Grace, he's here. I'll get the baby's diaper bag. You get your things."

Suddenly, Grace was flustered. During her short stay, she'd come to feel at home here in Mrs. Beabots's house. She liked the camaraderie, the closeness with her aunt, whom she loved dearly.

"Oh, I'm going to miss you, Aunt Louise!"

"Grace, I'll be in Paris in three days."

"I know. It seems a long time from now."

Mrs. Beabots smiled. "You are always welcome in this house, Grace." You have to know that. I'll miss you terribly." Mrs. Beabots hugged Grace and kissed Jules's cheek.

Jules grabbed Mrs. Beabots's hair and smiled. "Ba."

"We'll both miss you," Grace said as a wave of homesick tears crested her heart. "I can't believe I'm leaving."

Mica came to the door and Grace opened it. She felt every wound she'd inflicted on him. She wasn't sure how she'd live with herself. She felt glued to the floor, knowing that leaving was the worst decision. Staying was a choice riddled with misery as well.

"Ready to go?" he asked solemnly.

"Yes." She handed Jules to him.

While Mica buckled Jules into his carrier,

Grace turned to Louise. "I'll pick you up at Charles de Gaulle. You text me when you leave New York. I'll check with the airlines to make sure you're on time. Oh, Aunt Louise, thank you for coming over to help me. This means the world to me. Especially—" She looked over at Mica, who was coming back up the steps to help with her luggage. "Especially now."

"I know, dear. I love you."

"I love you, too. 'Bye."

Grace followed Mica to the truck and got in.

He backed out of the drive and started down Maple Boulevard.

"Thanks for letting me take you. I figured with me having the car seat for Jules and all…"

Grace couldn't find her voice.

"It's okay," she finally said.

They crossed the light at Main Street. She looked up at the sandstone county courthouse. She glanced down Main Street at all the pretty shops. She remembered how the town looked in spring, with the white pear blossoms. In a small-town way, it reminded her of Paris.

Paris. Her home.

Indian Lake. Her heart's home.

They pulled up to the train station. Most of the snow had been plowed and the large piles from the blizzard had been carted away by dump trucks and taken up to Lake Michigan, where the snow would turn back into water in the spring.

Mica left the truck running and the heater on. He turned to her.

"Grace. There's something I want…I mean, I *need* to say to you."

Grace felt a cold chill as if the winter wind had seeped through the truck's steel and glass. "And that is?"

"Your leaving is the best thing for us."

"What?" Her insides froze. And that stone her heart had become was heavy and painful.

Mica loved her. She was certain of it now. But she'd hurt him deeply. If he admitted his feelings to her, he undoubtedly thought he wouldn't be able to go on.

Their love had been doomed from the start.

"You deserve so much more than I can ever give you. You should have a guy like that Rene fellow. He lives in your world. Understands it and you. He's protective of you. I like that about him. And if not him, someone else even better."

"This isn't happening, Mica. You know I love you."

"Grace, I don't think I could take another heartbreak. I don't know how long it will take for me to really forgive you for keeping Jules a secret. I hope I'll overcome it someday. But then to take him away from me just when I start planning my life around him? You were going to leave two days from now anyway… but I'd planned for him to stay with me."

"You're right," she choked out.

She covered her face with her hands. "Mica, I'm so sorry. Deeply sorry. But I do love you."

"Grace, I meant it when I said that I had some things to work out for myself. The thing is…I'm going away, too."

She turned to face him. "Away? Where?"

"Florida."

"I don't understand."

"I've been tinkering around with designs to retrofit farm equipment for disabled folks like me."

She blinked as she took it all in. "Your design?"

"Yeah." He ran his hand through his hair. "Until now, it's only been a dream. Then when you and Jules showed up, I finally did something about it and sent my proposal to Peerless Farm Manufacturing. I got a call from them right before I left the house to come here. They want a meeting with me. For that, I have to thank you, Grace."

"I—I had no idea."

"Nobody did. I didn't want to tell anyone until it became a sure thing."

She stared at him, speechless.

"I have to do this, for me and for Jules and his future. I want him to be proud of his father. I need this. Do you understand?"

"I do, Mica."

"As it is, I wouldn't be able to watch him right now. I have to leave for Florida in a few days."

"That soon?"

"Yeah."

"And after that?"

"I'll find out if we mesh. I might have to move out there."

She gasped. "You? Would leave the farm?" She couldn't believe it. Mica had always been part of the land, part of the Barzonni legend in her mind.

"This is going to sound crazy, Grace, but I believe my accident showed me I needed to change course in my life. I needed to delve inside myself and find out what I wanted. Not what my father wanted for me or my mother. Florida is my chance to find myself."

Pursing her lips, she said, "I get that. I do."

"I thought you would. Even if no one else did."

"Oh, Mica, they're going to love your work."

"Don't be so sure. Besides, you have no idea what I've been doing."

"I believe in you. I know you wouldn't even begin a project if it didn't have true worth."

"That's exactly how I felt."

"You see? I do know you." Her smile was genuine, though it hurt her heart.

"You do." He reached out and traced her cheekbone.

"Mica, what if you have to move to Florida? What about Jules, I mean?" *And me. Is there any hope for me?*

"I'd make arrangements for him to visit me there, of course."

"Oh."

"Grace, we have to work together so that I can see Jules. Once I secure my career, we'll talk it out. Okay? We'll find a way."

"Yes, we'll do that," she said feeling empty inside.

Mica was being practical and realistic. It was amazing how quickly her Sunday morning dream had shattered. She'd been foolish to think that she could have a long-ago dream. She was a contemporary woman living in a high-charged world of commerce and competition. It was where she belonged.

Too many people depended on her. She couldn't and wouldn't chuck it all just to have a sweet home with Mica and Jules. Besides, she wouldn't be herself if she didn't have her work. She had to keep her head on straight and stay real.

He leaned over and kissed her cheek.

Grace didn't want to miss a nanosecond of the feel of him, the warmth and the bittersweet emotion that erupted inside her.

"Mica, I wish…"

"I wish a lot of things, too, Grace," he said huskily and kissed her.

This was a kiss she didn't like at all. It was filled with that same longing she'd felt before, but it was now riddled with finality. A goodbye kiss.

Grace wasn't sure she'd live through it.

This wasn't just goodbye, this was the final sting. The kill. The end.

"I admit to liking our times together. All of them. But both of us are realists. You live in Paris. Right now, I pretty much don't know where the next day is going to take me. I promise to help with Jules in any way I can. Like I said, we'll work out the logistics. Okay? You just tell me what you want."

Grace had to force herself to remember to breathe. She couldn't think.

She heard the train whistle blast.

She opened the door. "Train."

Mica rushed to jump out. "I'll get Jules."

Grace took her bags as Mica carried Jules toward the loading area.

The train came to a stop and the conductor got out. Mica and Grace hung back as another dozen or so passengers got on.

Mica handed Jules to Grace as the conductor took her bags. She walked up to the little metal steps.

"Goodbye, Grace," Mica said. He kissed Jules's cheek.

"Da!" Jules waved and then snuggled his face in Grace's shoulder.

"Goodbye, Mica," she replied, taking one last look at him. It was an image she knew she had to lock away. It had to last the rest of her life.

MICA STOOD ON the pavement and watched as the train pulled out of the station and headed west. The winter wind cut through his sheepskin jacket, but he didn't feel a thing. He'd been numb all day.

Ever since you told me that you loved me.

In less than a week, Mica had come to a lot of revelations and decisions. His mother was right. Grace lit up when he was around, an incandescence he'd never seen in anyone. Not that he'd paid attention to other people and their lives all that much. But once he knew what he was looking for, he'd found it.

Grace was everything any man in his right mind could ever want. And that was the problem.

Even if he'd gotten on that plane and flown back with her, he knew that they wouldn't stay together. She'd said she loved him, more than once, but then she'd taken Jules. If she loved him, how could she do that? She had to know how much she hurt him. Sure, Grace had had a crush on him when they were kids. Back then, her head was filled with rhinestone crowns, runways and finding a Prince Charming to her Cinderella.

Now they were adults and he was no prince. Not even close.

He had to make something of himself. He wanted Grace to be proud of him. He wanted his son to look up to him the way he'd admired his own father.

More than that, he wanted to know his son loved him. Really loved him. He would have to find a way to be present in Jules's life and that meant working around Grace's schedule. If she had to be in Paris, he would fly to her. He would not wait around for Grace to make the decisions and the plans. He would find a way.

And to make that happen, Mica had a great deal to do.

Mica went to his truck and backed away from the station.

"This was the right decision," he said to himself.

For a short time, he'd gotten lost in Grace's vibrancy, her joy, her caring for others and, yes, her love for him. He was going to miss her. Heck. He already missed her and she hadn't been gone more than a few minutes.

He didn't want to think how sharp this pain in his chest was going to get after a week apart. Months.

And what would his life be like years from now, not seeing Grace? Or once she did find another man? How would he deal with that when just this parting was killing him?

"Mica, you idiot. You're in love with her. Not a crush or infatuation. You love her—and it's taken her leaving you for you to realize it."

Mica kept driving south wondering when it had started to rain.

The laugh that escaped his mouth tasted bitter. "Not rain—tears."

CHAPTER TWENTY-FOUR

MICA WORE PROTECTIVE glasses as he stood next to Vincent Asmundi and Chip Hardesty and watched sparks fly from a flux welding torch at the Peerless Farm Manufacturing plant. Half a dozen workers wearing helmets, masks and heavy gloves barely noticed their presence.

"We've got the first prototype all set up in the next room, Mica," Vincent said.

"Yes, we're very excited about your design. We didn't have to make a single adjustment. The wiring and the motherboard specs you sent were letter-perfect."

"That's great news." Mica smiled as he followed them into a large warehouse. Here were tractors, bulldozers, large riding lawn mowers, trailers and trucks. All were being retrofitted with his voice-activated device.

Vincent began the demonstration. "Using a universal command device, as you suggested, was genius. Our code expert jumped right in as we'd hoped."

Chip motioned to Mica to follow him. "We'll go up to what we call the box. You can watch nearly everything in the warehouse from here."

Vincent began the demonstrations. One after another, he "drove" each vehicle with voice commands.

After nearly an hour of taking the vehicles through their paces, Vincent suggested they retire back to his office for the rest of the meeting.

Vincent's office was a sea of metal racks containing equipment pieces and engine parts.

"I keep my experimental jobs back here so they don't wind up where they shouldn't."

Chip laughed. "That's my fault. I'm always tinkering with things and I have a bad habit of using what I can find. Once I'm in that creative 'zone'…"

"I understand that," Mica said. "It's like living in another world."

Vincent nodded. "I think all creative types are like that, don't you? Doesn't matter if you're an artist, filmmaker or designer. Once that creative switch is turned on…" He raked his hand through his hair. "I find I forget to eat."

Mica nodded. "So true." Odd that at that moment he would think of Grace and her drawings. She could sketch all night long, she'd said. She understood about the lengths he would go to when an idea hit him. She understood what it was like to lie awake all night making notes on whatever scratch paper was at hand. He'd been doing that a lot for the past three weeks and had come up with even more ideas to present to Vincent and Chip. He would have liked to have told Grace about them. She would have been happy for him.

But he'd sent her away.

"So, Mica, here's the thing. You've got us to thinking. We'd like to delve more deeply into your ideas regarding accessible equipment. Vincent and I see several avenues we'd like to travel, but we need you on our team to accomplish this."

Mica straightened in his chair. This had never happened to him before. These experts, entrepreneurs, were asking his advice. He'd dipped a toe into his career, his chosen field, but he'd never taken the plunge. Well, he was diving in now.

"What do you have in mind?"

Vincent beamed and opened his drawer. "You won't believe this, but we've made some inquiries. Everything from motor scooters to motorcycles, quadrupeds and even airplanes."

"Airplanes?"

"Can you imagine if we went military with this?"

Mica dropped his jaw. "But disabled veterans…"

"That's what we were thinking. Normally, they're discharged. But what if we offered equipment, all kinds of equipment, they could run? What if we changed the landscape for them?"

Mica wanted to jump for joy. It was all he could do to contain his enthusiasm. "This is incredible."

"We could change the world for a lot of people, Mica," Chip said.

Vincent shoved the list across his desk. "We believe that with you on the team, there's no limit to what we could come up with—"

Chip interrupted. "We understand if you need time to think about it."

Mica picked up the paperwork, perusing it quickly. "I assume you'd want me to move here to Florida."

"That would be ideal, yes," Chip said.

Vincent leaned across the desk. "Mica, it goes without saying that if you joined us, you'd be a partner in the company. That would also mean that we would share in the profits of your ideas. You might want to keep the patent on your designs. That's up to you. But I can promise you this. We have contacts in the military. At all the major manufacturers you see represented in this warehouse. We have ten years of cultivating the relationships we bring to the table."

Mica looked from Chip's lean, scruffy face to Vincent's intense brown eyes. "It's a lot to think about."

"It is, but whatever your concerns, we want to work that out with you. There's nothing that we can't overcome—together."

Mica cocked his head. "Nothing?"

"I promise you. Where there's a will, there's a way. That's always been my motto."

Vincent rose and held out his hand. "You've been an inspiration to us, Mica."

"Ditto," Chip said as he shook Mica's hand as well.

Mica left the plant with his head swimming. Had those men said those things? Had they actually offered him a partnership? Was the excitement he felt from them real? Did they really think they could change the world for disabled workers?

"Why not?"

It was time for some real changes in the

world of accessibility and Mica wanted, no, craved, to be part of it all.

He'd followed in his father's footsteps for so long, he'd had no idea that this was the kind of elation, the solid satisfaction that comes from creating something worthy. That others valued and sought out.

This must be how Grace feels when she sells one of her designs. No wonder she flew back to Paris so quickly. Who could ever live an ordinary life after tasting this kind of success?

Rather than call for a cab to take him back to his hotel, he chose to walk along the palm-tree-lined sidewalk and enjoy the mild winter weather.

People cycled along wide bike paths. Up ahead was a park, where he saw two elderly men playing checkers. A young couple read books while holding hands on a blanket spread under a river birch tree. He saw jogging mothers pushing strollers. One mother had twins.

Twins. What must that be like?

His mind flew to Jules. He missed his baby more than he'd thought possible. During sleepless nights, he'd conjured plans of seeing Jules and Grace again. He'd imagined them at his mother's dining table for her Superbowl party. But the Superbowl had come and gone, and though Grace phoned him, he did not see Jules. Mica was amazed how much he wanted to hold his son.

He had to admit that Grace was very good about sending him pictures of Jules. Several of the photos, he'd printed and framed. He bought a new wallet for his favorites.

Mica had sent Grace plane tickets for her and Jules to visit him for Easter, but though the days moved closer to their visit, it seemed a lifetime away.

He thought Jules would like a sunny day like this under the palm trees, listening to the ocean waves crash on the beach. He wondered if Grace would ever want to come visit him in this pretty seaside town.

Then he stopped dead still.

Of course she wouldn't. You rejected her. She put her heart on the line and you crushed it.

He looked up at the cloudless blue sky. Talk about botching up a life. He'd really done it. He hadn't pushed Grace away, he'd thrown her across the ocean without so much as a thank-you.

Mica walked through the little park and across the wide concrete sidewalk that was filled with people on Rollerblades, skateboards and bicycles. When he got to the beach, he took off his dress shoes and socks. Feeling the warm sand slip between his toes, he realized how little of life he'd experienced.

He'd like to blame his accident for that fact, but the truth was, his accident had brought him to life. He'd shoved his dreams and possibilities for himself into a drawer along with his college diploma. It was his fault he hadn't had the courage to live. It was his sense of duty to his father, then to his mother, that had kept him tethered to a world that didn't serve him anymore.

Grace's return to Indian Lake with Jules had opened his heart and shown him that he was much more than the Mica Barzonni he thought he was.

Chip and Vincent saw something in him that he'd been afraid to face. Potential. Talent. He had these things.

Grace had seen them.

Mica had to admit he'd seen them, too. But time after time, he'd blocked them out.

Mica looked out across the Atlantic.

"She's an ocean away. She might as well be on the moon."

He would take Vincent and Chip's offer. He would make something of himself so he could become the kind of man worthy of a woman like Grace. Worthy of her love.

He had vowed to himself that he wouldn't see her until he'd made that happen. He knew that if he didn't try his wings, just like she had, he would sabotage their relationship in the future because he'd always feel inadequate. That much he knew about himself.

That's why it had taken her leaving for him to realize how deeply he loved her.

Grace deserved all the love this world had to give. And Mica knew he would love her forever.

He hoped she would want that from him, but after he'd pushed her away, he had serious doubts.

It was going to take time to make his mark.

He stared at the blue water and the enormous waves. *Grace...*

He took out his cell phone. He could text her. See if she was all right. Ask about Jules.

But if she didn't reply, his heart would break again.

He didn't know which was worse. The constant missing her or his fear that this time, *she'd* throw *him* across the ocean and he'd never see her again.

CHAPTER TWENTY-FIVE

GRACE WAS EXHAUSTED after interviews with Eloise's team, Fashion Week, then men's Fashion Week and finally a meeting with Eloise in person. She'd expected to be tongue-tied but she wasn't. Her days as a preteen on an Illinois runway had apparently prepared her to act professional and poised.

Now the pressure was on and no one felt it more than Grace, despite Etienne's eye-rolling and Jasminda's fluttering hands.

The atelier buzzed with activity and creative energy as Grace inspected a bolt of hand-painted chartreuse silk that she planned to lay over a slip of crepe de chine.

"That's gorgeous," Rene said, breezing through the room with a full-skirted, strapless dress in graduated aqua, lake-green and turquoise batiste.

"Put a coral belt on that dress," Grace said. "Leather with a shell buckle. Mother-of-pearl. Something shimmery."

"Will do," Rene replied. Out of the corner of her eye, she saw him stop dead in front of Jules's high chair. "When did he learn to do that?"

Grace glanced up. Jules was using his body front to back to make the chair move across the wood floor. "Yesterday."

"Is that safe?"

"It's a stable chair and he doesn't go far. And since I'm afraid to let him walk, which his father adores…"

"Oh, him again…" Jasminda groaned as she expertly cut a piece of silk.

Since she'd returned from Indian Lake, Jasminda had let everyone in the atelier know that she didn't approve of Mica's rejection of Grace. Every time Grace sent Mica a photo of Jules, Jasminda frowned. Though Grace appreciated the young woman's loyalty, she also wanted her team to understand that Mica would always be a part of Jules's life.

"Aunt Louise will be back from the *boulanger* in a few minutes with lunch. When she gets back, I'll take Jules for a walk and get some fresh air."

"Oh? Where are you going?" Etienne asked.

"I should go by my apartment and get some diapers and something for his supper, since it

looks like we'll be working late again tonight."
She sighed.

"Ah, yes." Rene chuckled. "Darn the bad
luck, huh? We simply have to work longer
hours now that we're under contract for Eloise!" He fist-bumped Jules. Rene glanced at
Grace. "At least his daddy taught him some
fun things."

"Da!" Jules said and clapped his hands.

Grace's face fell. Trying not to think about
Mica was like pretending the sun didn't come
up or go down. Useless. She'd finally come to
the decision that she had to work through her
broken heart. As they worked out their co-
parenting schedules, she'd see Mica. Be with
him. And her heart would break again.

Grace went over to Jules and lifted him out
of the high chair. She picked up a yellow shirt
she'd made and tried it on him. He scrunched
his nose and blew her a raspberry. "It's not
right, is it, Jules? I think I should go with the
yellow-and-white-striped collar and cuffs on
the sleeves. What do you think, Jasminda?"

"*Oui*. I made a yellow-and-white-striped tam
with a green ball at the top. It's over here," she
said, retrieving the hat.

Etienne walked up and looked at Jules, who

was chewing on his hands. "Why do I get the feeling you're going after a baby Eloise line?"

Grace raised her eyebrows. "Because it would make money? Duh."

Everyone burst into laughter just as Louise walked through the door. "Am I missing something?"

Rene walked over and kissed both her cheeks. "Your niece is going to work us to an early death."

Louise laughed. "Ah, but now that I've been here for three weeks, I know that none of you would have it any other way. Am I right?"

"Oui," they said in unison.

"Aunt Louise, you're so sweet to get lunch for everyone. Listen, I'm going to take Jules out for a break, get some fresh air. I'll stop at the apartment and change him. We're going to have to work late tonight. I know you have a ticket to see the opera."

"I could go to the apartment for you, Grace," Louise offered. "Although, it's a lovely day out there and a little break from the workroom might be good for you both."

Grace hugged her aunt and went to the hall where she kept Jules's stroller. She came back and took Jules from Jasminda, who had slipped a pair of dark emerald green pants on him. She stood back and wrinkled her nose.

"*Non. Non.* The pants aren't right, Grace."

"They should be navy blue." She took the tam off Jules's head. "And change the pompom to navy as well."

"Ah!" Jasminda's eyes rounded. "Of course."

Grace left the atelier with Jules and stepped into the sunshine.

She lifted her face to the warming rays and inhaled. There was something about these last days of January that she loved. The trees were still bare, allowing every facet of the stunning Parisian architecture to be on display. The hotels decked their window boxes and planters with flowers, but the parks were still devoid of foliage.

Grace loved it all. This was her town, her home. And now that she was back she couldn't imagine living anywhere in the world but Paris.

Not even Indian Lake.

She trundled Jules's stroller over the cobbled streets of Montmartre, and he giggled and clapped with each bump as if he was in an amusement park. Close to the famous Lapin Agile was a café she loved, La Maison Rose. The pink stucco walls and kelly green shutters always beckoned to her. She should take a seat at one of the little tables on the sidewalk, she thought. She should order a café au lait and stop for a moment to drink in this gorgeous day.

"Madame?"

Grace hadn't realized she'd been standing still, staring at the empty table.

"Une table, s'il vous plait."

The waiter nodded and gestured to the table.

Grace rolled Jules up to the little table and sat in the chair facing down the street. A Fiat rounded the corner, honked the horn and stopped. A young girl jumped up from the table next to Grace and rushed over to the car. She opened the door and threw herself into the driver's arms. She raced around to the passenger side and they drove off.

From across the street she heard someone playing "April in Paris." A couple a few tables away from her kissed each other, then held up their glasses of Pernod and clinked the rims.

"Grace?"

Her shoulders stiffened.

"Grace?"

It was the voice she'd heard in a thousand dreams on a thousand nights. It was the voice that invaded her daytime concentration. It was the voice she'd thought she'd go the rest of her life without hearing again.

His shadow loomed over her as he walked up from behind. Her heart stopped beating. Her breath stuck in her lungs. She didn't dare speak or this magic would end.

"I found you," Mica said as he walked around Jules's stroller and sat in the chair close to the pink stucco wall. He reached out to touch Jules's outstretched hand, then leaned over and kissed Jules on the forehead. He looked back to her.

"How?" She swallowed and tried to think. "How did you find me?"

His smile was nearly imperceptible, but his tanned face seemed to glow. Grace wondered if the day would ever come when she wasn't completely shattered by him. All of him. His blue eyes looked twice as intense as she remembered them. His raven hair was longer, as if he hadn't had time to cut it.

"Da! Da! Dada!" Jules squealed and kept stretching his hand to Mica and banging his legs against the stroller.

"I think he's happy to see me. Are you?"

Grace glanced at Jules, then back at Mica. She was in shock. Mica. Here. In Paris. "You didn't answer me."

"I had help."

"My aunt?" Grace couldn't believe Louise would betray her like this. What if Mica was here to take Jules away?

"Uh, no. But she was an unwitting participant. She wrote to Mrs. Beabots."

"And Mrs. Beabots told you where I was?"

"Yes." He reached toward Grace's hand. "Don't be mad at her. I had to find you, Grace."

Hot, liquid fire slid down Grace's throat as she stared at him. Was he kidding? He was back to make her feel like a fool again? What could he want? The only reason he would be here wasn't good. She felt like she was readying for battle. No one, not even Mica, could separate her from Jules. For a long moment, her mind went black. She couldn't think. His face swam in front of her. She forced herself to breathe.

You can do this, Grace. Be strong. He's only a Barzonni. He can't hurt you any more than he already has.

"Why is it so important you see me?" She braced for the truth.

"Because I found out some things after you left, Grace," he said huskily, without a trace of reproach or arrogance.

His eyes softened. She remembered that

look. She'd only seen it briefly, once, when he'd looked at her in the moonlight. She'd had her eyes closed and she'd opened them suddenly, and she'd caught him. She realized now that it had been that look that she'd pinned hopes on all these months. That look had spurred her to book a ticket to America and take Jules to meet him. It was that look that she'd desperately wanted to see—even if it was only one more time.

"Such…as?"

"I learned I can't live without you. I don't want to live without you or Jules. I was stupid and blind. I was afraid that if I couldn't give you the world, you wouldn't want me, Grace."

Stunned, Grace was terrified to believe him. Her mouth had gone dry and her heart hammered in her chest. "Mica, what—what are you saying?"

"I love you, Grace." He rose from the chair and came over to her. "I love you with all my heart and soul. I should have told you before, but I was too bitter, too arrogant and afraid."

"You love me?"

He pulled her up from the chair. He stood so close she could feel his breath on her face.

"I do. I do. I know I deserve to be turned away. But please don't. Please give me a chance to make it all up to you. All the things I didn't say when I should have said them. Give me a chance."

Tears filled Grace's eyes. She felt weak and strong at the same time. "Mica, you can't just fly across an ocean and surprise me like this and expect me to drop everything and come back to Indian Lake with you."

He cupped her face in his hands and kissed her cheeks, her nose, her lips, and started laughing. "Oh, Grace, how I love you! I never said anything about taking you and Jules out of Paris."

"But you said…"

"Grace, you *are* Paris to me. You are its light and beauty and love. It's in your blood as surely as if you'd been born here. I've been walking this area for hours. I found your apartment but you weren't there. I wandered around and I fell in love with every lamppost and café. I can't believe I'm saying this, but I feel as if I've come home, too, Grace."

"But…you were going to Florida and—"

"I went to Florida. It's gorgeous there. Palm trees and the beach. But when I looked out on that ocean and knew you were on the other side of the Atlantic, I couldn't take it. It took me a few weeks to get things squared away legally—"

"What do you mean, 'legally'?" she interrupted. His words were coming at her like a tsunami. A wonderful, powerful, emotion-packed wave.

"My work contracts. It's all done. I'm a partner in Peerless. The company I told you about."

"Partner?"

"Uh-huh." He pushed back a lock of hair from her face. "We worked it out. I'll email my designs and a few times a year I'll fly to Miami and conference with Vince and Chip, my colleagues. I'll take you and Jules with me. He's gonna love the beach and the park—"

"So, you have it all worked out."

"Just about. Except for one thing." He reached into his pocket and withdrew a sparkling diamond ring in a platinum setting. "All my brothers told me the reason you refused me was because I didn't have a ring. This time I took their advice."

"Mica, it was never the ring," she said softly as he moved even closer to her. He put his arm around her and pulled her to his chest.

"I know that."

"I wanted you to love me," she said through her tears.

"And I do. More than you can possibly know. I intend to spend the rest of my life showing you how much."

"Show me now," she said, putting her arms around his neck and leaning into his kiss.

His lips were filled with the promise of love that Grace had dreamed about for years. The sun beat down on them and though Grace knew it was her imagination, oddly, she thought she smelled suntan lotion and chlorine on him.

Maybe it was the wish she'd made all those years ago in the swimming pool coming true.

Mica loved her. He wanted to be hers. It was the only wish that mattered.

EPILOGUE

Mica hung up the phone and turned to Grace. "They're all mad," he said handing the phone to Grace and taking Jules in his arm.

"How can they be mad that we're engaged? Wait a minute. Your mother said that?"

"No, Gabe." Mica walked up to the street light across from the Eiffel Tower.

Frowning, Grace said, "Your brother is mad because you asked me to marry you or because I said 'yes'?"

Mica burst into laughter and as he did, Jules put his hand over Mica's mouth and laughed along with him.

Mica shrugged. "Actually, Nate was on the phone with him. He and Maddie were out at Gabe and Liz's for dinner. Then I called Mom and conferenced her and Sam in as well."

"That's practically the whole family," Grace replied as the light turned.

"Da!" Jules pointed to the green light.

"Hey!" Mica kissed Jules's cheek. "I thought I was 'Da.'"

Grace put her arm around Mica's waist, liking the feeling of the three of them blending together. It hit her that she was living her dreams. Mica was here, in Paris, and he wasn't leaving. He wanted to make a life with her. No wonder people thought Paris was paradise. "Oh, Mica, he's been calling everything 'Da' since we returned."

"And I thought I was special."

"You are special," Grace said earnestly. "To both of us."

"Keep telling me that," he said as they walked past a street vendor selling flowers.

"Back to your brothers..."

"Sorry. Gabe said he was hoping they'd be around for the engagement party. Then when Mom realized I wasn't coming back anytime soon, she wasn't happy. She's thrown engagement parties for all her daughters-in-love."

"In-law, you mean."

"That's not what Mom will call you."

"Hmm. I like that," Grace said stopping to inspect a nosegay of lily of the valley. She held them up to her face, smelled them and then held them out to Jules, who stared at them and then sniffed. Then he grabbed one and licked it."

Mica turned to the woman vendor. "We'll take these."

Grace laughed as she dug in Mica's back pocket for his wallet. She paid the vendor and as she closed the wallet, she saw the pictures of Jules.

Mica rested his chin on her shoulder. "You didn't send one of yourself. I would have put yours in there as well."

"So we'll take a selfie by the Eiffel Tower."

"Done," he said. "Hey, I figured out how to appease everyone in my family."

Grace raised an eyebrow. "They all have their own opinions. I don't see how..."

Mica dropped to his knee and balanced Jules next to him so that it looked as if Jules was standing. "Grace. The men in your life hope you will grant our request. We would like to fly back to Indian Lake to have our wedding there."

"That's a great idea!"

Mica stood instantly. "You're kidding. I thought you'd want the wedding here with all your friends."

"But what about all your family? Rafe and Olivia? And all your friends? Not to mention Aunt Louise and Mrs. Beabots. No, it should be Indian Lake."

Mica's expression fell. "I really wanted it

to be in Paris. Who doesn't want to get married in Paris?"

Grace took Jules in her arms and handed Mica her purse. "Seriously, Mica. We need to have it in Indian Lake."

Jules looked from his mother to his father. "Paris." Mica shook his head.

Jules looked back to Grace, but before she could say another word, the baby put his hand over her mouth.

Jules looked at his father. Then he smiled.

Grace laughed and Mica laughed along with her. "I guess Jules has the last word."

Grace kissed Mica and then kissed Jules. She was outnumbered. It didn't matter. All these years, she'd loved Mica and only him. In her darkest hours, she'd wondered what had become of all that love she'd given. Now she knew. It had come back to her a thousand times over.

And her dreams of being loved by Mica had not come close to this immeasurable happiness.

* * * * *

For more stories from the
SHORES OF INDIAN LAKE,
check out Catherine Lanigan's
FAMILY OF HIS OWN and
PROTECTING THE SINGLE MOM.

Get 2 Free Books,

Plus 2 Free Gifts—

just for trying the Reader Service!

Love Inspired®

HHBPA17

Get 2 Free Books,
Plus 2 Free Gifts —
just for trying the Reader Service!

HARLEQUIN *superromance*

YES! Please send me 2 FREE LARGER-PRINT Harlequin® Superromance® novels and my 2 FREE gifts (gifts are worth about $10 retail). After receiving them, if I don't wish to receive any more books, I can return the shipping statement marked "cancel." If I don't cancel, I will receive 4 brand-new novels every month and be billed just $6.19 per book in the U.S. or $6.49 per book in Canada. That's a savings of at least 11% off the cover price! It's quite a bargain! Shipping and handling is just 50¢ per book in the U.S. or 75¢ per book in Canada.* I understand that accepting the 2 free books and gifts places me under no obligation to buy anything. I can always return a shipment and cancel at any time. The free books and gifts are mine to keep no matter what I decide.

132/332 HDN GLWS

Name	(PLEASE PRINT)	

Address		Apt. #

City	State/Prov.	Zip/Postal Code

Signature (if under 18, a parent or guardian must sign)

Mail to the **Reader Service:**
IN U.S.A.: P.O. Box 1341, Buffalo, NY 14240-8531
IN CANADA: P.O. Box 603, Fort Erie, Ontario L2A 5X3

Want to try two free books from another line?
Call 1-800-873-8635 today or visit www.ReaderService.com.

* Terms and prices subject to change without notice. Prices do not include applicable taxes. Sales tax applicable in N.Y. Canadian residents will be charged applicable taxes. Offer not valid in Quebec. This offer is limited to one order per household. Books received may not be as shown. Not valid for current subscribers to Harlequin Superromance Larger-Print books. All orders subject to approval. Credit or debit balances in a customer's account(s) may be offset by any other outstanding balance owed by or to the customer. Please allow 4 to 6 weeks for delivery. Offer available while quantities last.

Your Privacy—The Reader Service is committed to protecting your privacy. Our Privacy Policy is available online at www.ReaderService.com or upon request from the Reader Service.

We make a portion of our mailing list available to reputable third parties that offer products we believe may interest you. If you prefer that we not exchange your name with third parties, or if you wish to clarify or modify your communication preferences, please visit us at www.ReaderService.com/consumerschoice or write to us at Reader Service Preference Service, P.O. Box 9062, Buffalo, NY 14240-9062. Include your complete name and address.

HSRLP17R

Get 2 Free Books,
Plus 2 Free Gifts—
just for trying the Reader Service!

YES! Please send me 2 FREE Harlequin® Romance LARGER PRINT novels and my 2 FREE gifts (gifts are worth about $10 retail). After receiving them, if I don't wish to receive any more books, I can return the shipping statement marked "cancel." If I don't cancel, I will receive 4 brand-new novels every month and be billed just $5.34 per book in the U.S. or $5.74 per book in Canada. That's a savings of at least 15% off the cover price! It's quite a bargain! Shipping and handling is just 50¢ per book in the U.S. and 75¢ per book in Canada.* I understand that accepting the 2 free books and gifts places me under no obligation to buy anything. I can always return a shipment and cancel at any time. The free books and gifts are mine to keep no matter what I decide.

119/319 HDN GLWP

Name _____ (PLEASE PRINT)

Address _____ Apt. #

City _____ State/Prov. _____ Zip/Postal Code

Signature (if under 18, a parent or guardian must sign)

Mail to the **Reader Service:**
IN U.S.A.: P.O. Box 1341, Buffalo, NY 14240-8531
IN CANADA: P.O. Box 603, Fort Erie, Ontario L2A 5X3
Want to try two free books from another line?
Call 1-800-873-8635 or visit www.ReaderService.com.

* Terms and prices subject to change without notice. Prices do not include applicable taxes. Sales tax applicable in N.Y. Canadian residents will be charged applicable taxes. Offer not valid in Quebec. This offer is limited to one order per household. Books received may not be as shown. Not valid for current subscribers to Harlequin Romance Larger-Print books. All orders subject to approval. Credit or debit balances in a customer's account(s) may be offset by any other outstanding balance owed by or to the customer. Please allow 4 to 6 weeks for delivery. Offer available while quantities last.

Your Privacy—The Reader Service is committed to protecting your privacy. Our Privacy Policy is available online at www.ReaderService.com or upon request from the Reader Service.

We make a portion of our mailing list available to reputable third parties that offer products we believe may interest you. If you prefer that we not exchange your name with third parties, or if you wish to clarify or modify your communication preferences, please visit us at www.ReaderService.com/consumerschoice or write to us at Reader Service Preference Service, P.O. Box 9062, Buffalo, NY 14240-9062. Include your complete name and address.

HRLP17R2